THE BOOK EVERYONE IS TALKING ABOUT

GOVERNOR GENERAL'S LITERARY AWARD WINNER

ROGERS WRITERS' TRUST FICTION PRIZE WINNER

STEPHEN LEACOCK MEMORIAL MEDAL FOR HUMOUR WINNER

OREGON BOOK AWARDS: KEN KESEY AWARD FOR FICTION WINNER

CANADIAN BOOKSELLERS ASSOCIATION: FICTION BOOK OF THE YEAR WINNER

SCOTIABANK GILLER PRIZE FINALIST

MAN BOOKER PRIZE FINALIST

WALTER SCOTT PRIZE FINALIST

GOOGLE PLAY™ INTERNATIONAL AUTHOR OF THE YEAR FINALIST

GLOBE AND MAIL TOP 100 BOOK

TORONTO STAR TOP 100 BOOK

MACLEAN'S BEST BOOKS OF THE YEAR

PUBLISHERS WEEKLY BEST BOOKS OF THE YEAR

QUILL & QUIRE BEST BOOKS OF THE YEAR

#1 AMAZON BEST BOOK OF 2011

#1 NATIONAL BESTSELLER

★ "A quirky and stylish revisionist western…With nods to Charles Portis and Frank Norris, deWitt has produced a genre-bending frontier saga that is exciting, funny, and, perhaps unexpectedly, moving." — *Publishers Weekly*, starred review

"Written with the parsed force of the best of Elmore Leonard, deWitt's closest CanLit antecedent seems to be Michael Ondaatje's *The Collected Works of Billy the Kid*. The influence comes through not only in his attention to every word, every detail, but also in the deadpan, unflinching depiction of violence…A bold, original, powerfully compelling work." — *Globe and Mail*

"*The Sisters Brothers* confirms Patrick deWitt as one of the most talented young writers around. A playful often surreal take on the classic western, it is as funny as *Ablutions*, but has a much stronger narrative line, deeper characters, and a vision of searing originality…DeWitt's great achievement is to match a narrator of such simple humanity to a tale of such lurid brutality. Eli is perhaps the most endearing killer you will ever meet. His narrative is unique and bestows the whole range of novelistic pleasures." — *Sunday Times*

"A witty noir version of *Don Quixote*…Hugely entertaining." — *Financial Times*

"There was never a more engaging pair of psychopaths than Charlie and Eli Sisters…So subtle is deWitt's prose, so slyly note-perfect his rendition of Eli's voice in all its earnestly charming nineteenth-century syntax, and so compulsively readable his bleakly funny western noir story." — *Maclean's*

"A triumphantly dark, comic anti-western…A devastating sense of confidence and glittering prose…The writing is superb… Both cinematic and schematic, with a swaggering, poetic feel reminiscent of a Bob Dylan lyric…In *The Sisters Brothers*, a diabolical combination of *Laurel and Hardy* and *Butch Cassidy and the Sundance Kid* (with a touch of Don Quixote and Sancho Panza, just to emphasize the high literary stakes), deWitt has ensured another unforgettable pair their place in fictive lore." — *Telegraph*

"*The Sisters Brothers* is surely gritty, as well as deadpan and often very comic...A narrative voice so sharp and distinctive...[it] opens new doors in the imagination." — *New York Times*

"Marvellous...deWitt has deliberately flouted the rules of straight-laced historical realism here, to stunning effect...Just imagine John Wayne from *The Searchers* declining a rasher of campfire-crisped bacon and opting for boiled carrots if you still need confirmation that we are indeed in uncharted territory... Fresh, hilariously anti-heroic, often genuinely chilling, and relentlessly compelling. Yes, this is a mighty fine read, and deWitt a mighty fine writer." — *National Post*

"Thrilling...A lushly voiced picaresque story...A kind of *True Grit* told by Tom Waits." — *Esquire*

"A bright, brutal revision of the Western, *The Sisters Brothers* offers an unexpected meditation on life, and on the crucial difference between power and strength." — Gil Adamson, author of *The Outlander*

"Combine the casual, brutal violence of Cormac McCarthy with an English comedy of manners — P. G. Wodehouse works — add a dash of *Heart of Darkness*, and you get the gist of what Patrick deWitt has done, to brilliant effect...I doubt very much I'll read a funnier, more original book than this picaresque, Wild West tale... The western has been spoofed perhaps more than any other genre, but never quite in such a masterfully strange and wonderful way as this." — *Toronto Star*

"Sheer brilliance." — *Chatelaine*

"DeWitt's inspired, many-layered yarn is as entertaining and as stylistically accomplished as it is unsettling and most original in its revisiting of what remains a glorious genre." — *Irish Times*

"Original, entrancing, and entertaining." — *Denver Post*

"If Cormac McCarthy had a sense of humour, he might have concocted a story like Patrick deWitt's bloody, darkly funny western *The Sisters Brothers*...Smooth and seamless, shot through with dark humour, pared and antique without being baroque...As easy to slip into as the HBO series *Deadwood*." — *Los Angeles Times*

"*The Sisters Brothers* practically holds a Colt to your head and growls: read me." — *Winnipeg Review*

"Every so often, a novel arrives so worthy of praise that I can't help feeling a bit inadequate to the task...Patrick deWitt's new frontier saga is such a book. I devoured the novel over consecutive enchanted evenings. Violent, funny, and strangely touching, it's destined for a spot on many best-of-2011 lists...With nods to Charles Portis and Cormac McCarthy and the classic cinematic western, this is a quirky, lustful tale that clips along at precisely the sort of pace deWitt so rarely encountered on those long nights on Bainbridge." — *Edmonton Journal*

"Patrick deWitt rides parallel to the trails of Jack Schaefer, James Carlos Blake, and Cormac McCarthy, but he frequently crosses into comic territory to produce a story that's weirdly funny, startlingly violent, and steeped in sadness...Miraculously lovely."
— *Washington Post*

"Bursting with vitality and driven along by a terrific pulpy energy, *The Sisters Brothers* is the kind of book you may well end up wholeheartedly recommending to friends." — *Herald Scotland*

THE SISTERS BROTHERS

THE SISTERS BROTHERS

Patrick deWitt

ANANSI

This edition published in 2013 by
House of Anansi Press Inc.
110 Spadina Avenue, Suite 801
Toronto, ON, M5V 2K4
Tel. 416-363-4343
Fax 416-363-1017
www.houseofanansi.com

Distributed in Canada by
HarperCollins Canada Ltd.
1995 Markham Road
Scarborough, ON, M1B 5M8
Toll free tel. 1-800-387-0117

House of Anansi Press is committed to protecting our natural environment. As part of our efforts, the interior of this book is printed on paper that contains 30% post-consumer recycled fibres, is acid-free, and is processed chlorine-free.

17 16 15 14 13   1 2 3 4 5

Library and Archives Canada Cataloguing in Publication

DeWitt, Patrick, 1975–
The sisters brothers / Patrick deWitt.

Issued also in electronic format.
ISBN: 978-1-77089-335-1

I. Title.

PS8607 E9825 S57 2013   C813'.6   C2012-906451-3

Jacket art and design: Dan Stiles
Text design and typesetting: Suet Yee Chong

Canada Council   Conseil des Arts
for the Arts   du Canada

ONTARIO ARTS COUNCIL
CONSEIL DES ARTS DE L'ONTARIO

We acknowledge for their financial support of our publishing program the Canada Council for the Arts, the Ontario Arts Council, and the Government of Canada through the Canada Book Fund.

Printed and bound in Canada

MIX
Pulp from
responsible sources
FSC® C107923
www.fsc.org

For my mother

OREGON CITY, 1851

one

TROUBLE
WITH THE
HORSES

I was sitting outside the Commodore's mansion, waiting for my brother Charlie to come out with news of the job. It was threatening to snow and I was cold and for want of something to do I studied Charlie's new horse, Nimble. My new horse was called Tub. We did not believe in naming horses but they were given to us as partial payment for the last job with the names intact, so that was that. Our unnamed previous horses had been immolated, so it was not as though we did not need these new ones but I felt we should have been given money to purchase horses of our own choosing, horses without histories and habits and names they expected to be addressed by. I was very fond of my previous horse and lately had been experiencing visions while I slept of his death, his kicking, burning legs, his hot-popping eyeballs. He could cover sixty miles in a day like a gust of wind and I never laid a hand on him except to stroke him or clean him, and I tried not to think of him burning up in that barn but if the vision arrived uninvited how was I to guard against it? Tub was a healthy enough animal but would have been better suited to some other, less ambitious owner. He was portly and low-backed and could not travel more than fifty miles in a day. I was often forced to whip him, which some men do not mind doing and which in fact some enjoy doing, but which I did not like to do; and afterward he, Tub, believed me cruel and thought to himself, Sad life, sad life.

I felt a weight of eyes on me and looked away from Nimble. Charlie was gazing down from the upper-story window, holding up five fingers. I did not respond and he distorted his face to make me smile; when I did not smile his expression fell slack and he moved backward, out of view. He had seen me watching his horse, I knew. The morning before I had suggested we sell Tub and go halves on a new horse and he had agreed this was fair but then later, over lunch, he had said we should put it off until the new job was completed, which did not make sense because the problem with Tub was that he would impede the job, so would it not be best to replace him prior to? Charlie had a slick of food grease in his mustache and he said, 'After the job is best, Eli.' He had no complaints with Nimble, who was as good or better than his previous horse, unnamed, but then he had had first pick of the two while I lay in bed recovering from a leg wound received on the job. I did not like Tub but my brother was satisfied with Nimble. This was the trouble with the horses.

Charlie climbed onto Nimble and we rode away, heading for the Pig-King. It had been only two months since our last visit to Oregon City but I counted five new businesses on the main street and each of these appeared to be doing well. 'An ingenious species,' I said to Charlie, who made no reply. We sat at a table in the back of the King and were brought our usual bottle and a pair of glasses. Charlie poured me a drink, when normally we pour our own, so I was prepared for bad news when he said it: 'I'm to be lead man on this one, Eli.'

'Who says so?'

'Commodore says so.'

I drank my brandy. 'What's it mean?'

'It means I am in charge.'

'What's it mean about money?'

'More for me.'

'My money, I mean. Same as before?'

'It's less for you.'

'I don't see the sense in it.'

'Commodore says there wouldn't have been the problems with the last job if there had been a lead man.'

'It doesn't make sense.'

'Well, it does.'

He poured me another drink and I drank it. As much to myself as to Charlie I said, 'He wants to pay for a lead man, that's fine. But it's bad business to short the man underneath. I got my leg gouged out and my horse burned to death working for him.'

'I got my horse burned to death, too. He got us new horses.'

'It's bad business. Stop pouring for me like I'm an invalid.' I took the bottle away and asked about the specifics of the job. We were to find and kill a prospector in California named Hermann Kermit Warm. Charlie produced a letter from his jacket pocket, this from the Commodore's scout, a dandy named Henry Morris who often went ahead of us to gather information: 'Have studied Warm for many days and can offer the following in respects to his habits and character. He is solitary in nature but spends long hours in the San Francisco saloons, passing time reading his science and mathematics books or making drawings in their margins. He hauls these tomes around with a strap like a schoolboy, for which he is mocked. He is small in stature, which adds to this comedy, but beware he will not be teased about his size. I have seen him fight several times, and though he typically loses, I do not think any of his opponents would wish to fight him again. He is not above biting, for example. He is bald-headed, with a wild red beard, long, gangly arms, and the protruded belly of a pregnant woman. He washes infrequently and sleeps where he can—barns, doorways, or if need be, in the streets. Whenever he is engaged to speak his manner is brusque and uninviting. He carries a baby dragoon, this tucked into a sash slung around his waist. He does not drink often, but when he finally lifts his bottle, he lifts it to become completely drunken. He pays for his whiskey with raw gold dust that he keeps in a leather pouch worn on a long string, this hidden in the folds of his many-layered clothing. He has not once left the town since I have been here and I do not know if he plans to return to his claim, which sits some ten miles east of Sacramento (map enclosed). Yesterday in a saloon he asked me for a match, addressing me politely and by name. I have no idea how he knew this, for he never seemed to notice that I was following him. When I asked how he had come to learn my identity he became abusive, and I left. I do not care for him, though there are some who say his mind is uncommonly strong. I will admit he is unusual, but that is perhaps the closest I could come to complimenting him.'

Next to the map of Warm's claim, Morris had made a smudged drawing of the man; but he might have been standing at my side and I would not have known it, it was so clumsy a rendering. I mentioned this to Charlie and he said, 'Morris is waiting for us at a hotel in San Francisco. He will point Warm out and we will be on our way. It's a good place to kill someone, I have heard. When they are not busily burning the entire town down, they are distracted by its endless rebuilding.'

'Why doesn't Morris kill him?'

'That's always your question, and I always have my answer: It's not his job, but ours.'

'It's mindless. The Commodore shorts me my wage but pays

this bumbler his fee and expenses just to have Warm tipped off that he is under observation.'

'You cannot call Morris a bumbler, brother. This is the first time he has made a mistake, and he admits his error openly. I think his being discovered says more about Warm than Morris.'

'But the man is spending the night in the streets. What is holding Morris back from simply shooting him as he sleeps?'

'How about the fact that Morris is not a killer?'

'Then why send him at all? Why did he not send us a month ago instead?'

'A month ago we were on another job. You forget that the Commodore has many interests and concerns and can get to them but one at a time. Hurried business is bad business, these are words from the man himself. You only have to admire his successes to see the truth in it.'

It made me ill to hear him quote the Commodore so lovingly. I said, 'It will take us weeks to get to California. Why make the trip if we don't have to?'

'But we do have to make the trip. That is the job.'

'And what if Warm's not there?'

'He'll be there.'

'What if he's not?'

'Goddamnit, he will be.'

When it came time to settle I pointed to Charlie. 'The lead man's paying.' Normally we would have gone halves, so he did not like that. My brother has always been miserly, a trait handed down from our father.

'Just the one time,' he said.

'Lead man with his lead man's wages.'

'You never liked the Commodore. And he's never liked you.'

'I like him less and less,' I said.

'You're free to tell him, if it becomes an unbearable burden.'

'You will know it, Charlie, if my burden becomes unbearable. You will know it and so will he.'

This bickering might have continued but I left my brother and retired to my room in the hotel across from the saloon. I do not like to argue and especially not with Charlie, who can be uncommonly cruel with his tongue. Later that night I could hear him exchanging words in the road with a group of men, and I listened to make sure he was not in danger, and he was not—the men asked him his name and he told them and they left him alone. But I would have come to his aid and in fact was putting on my boots when the group scattered. I heard Charlie coming up the stairs and jumped into bed, pretending I was fast asleep. He stuck his head in the room and said my name but I did not answer. He closed the door and moved to his room and I lay in the dark thinking about the difficulties of family, how crazy and crooked the stories of a bloodline can be.

In the morning it was raining—constant, cold drops

that turned the roads to muddy soup. Charlie was stomach-sick
from the brandy, and I visited the chemist's for a nausea rem-
edy. I was given a scentless, robin's-egg-blue powder which I
mixed into his coffee. I did not know the tincture's ingredients,
only that it got him out of bed and onto Nimble, and that it
made him alert to the point of distraction. We stopped to rest
twenty miles from town in a barren section of forest that had
the summer prior been burned through in a lightning fire. We
finished our lunch and were preparing to move on when we saw
a man walking a horse a hundred yards to our south. If he had
been riding I do not think we would have commented but it

was strange, him leading the horse like that. 'Why don't you go see what he is doing,' Charlie said.

'A direct order from the lead man,' I said. He did not respond and I thought, The joke is wearing thin. I decided I would not tell it again. I rode Tub out to meet the walker. When I swung around I noticed he was weeping and I dismounted to face him. I am a tall and heavy and rough-looking man and could read the alarm on his face; to soothe his worries, I said, 'I don't mean you any harm. My brother and I are only having our lunch. I prepared too much and thought to ask if you were hungry.'

The man dried his face with his palm, inhaling deeply and shivering. He attempted to answer me—at least he opened his mouth—but no words or sound emerged, being distraught to the degree that communication was not possible.

I said, 'I can see you're in some distress and probably want to keep traveling on your own. My apologies for disturbing you, and I hope you are heading for something better.' I remounted Tub and was halfway to camp when I saw Charlie stand and level his pistol in my direction. Turning back, I saw the weeping man riding quickly toward me; he did not seem to wish to hurt me and I motioned for Charlie to lower his gun. Now the weeping man and I were riding side by side, and he called over: 'I will take you up on your offer.' When we got to camp, Charlie took hold of the man's horse and said, 'You should not chase someone like that. I thought you were after my brother and nearly took a shot.' The weeping man made a dismissive gesture with his hands indicating the irrelevance of the statement. This took Charlie by surprise—he looked at me and asked, 'Who is this person?'

'He has been upset by something. I offered him a plate of food.'

'There's no food left but biscuits.'

'I will make more then.'

'You will not.' Charlie looked the weeping man up and down. 'Isn't he the mournful one, though?'

Clearing his throat, the weeping man spoke: 'It is ignorant behavior, to talk about a man as though he was not present.'

Charlie was not sure whether to laugh or strike him down. He said to me, 'Is he crazy?'

'I will ask you to watch your words,' I told the stranger. 'My brother isn't feeling well today.'

'I am fine,' said Charlie.

'His charity is strained,' I said.

'He looks sick,' said the weeping man.

'I said I'm fine, damn you.'

'He *is* sick, slightly,' I said. I could see that Charlie's patience had reached its limit. I took some of the biscuits and put them in the hand of the weeping man. He gazed upon them for a long moment, then began to weep all over again, coughing and inhaling and shivering pitifully. I said to Charlie, 'This was how it was when I found him.'

'What's the matter with him?'

'He didn't say.' I asked the weeping man, 'Sir, what's the matter with you?'

'They're gone!' he cried. 'They're all gone!'

'Who's gone?' asked Charlie.

'Gone without me! And I wish I was gone! I want to be gone with them!' He dropped the biscuits and walked away with his horse. He would take ten steps and throw back his head to moan.

He did this three times and my brother and I turned to clean our camp.

'I wonder what was the matter with him,' said Charlie.

'Some kind of grief has made him insane.'

By the time we mounted our horses, the weeping man was out of sight, and the source of his worry would remain forever a mystery.

We rode along in silence, thinking our private thoughts. Charlie and I had an unspoken agreement not to throw ourselves into speedy travel just after a meal. There were many hardships to our type of life and we took these small comforts as they came; I found they added up to something decent enough to carry on.

'What has this Hermann Warm done?' I asked.

'Taken something of the Commodore's.'

'What has he taken?'

'This will be revealed soon enough. To kill him is the thing.' He rode ahead and I rode after. I had been wanting to talk about it for some time, before the last job, even.

'Haven't you ever found it strange, Charlie? All these men

foolish enough to steal from the Commodore? As feared a man as he is?'

'The Commodore has money. What else would attract a thief?'

'How are they getting the money? We know the Commodore to be cautious. How is it that all these different men have access to his wealth?'

'He does business in every corner of the country. A man cannot be in two places at once, much less a hundred. It only stands to reason he'd be victimized.'

'Victimized!' I said.

'What would you call it when a man is forced to protect his fortune with the likes of us?'

'Victimized!' I found it amusing, genuinely. In honor of the poor Commodore, I sang a mawkish ballad: *'His tears behind a veil of flowers, the news came in from town.'*

'Oh, all right.'

'His virgin seen near country bower, in arms of golden down.'

'You are only angry with me for taking the lead position.'

'His heart mistook her smile for kindness, and now he pays the cost.'

'I'm through talking with you about it.'

'His woman lain in sin, her highness, endless love is lost.'

Charlie could not help but smile. 'What is that song?'

'Picked it up somewhere.'

'It's a sad one.'

'All the best songs are sad ones.'

'That's what Mother used to say.'

I paused. 'The sad ones don't actually *make me sad.*'

'You are just like Mother, in many ways.'

'You're not. And you're not like Father, either.'

'I am like no one.'

He said this casually, but it was the type of statement that eclipsed the conversation, killed it. He pulled ahead and I watched his back, and he knew I was watching his back. He stuck Nimble's ribs with his heels and they ran off, with me following behind. We were only traveling in our typical fashion, at our typical pace, but I felt all the same to be chasing him.

Short, late-winter days, and we stopped in a dried ravine to make up camp for the night. You will often see this scenario in serialized adventure novels: Two grisly riders before the fire telling their bawdy stories and singing harrowing songs of death and lace. But I can tell you that after a full day of riding I want nothing more than to lie down and sleep, which is just what I did, without even eating a proper meal. In the morning, pulling on my boots, I felt a sharp pain at the long toe of my left foot. I upended and tapped at the heel of the boot, expecting a nettle to drop, when a large, hairy spider thumped to the ground on its back, eight arms pedaling in the cold air. My pulse was sprinting and I became weak-headed because I am very much afraid of spiders and snakes and crawling things, and Charlie, knowing this, came to my aid, tossing the creature into the fire with his knife. I watched the spider curl up and die, smoking like balled paper, and was happy for its suffering.

Now a shimmering cold was traveling up my shinbone like a frost and I said, 'That was a powerful little animal, brother.' A fever came over me at once and I was forced to lie down. Charlie became worried by my pale coloring; when I found I could no longer speak he stoked up the fire and rode to the nearest town for a doctor, whom he brought to me against or partially against the man's will—I was in a fog but recall his cursing each time Charlie walked out of earshot. I was given a kind of medicine or antivenom, some element of which made me glad and woozy as when drunk, and all I wanted to do was forgive everyone for everything and also to smoke tobacco ceaselessly. I soon dropped off into dead-weighted sleep and remained untouchable all through that day and night and into the next morning. When I awoke, Charlie was still at the fire, and he looked over to me and smiled.

'Can you remember what you were dreaming of just now?' he asked.

'Only that I was being restricted,' I said.

'You kept saying, "I am in the tent! I am in the tent!"'

'I don't remember.'

'"I am in the tent!"'

'Help me stand up.'

He assisted me and in a moment I was circling the camp on wooden-feeling legs. I was slightly nauseated but ate a full meal of bacon and coffee and biscuits and managed to keep this down. I decided I was well enough to travel and we rode easy for four or five hours before settling down again. Charlie asked me repeatedly how I was feeling and I attempted each time to answer, but the truth of it was that I did not exactly know. Whether it was the poison from the spider or the harried doctor's antivenom, I was not entirely in my body. I passed a night of fever and starts and in the morning, when I turned to meet Charlie's good-day greeting, he took a look at me and emitted a shriek of fright. I asked him what was the matter and he brought over a tin plate to use as a looking glass.

'What's that?' I asked.

'That's your head, friend.' He leaned back on his heels and whistled.

The left side of my face was grotesquely swollen, from the crown of my skull all the way to the neck, tapering off at the shoulder. My eye was merely a slit and Charlie, regaining his humor, said I looked like a half dog, and he tossed a stick to see if I would chase it. I traced the source of the swelling to my teeth and gums; when I tapped a finger on the lower left row, a singing pain rang through my body from top to bottom and back again.

'There must be a gallon of blood sloshing around,' said Charlie.

'Where did you find that doctor? We should revisit him and have him lance me.'

Charlie shook his head. 'Best not to search *him* out. There was an unhappy episode regarding his fee. He would be glad to see me again, it's true, but I doubt he would be eager to assist us further. He mentioned another encampment a few miles farther to the south. That might be our wisest bet, if you think you can make it.'

'I don't suppose I have a choice.'

'As with so many things in a life, brother, I don't suppose you do.'

It was slow going, though the terrain was easy enough—a mild downhill grade over firm, forested earth. I was feeling strangely happy, as though involved in a minor amusement, when Tub made a misstep and my mouth clacked shut. I screamed out from the pain, but in the same breath was laughing at the ridiculousness of it. I stuck a wad of tobacco between my uppers and lowers for cushioning. This filled my head with brown saliva but I could not spit, as it proved too painful, so I merely leaned forward and let the liquid leak from my mouth and onto Tub's neck. We passed through a quick flurry of snow; the flakes felt welcome and cool on my face. My head was listing and Charlie circled me to stare and ogle. 'You can see it from behind, even,' he said. 'The scalp itself is swollen. Your *hair* is swollen.' We passed widely around the unpaid doctor's town and located the next encampment some miles later, a nameless place, a quarter mile long and home to a hundred people or less. But luck was with us, and we found a tooth doctor there named Watts smoking a pipe outside his storefront. As I approached the man he smiled and said, 'What a profession to be involved in, that I'm actually happy to see someone so distorted.' He ushered me into his efficient little work space, and toward a cushioned leather chair that squeaked and sighed with newness as I sat. Pulling up a tray of gleaming tools, he asked tooth-history questions I had no satisfactory answers for. At any rate I got the impression he did not care to know the answers but was merely pleased to be making his inquiries.

I shared my theory that this tooth problem was linked to the spider bite, or else the antivenom, but Watts said there was no medical evidence to support it. He told me, 'The body is an actual miracle, and who can dissect a miracle? It may have been the spider, true, and it may have been a reaction to the doctor's so-called antivenom, and it may have been neither one. Really, though, what difference does it make *why* you're unwell? Am I right?'

I said I supposed he was. Charlie said, 'I was telling Eli here, Doc, that I bet there's a gallon of blood sloshing loose in his head.'

Watts unsheathed a polished silver lance. Sitting back, he regarded my head as a monstrous bust. 'Let's find out,' he said.

The story of Reginald Watts was a luckless one dealing in every manner of failure and catastrophe, though he spoke of this without bitterness or regret, and in fact seemed to find humor in his numberless missteps: 'I've failed at straight business, I've failed at criminal enterprise, I've failed at love, I've failed at friendship. You name it, I've failed at it. Go ahead and name something. Anything at all.'

'Agriculture,' I said.

'I owned a sugar beet farm a hundred miles northeast of here. Never made a penny. Hardly saw one sugar beet. A devastating failure. Name something else.'

'Shipping.'

'I bought a share in a paddle-wheel steamboat running goods

up and down the Mississippi at an obscene markup. Highly profitable enterprise until I came along. Second trip she made with my money in her, sank to the bottom of the river. She was uninsured, which was my bright idea to save us a few dollars on overhead. Also I had encouraged a name change, from *The Periwinkle*, which I thought bespoke frivolity, to the *Queen Bee*. An unmitigated failure. My fellow investors, if I'm not mistaken, were going to lynch me. I pinned a suicide note to my front door and left town in one hell of a shameful hurry. Left a good woman behind, too. Still think of her, these many years later.' The doctor took a moment and shook his head. 'Name something else. No, don't. I'm tired of talking about it.'

'That's two of us,' said Charlie. He was sitting in the corner reading a newspaper.

I said, 'Looks like you're making a go of it here, Doc.'

'Hardly,' he said. 'You're my third customer in three weeks. It would appear that oral hygiene is low on the list of priorities in this part of the world. No, I expect I'll fail in dentistry, also. Give it another two months on the outside and the bank'll shut me down.' He held a long, dripping needle next to my face. 'This is going to pinch, son.'

'Ouch!' I said.

'Where did you study dentistry?' Charlie asked.

'A most reputable institution,' he answered. But there was a smirk on his lips I did not care for.

'I understand the course of study takes several years,' I said.

'Years?' said Watts, and he laughed.

'How long then?'

'Me personally? Just as long as it took to memorize the nerve chart. As long as it took those fools to ship me the tools on credit.' I looked over to Charlie, who shrugged and returned to his reading. I reached up to check the swelling of my cheek and was startled to find I had no feeling in my face.

Watts said, 'Isn't that something? I could pull every tooth you've got and you wouldn't feel the slightest pain.'

Charlie's eyes peered over the paper. 'You really can't feel anything?' I shook my head and he asked Watts, 'How do you get ahold of that?'

'Can't, unless you're in the profession.'

'Might prove handy, in our line of work. What would you say to selling us some?'

'They don't hand it over by the barrel,' Watts said.

'We'd give you a fair price.'

'I'm afraid the answer is no.'

Charlie looked at me blankly; his face disappeared behind the paper.

Watts lanced my face in three different places and the colorful fluids came trickling out. There was some remaining in the head but he said it would go down of its own accord, and that the worst of it was passed. He extracted the two offending teeth and I laughed at the painless violence of it. Charlie became uneasy and retired to the saloon across the road. 'Coward,' called Watts. He stitched the hole closed and filled my mouth with cotton, afterward leading me to a marble basin where he showed me a dainty, wooden-handled brush with a rectangular head of gray-white bristles. 'A toothbrush,' he said. 'This will keep your teeth clean and your breath pleasant. Here, watch how I do it.' The doctor demonstrated the proper use of the tool, then blew mint-smelling air on my face. Now he handed me a new brush, identical to his own, and also a packet of the tooth powder that produced the minty foam, telling me they were mine to keep. I protested this but he admitted he had been sent a complimentary box from the manufacturer. I paid him two dollars for the removal of the teeth and he brought out a bottle of whiskey to toast what he called our mutually beneficial transaction. Altogether I found the man quite charming, and I was remorseful when Charlie reentered the office with his pistol drawn, leveling it at the good doctor. 'I tried to bargain with you,' he said, his face flushed with brandy.

'I wonder what I will fail at next,' Watts said forlornly.

'I don't know, and I don't care. Eli, gather the numbing medicine and needles. Watts, find me a piece of rope, and quickly. If you get shifty on me I will put a hole in your brain.'

'At times I feel one is already there.' To me he said, 'The pursuit of money and comfort has made me weary. Take care of your teeth, son. Keep a healthy mouth. Your words will only sound that much sweeter, isn't that right?'

Charlie cuffed Watts on the ear, thus bringing his speech to a close.

We rode through the afternoon and into the evening, when I became dizzy to the point I thought I might fall from the saddle. I asked Charlie if we could stop for the night and he agreed to this, but only if we should find a sheltered place to camp, as it was threatening to rain. He smelled a fire on the air and we traced it to a one-room shack, wispy cotton-smoke spinning from its chimney, a low light dancing in the lone window. An old woman wrapped in quilting and rags answered the door. She had long gray hairs quivering from her chin and her half-opened mouth was filled with jagged, blackened teeth. Charlie, crushing his hat in his hand, spoke of our recent hardships in a stage actor's dramatic timbre. The woman's oyster-flesh eyes fell on me and I grew instantly colder. She walked away from the door without a word. I heard the scrape of a chair on the floor. Charlie turned to me and asked, 'What do you think?'

'Let's keep on.'

'She's left the door open for us.'

'There is something not right with her.'

He kicked at a patch of snow. 'She knows how to build a fire. What more do you want? We're not looking to settle down.'

'I think we should keep on,' I repeated.

'Door!' cried the woman.

'A couple of hours in a warm room would suit me fine,' said Charlie.

'I am the sick one,' I said. 'And I am willing to move on.'

'I am for staying.'

The shadow of the woman crept along the far interior wall and she stood at the entrance once more. 'Door!' she shrieked. 'Door! Door!'

'You can see she wants us to enter,' said Charlie.

Yes, I thought, past her lips and into her stomach. But I was too weak to fight any longer, and when my brother took me by the arm to enter the cabin I did not resist him.

In the room was a table, a chair, and an unclean mattress. Charlie and I sat before the stone fireplace on the twisted wooden floorboards. The heat stung pleasantly at my face and hands and for a moment I was happy with my new surroundings. The woman sat at the table speaking not a word, her face obscured in the folds of her rags. Before her lay a mound of dull red and black beads or stones; her hands emerged from her layers and nimbly took these up one by one, stringing them onto a piece of thin wire to fashion a long necklace or some other manner of elaborate jewelry. There was a lamp on the table, lowly lit and flickering yellow and orange, a tail of black smoke slipping from the tip of the flame.

'We are obliged to you, ma'am,' said Charlie. 'My brother is feeling poorly, and in no condition to be sleeping out of doors.' When the woman did not respond, Charlie said to me he supposed she was deaf. 'I am *not* deaf,' she countered. She brought a piece of the wire to her mouth and chewed it back and forth to snap it.

'Of course,' said Charlie. 'I didn't mean any offense to you. Now I can see how able you are, how sharp. And you keep a fine home, if you don't mind my saying.'

She laid her beads and wire on the table. Her head swiveled to face us but her features remained hidden in slipping shadows. 'Do you think I don't know what type of men you are?' she asked, pointing a broken-looking finger at our gun belts. 'Who are you pretending to be, and why?'

Charlie's demeanor changed, or resumed, and he was once more himself. 'All right,' he said, 'who are we then?'

'Would you not call yourselves killers?'

'Just because of our guns, and you assume it?'

'I assume nothing. I know by the dead men following behind you.'

The hair on my neck stood up. It was ridiculous, but I dared not turn around. Charlie's tone was even: 'Do you fear we will kill you?'

'I fear nothing, least of all your bullets and talk.' She looked at me and asked, 'Do you fear I will kill *you*?'

'I am very tired,' came my lame reply.

'Take the bed,' she instructed.

'Where will you sleep?'

'I will not. I must finish my work. In the morning, I will be mostly gone.'

Charlie's face had grown hard. 'This isn't your cabin, is it?'

At this she stiffened, and did not look to be breathing. She pulled back her rags, and in the firelight and lamplight I saw she had almost no hair on her head, only white tufts here and there, and her skull was dented, appearing soft in places, pushed in like an old piece of fruit. 'Every heart has a tone,' she said to Charlie, 'just as every bell has one. Your heart's tone is most oppressive to hear, young man. It is hurtful to my ears, and your eyes hurt my eyes to look at them.'

A long silence followed with Charlie and the old witch simply staring at each other. I could not, from either of their expressions, understand what they were thinking. Eventually the woman rewrapped her skull and resumed her work, and Charlie lay down on the floor. I did not climb onto the bed, but lay down beside him, because I was frightened by the woman and thought it safest for us to sleep close together. I was so weak that despite my uneasiness I soon fell away into a dream state wherein I envisaged the room just as it was, though I was standing by, watching my own sleeping body. The old woman rose and came upon us; my body began to fidget and sweat but Charlie's was calm and still and the old woman leaned over him, opening his mouth with her hands. From the dark space in her folds there flowed a slow and heavy black liquid; this dropped into his mouth and I, not the sleeping I but the watching I, began to scream that she should leave him alone. With this the dream abruptly ended and I came to. Charlie was beside me, looking at me, eyes open though he was sleeping, as was his unnerving habit. Behind him sat the old woman, her bead pile significantly smaller—a good deal of time had passed. She remained at her table but her head was turned all the way around, looking in the far dark corner. I do not know what had caught her attention but she stared for such a time that I gave up wondering and returned my head to the floor. In a jump I was dead asleep once more.

In the morning I awoke on the floor, and Charlie was not beside me. I heard a footfall at my back and turned to find him standing before the open doorway, looking out at the field before the cabin. It was a bright day and the horses stood in the distance, tied to the root of an upended snag. Nimble nosed about in the frost for a mouthful of grass; Tub shivered and stared at nothing. 'The woman has left,' Charlie said.

'That is all right by me,' I replied, standing. The room stunk of ash and charcoal and my eyes were raw and burning. I had to make water and moved to exit the cabin but Charlie blocked my way, his face gaunt and unrested. 'She has left,' he said, 'but has kept us with something as a remembrance.' He pointed and I followed the line of his finger. The woman had hung the string of beads around the jamb of the door. *I will be mostly gone,* I recalled her saying—mostly but not completely.

'What do you make of it?' I asked.

Charlie said, 'It's no decoration.'

'We could take it down,' I said, reaching.

He caught my hand. 'Don't touch it, Eli.'

We stood back to consider the options. The horses heard our voices and were watching us from the field. 'We won't walk beneath it,' said Charlie. 'The only thing is to knock out the window and climb through.' Feeling my middle section, which is and always has been bountiful, I said I did not think I would fit in the small opening. Charlie mentioned it was worth a try but the idea of failing—of climbing back away from the hole red-faced—was not something I was eager to experience, and I said I would not attempt it.

'Then I will go alone,' said Charlie, 'and return to you with some tools to cut a larger piece away.' Standing on the old woman's wobbly chair, he knocked out the glass with the handle of his revolver and I boosted him up and out the window. Now we faced each other on opposite sides of the door. He was smiling, and I was not. 'There you are,' he said, patting the glass shards from his belly.

I said, 'I don't like this plan. Striking out into the wild with hopes of finding a gentle soul eager to loan out his tools. You will ride aimlessly while I stew in this hovel. What if the old woman returns?'

'She has left us her evil tidings, and there is no reason for her to come back.'

'That's easy for you to say.'

'I believe it to be true. And what else can I do? If you have another plan, now is the time to share it.'

But no, I did not have one. I asked him to bring me my food bag and I watched him walk out to the horses. 'Don't forget a pan,' I called. 'What man?' he asked. 'A pan! A pan!' I mimed a cooking-with-a-pan motion, and he nodded. He returned and pushed my effects through the window, wishing me a happy breakfast before mounting Nimble and riding away. I experienced a miserable feeling at their leaving; staring at the opening in the tree line where they had disappeared, I felt a premonitory concern they would never revisit it.

I gathered up my reserves of cheer and decided to make a temporary home of the cabin. There was no chopped wood or kindling available but the ashes and coals were still glowing hot so I demolished the old woman's chair by swinging it widely and crashing it over the floor. I stacked its legs, seat, and back into the fireplace in an upside down V shape, pouring some of the lamp's oil over top of the pile. A moment passed and the chair ignited all at once. I was heartened by its light and fragrance. It was made of hard oak and would burn well. 'Little victories,' my mother used to say, and which I then said aloud, to myself.

I spent some minutes standing in the doorway, looking out at the world. There was not a cloud in sight and it was one of those purple-blue days where the sky appears taller and deeper than usual. Melted snow-water came draining off the roof in rivulets and I held my tin cup out the window to fill it. The tin turned frigid in my hand and small islands of translucent ice floated on the water's surface, stinging my lip as I drank. It was a relief to wash away my mouth's ghastly coffin-taste of stale blood leftover from the day before. I warmed the cold liquid over my tongue, pushing it back and forth in hopes of cleansing my wound. I became alarmed when I felt something solid come loose, knocking around in my water-filled skull. Thinking the object a flap of skin, I spit it out onto the floor. It landed with a sickening slap, and I crouched down close to inspect it. It was cylindrical and black, which brought my heart to a trot: Had Doctor Watts slid a leech into my mouth without my knowing it? But when I nudged the thing with my thumb it unraveled, and I recalled the cotton he had tucked beside my gums. I flung it into the fire and it slithered down a flaming chair leg, bubbling and smoking and leaving a trail of blood and saliva.

Staring out at the steam rising in the field, I felt a gladness at having survived the recent series of happenings: The spider, the bloated head, the curse averted. I filled my lungs with all the cold air they could hold. 'Tub!' I shouted into the wilderness. 'I am stuck inside the cabin of the vile gypsy-witch!' He raised his head, his jaw working on a mouthful of crunchy grass. 'Tub! Assist me in my time of need!'

I made myself a modest breakfast of bacon, grits, and coffee. A piece of gristle lodged itself into my tooth-hole and I had no small amount of trouble removing it, thus irritating the wound and causing bleeding. I thought of the toothbrush then, which I retrieved from my vest pocket along with the powder, laying these neatly on the table beside the tin cup. Watts had not said whether I should wait for my mouth to heal entirely before using the tool but I thought to go ahead, albeit cautiously. I dampened the bristles and tapped out a thimbleful of the powder. 'Up, down, side to side,' I said, for these were the words the doctor had spoken. My mouth was filled with the mint-smelling foam and I scrubbed my tongue raw. Pulling myself up to the window, I spit the bloody water into the dirt and snow. My breath was cool and fine-smelling and I was greatly impressed with the tingling feeling this toothbrush gave me. I decided I would use it every day, and was tapping the tool on the bridge of my nose, thinking of nothing, or of several vague things simultaneously, when I saw the bear lumber out of the woods, toward Tub.

It was a grizzly. He was large but rangy and had likely just awoken from hibernation. Tub saw him or smelled him and began bucking and jumping but could not loose himself from the tree root. Standing shy of the doorway, I raised my pistol, firing six quick shots, but these were taken in a panic and none of them hit their mark. The bear was unimpressed with the gun's report and continued on; by the time I took up my second pistol he was standing over Tub. I fired twice but missed and he lunged, knocking Tub to the ground with a heavy blow to the eye. Now he was standing on the far side of Tub and I could not get a clean shot without putting the horse in danger, and so with no other option but to watch my animal slaughtered, I crossed the cursed threshold, running into the fray and screaming just as loud as I was able. The grizzly took notice of my approach and became confused—should he continue the killing of the horse, already under way, or should he address this noisy new two-legged animal? While he pondered this I put two bullets in his face and two in his chest and he fell dead on the ground. Whether Tub was alive or not, I could not tell. He did not appear to be breathing. I turned back to face the black mouth of the cabin. A trembling grew in my hands and in the flesh of my legs. I was ringing all over.

I returned to the cabin. Cursed or not I did not see the
point of letting Charlie in on the news. I took stock of my health
but could not pinpoint any particular feeling besides the ringing,
which I decided was nerves, and which at any rate was abating.
Tub was still not moving and I was certain he was dead when a
nuthatch lit upon his nose and he leapt up, shaking his head and
panting. I walked away from the door and lay on the bed. It was
damp and lumpy and smelled of sod. I cut away a hole to look
inside and saw it was full of grass and earth. Some kind of witch
preference, perhaps. I moved to sleep on the floor before the fire.
I woke up an hour later. My brother was shouting my name and
attacking the window frame with an ax.

I crawled out the hole and we walked over and sat on the ground next to the dead bear. Charlie said, 'I saw this gentleman lying here and called your name, but you didn't answer. Then I looked in the doorway and saw you on your back on the floor. That is an unpleasant feeling, wanting to cross into a house but not being able to.' He asked me what had happened and I said, 'There's not a lot to it. The bear came out of the woods and knocked Tub to the ground. I took careful aim and killed him dead.'

'How many shots did you fire?'

'I emptied both pistols and hit him two with one and two the other.'

Charlie examined the bear's wounds. 'You fired from the window or the door?'

'Why are you asking all these questions?'

'No reason.' He shrugged. 'That's some nice shooting, brother.'

'Lucky, is all.' Hoping to change the subject, I asked about the ax.

'Prospectors heading south,' he said. There was a divot of skin gone from one of his knuckles and I asked how he came to be injured. 'The men were hesitant to loan me their equipment. Well, they'll not need the ax, now.' He returned to the cabin, entering through his hole. I did not know what he was doing at first, but soon saw the smoke issuing from inside. Next, my bag and pan jumped out the window, with Charlie following closely behind and wearing a wide smile. As we rode away the structure was a whirling tornado of whistling heat and flames and the bear, which Charlie had coated in lamp oil, was likewise burning—an impressive sight, but sad, and I was grateful to take leave of the place. It occurred to me that I had crossed the threshold for a horse I did not want but Charlie had not done the same for his own flesh and blood. A life of ups and downs, I thought.

Tub's eye was red and swollen and dead-looking, and he was acting strangely, turning right when I pulled left, stopping and starting of his own accord, and walking sideways. I said to Charlie, 'I think there's been some damage done to Tub's brain by that grizzly's paw.'

Charlie said, 'He is probably only dazed temporarily.' Tub walked headfirst into a tree and began loudly to urinate. 'You're too kind with him. Stab him in the ribs with your heels. This will give him all the focus you could want.'

'The last horse didn't need such prodding.'

Charlie shook his head. 'Let's not talk about that again, thank you.'

'The last horse was smarter than many grown men I've known.'

Charlie shook his head; he would not speak of it anymore. We came to the camp of the dead prospectors, or to-be prospectors, or never-to-be prospectors. I counted five bodies facedown on the ground, and none of them was lying next to another. Charlie told me the story while emptying their pockets and bags of valuables: 'This fat fellow here, he was the tough one. I tried to reason with him but he wanted to make a show for his friends. I shot him in the mouth and everyone ran. That's why they're all scattered and back wounded, see?' He squatted before a slight body. 'This one here can't be more than sixteen, I'd say. Well, he should have known better than to travel with such hotheads.'

I said nothing. Charlie looked at me for a reaction and I shrugged.

'What's that mean?' he said. 'You had a hand in this, let's not forget.'

'I don't see how you can say that. I did not want to stay the night in that old woman's cabin, remember.'

'But it was your illness that made such a stop necessary.'

'A spider crawled into my boot, there is the cause of my illness.'

'You're saying you wish to blame the spider?'

'I don't wish to blame anyone. You're the one who brought it up.'

Speaking to the assembled dead, Charlie said, 'My good men, it is a spider to blame for the early demise of your group. A woolly, fat-bottomed spider in search of warmth—here is the cause of your deaths.'

I said, 'All I am telling you, brother, is that it's a shame they had to go. And it *is* a shame. And that's all.' I rolled the boy over with my boot. His mouth was slack and a pair of hugely bucked upper teeth pushed past his lips.

'There's a handsome lad,' Charlie offered drolly. But he was feeling remorseful, I could see it. He spit on the ground and tossed a handful of dirt over his shoulder. 'All these people searching out their fortunes in California would do better to stay where they are and work their own land.'

'I understand it. They are looking for adventure.'

'These men found theirs.' He resumed rifling their pockets. 'This one has a fine watch and fob. Do you want it? Here, feel how heavy it is.'

'Leave the man his watch,' I said.

'I would feel better about this if you took something.'

'And I'd feel worse. Leave the watch, or take it for yourself, but I won't have it.'

He had also killed their horses. These lay in a group at the bottom of a gully past the camp. Normally this would not have bothered me but two of them were fine animals, greatly superior to Tub; I pointed this out to Charlie and he became bitter and told me, 'Yes, and their marks are here for anyone to see. Would you be so stupid as to ride a murdered man's horse into California, where his arrival is expected?'

'No one is expecting these men. And you know as well as I do there's no better place in the world to hide than California.'

'I'm done talking about your horse, Eli.'

'If you think it will not come up again, you are mistaken.'

'Then I'm done talking about your horse *today*. Now, let us divide the money.'

'This is your killing. You keep it.'

'I killed these men to free you from the cursed shack,' he complained. But I would not accept the coins and he said, 'Don't think I'm going to force it on you. I am overdue for some new clothes anyway. Do you think your mangled, brainless horse can make it to the next town without hurtling itself off a cliff? What's that? You're not smiling, are you? We're in a quarrel and you mustn't under any circumstances smile.' I was not smiling, but then began to, slightly. 'No,' said Charlie, 'you mustn't smile when quarreling. It's wrong, and I dare say you know it's wrong. You must stew and hate and revisit all the slights I offered you in childhood.'

We mounted to leave the camp. I kicked Tub in his ribs and he lay down flat on the ground.

It was after dark by the time we came to the next town, and the trading post did not look to be open for business. But the door was unlocked and the chimney was smoking, and we knocked and entered. The room was warm and still, the smell of new goods strong in my nostrils—pants and shirts and un-dershirts and stockings and hats filled the shelves in neat piles. Charlie knocked his boot heel on the floor and a spry old man in a sagging undershirt emerged from behind a heavy black-velvet curtain. He did not return our greeting but moved silently from place to place, lighting the lamps on the counter with a thin stick of pine, its end glowing and bobbing in his hand. Soon the room was bright in the golden glow, and the old man laid his hands on the countertop, blinking and smiling inquisitively.

'I am looking for some new clothes,' said Charlie.

'Top to bottom?' said the old man.

'I am thinking of a new shirt, foremostly.'

'Your hat is tattered.'

'What do you have in the way of shirts?' asked Charlie.

The old man studied Charlie's torso, reading his measurements with a trained eye, then turned and scurried up a ladder just behind him, pulling from the shelves a short stack of folded shirts. He descended and laid the stack before Charlie; as my brother sorted through these, the old man asked me, 'And you, sir?'

'I am not looking for anything this evening.'

'Your hat is tattered, also.'

'I like my hat.'

'You seem to have known each other a long while, judging by the sweat rings.'

My face darkened and I said, 'It is impolite to speak of other people's clothing like that.'

The man's eyes were black and slick and he reminded me of a mole or some other type of burrowing animal: Quick and sure and single-minded. He said, 'I did not intend to be impolite. I blame my line of work. Whenever I see a man in compromised attire I am drawn to him in sympathy.' His eyes grew wide and innocent but while he spoke his hands, working independently, laid three new hats out on the counter.

'Did you not hear me when I said I wanted nothing?' I asked.

'What will putting one on hurt you?' he wondered, propping up a looking glass. 'You're just passing time while your friend here tries out shirts.' The hats were black, chocolate, and dark blue. I laid mine next to them and had to admit it was in poor shape by comparison. I said I might try one on and the old man called out sharply, 'Rag!' Now a pregnant and markedly ugly young girl emerged from behind the curtain with a steaming cloth in her hand. She flung this at me and returned without a word from whence she came. I stood handling the hot rag, tossing it back and forth to cool it, and the old man offered his explanation: 'If you wouldn't mind wiping down your hands and brow, sir. We can't have the merchandise sullied by every fellow who enters the room.' I set about cleaning myself while he turned his attention to Charlie, busily buttoning up a black cotton shirt with pearl snap buttons. 'Now, *that* is a beautiful fit,' the old man said. Charlie stood before a long looking glass, moving this way and that to view the shirt from each angle. He turned to me and pointed at the garment, his eyebrows slightly raised.

'It is a handsome one,' I said.

'I'll take it,' Charlie said.

'And what do you think of your friend in this?' the old man asked as he put the chocolate hat atop my head. Charlie considered my profile, then asked to see what the black one looked like. When the old man swapped them out, Charlie nodded. 'If you were after a hat, you could stop right there. It's not going to get much better than that. And I think I might like to see the blue one, while they're out.'

'Rag!' said the old man, and again the pregnant girl emerged to hurl a steaming cloth over the counter, and again she returned, saying nothing. Wiping his forehead, Charlie smiled. 'That your woman, old man?'

'She is,' he said proudly.

'That your child in her belly?'

His face puckered to a scowl. 'You doubt the quality of my seed?'

'I had no plans to discuss your seed.'

'It is impertinent.'

Charlie raised his hands to make peace. 'I am impressed with you, is all. I meant you no offense, and wish the both of you a long and happy life together.' In this way the matter was settled, and whatever hard feelings that remained were put to rest by our purchases: I bought the hat and also a shirt, and Charlie, in a frenzy of commerce, was outfitted from head to toe. The old man went to bed forty dollars richer, and was glad to have risen from his slumber and seen to our needs. As we rode away in all our finery I said to Charlie, 'That is a tidy business.'

'It is tidier than killing,' he agreed.

'I believe I could settle into a life like that. I sometimes think about slowing down. Didn't it seem pleasant in there? Lighting the lamps? The smell of all the brand-new goods?'

Charlie shook his head. 'I would go out of my mind with boredom. That mute girl would come rushing out of her hole for the hundredth time and I'd shoot her dead. Or I would shoot myself.'

'It struck me as restful industry. I'll wager that old man sleeps very well at night.'

'Do you not sleep well at night?' Charlie asked earnestly.

'I do not,' I said. 'And neither do you.'

'I sleep like a stone,' he protested.

'You whimper and moan.'

'Ho ho!'

'It's the truth, Charlie.'

'Ho,' he said, sniffing. He paused to study my words. He wished to check if they were sincere, I knew, but could not think of a way to ask without sounding overly concerned. The joy went out of him then, and his eyes for a time could not meet mine. I thought, We can all of us be hurt, and no one is exclusively safe from worry and sadness.

We set up in a drafty, lopsided hotel at the southern-most end of town. There was but a single vacancy and Charlie and I were forced to share a room, when we typically kept individual quarters. Sitting before the washbasin I laid out my toothbrush and powder and Charlie, who had not seen these before, asked me what I was doing. I explained and demonstrated the proper use of the tool and afterward smacked my jaws and breathed in deeply. 'It is highly refreshing to the mouth,' I told him.

Charlie considered this. 'I don't like it,' he said. 'I think it's foolish.'

'Think what you like. Our Dr. Watts says my teeth will never rot if I use the brush dependably.'

Charlie remained skeptical. He told me I looked like a rabid beast with my mouth full of foam. I countered that I would prefer to look like one for minutes each day rather than smell like one all through my life, and this marked the end of our toothbrush conversation. My talk of Watts reminded him of the stolen numbing medicine, and he retrieved the bottle and needle from his saddlebags. He wanted to try it on himself, he said, and I watched him inject a goodly amount into his cheek. Once the medicine settled in he began to pinch and wrench his face. 'I will be goddamned,' he said. He beckoned me to slap him, which I did, lightly.

'I feel nothing,' he said.

'Your face is hanging like a griddle cake.'

'Slap me again, but harder,' he instructed, and I did this. 'Remarkable,' he said. 'Slap me again, one last time, only do it hard as you please.'

I pulled my arm back and slapped him with such force that it stung my hand. 'You felt that one. Your hair jumped. I could see the pain in your eyes.'

'A recoil from the blow, but no pain,' he said in wonderment. 'A smart man could make use of this.'

'Perhaps you could go from one town to the next, inviting frustrated citizens to clobber your head for a fee.'

'I'm being serious. We have in this bottle something which makes the impossible, possible. There is a profit in there somewhere.'

'We will see how you feel about the miracle solution when the effects wear off.'

His mouth was slack and a stringy length of spittle ran down his chin. 'Makes me drool,' he said, sucking this up. Shrugging, he put the bottle and needle away and said he wished to cross the street to the saloon. He invited me along, and though I did not much want to watch him grow hoggish with brandy I likewise did not wish to spend my time in the hotel room by myself, with its warped wallpaper, its drafts and dust and scent of previous boarders. The creak of bed springs suffering under the weight of a restless man is as lonely a sound as I know.

I awoke at dawn with a nagging pain in my head, not so much brandy-sickness as general fatigue, though the drinking had not helped the situation. I dunked my face in the water basin and brushed my teeth, standing beside an open window to feel the breeze against my skull. It was cool out but the air was enveloped in warmth; here was the first taste of spring, which brought me a satisfaction, a sense of rightness and organization. I crossed the room to check on Charlie's progress against the day, which I found to be poorer than my own.

'I was feeling shaky myself,' I told him, 'though I am better all the while. I believe there is some healing element to that tooth powder.'

'Call me a bath,' he croaked, hidden in quilts and sheets. 'Tell the woman I want it scorching.'

'A bath cost twenty-five cents,' I said. I knew this because I had seen the sign in the lobby; I mentioned it because back home a bath cost a nickel. But Charlie was not concerned with the price: 'If it costs twenty-five dollars, I don't care. It will save my life, if it's possible to save my life. I want the water hot enough to cook a bird. And I will ask you to fetch me medicine from the chemist's.'

I said, 'I wonder what the Commodore would think of a lead man so frequently sick from alcohol.'

'No more talking,' he pleaded. 'Go and find the woman. Scorching, tell her.'

'I will be back after the chemist's.'

'Hurry, please.'

I found the woman downstairs in the lobby, sitting behind her counter, mending a pillowcase with a long needle and thread. I had noticed her only perfunctorily when we checked in, but now I could see she was somewhat pretty, young and pale and plump and firm. Her hair was sweat-pasted to her forehead and her arm worked speedily, extending to its limit as she pulled the needle back. I knocked on the countertop and her eyes landed upon me with undisguised annoyance.

'My brother is brandy-sick and in need of a scorching hot bath.'

'Thirty cents,' she said monotonously. I looked at the sign above her, which still read twenty-five cents, but before I could speak she told me, 'It was twenty-five yesterday. It is thirty, now. Someday soon it will be thirty-five.'

'A boom time for the painters of signs,' I said. But the woman only continued her sewing. Pushing on, then: 'I had better pay immediately, before the prices get away from me.' Not so much as a smile from the overworked hotel maiden. To irritate her further I paid with a twenty-dollar piece. She regarded the heavy coin for several long seconds before sweeping it into her filthy smock pocket and fishing out the change. She made no effort to camouflage her dislike of me and I thought it prudent to warn her, 'My brother is not so patient as I am, ma'am, and he is in poor spirits this morning. He asks for a scorching hot bath and he had better get one. He is not one you will wish to upset, and you can take my word for it.'

'It will be scorching,' she said. Tucking the pillow under her arm, she turned to fulfill her duties. As she ducked behind the beaded curtain separating the lobby from the kitchen and boilers, I noticed a sliver of her dress was stuck between her buttocks. She removed this with a single dainty tug—a thoughtless, automatic action on her part, but I felt a great fortune to have witnessed it and began whistling a wild, snappy tune.

I left the hotel, searching distractedly for a chemist's or a doctor's, but found myself focusing mainly on the subject of women, and love. I had never been with a woman for longer than a night, and they had always been whores. And while throughout each of these speedy encounters I tried to maintain a friendliness with the women, I knew in my heart it was false, and afterward always felt remote and caved in. I had in the last year or so given up whores entirely, thinking it best to go without rather than pantomime human closeness; and though it was unrealistic for a man in my position to be thinking such thoughts, I could not help myself: I saw my bulky person in the windows of the passing storefronts and wondered, When will that man there find himself to be loved?

I located the chemist's and purchased a small bottle of morphine. Returning to the hotel, I met with the woman clomping down the stairs. She held a tin tub under her arm and her side was damp with bathwater. She paused a moment; I thought she wished to greet me and I took off my hat, offering my version of a smile. But now I saw she was breathing heavily and harboring some bitterness or unhappy feelings. When I asked her what was the matter she declared, and loudly, that my brother was a heathen, and that the hottest waters of hell would not cleanse him. I asked what he had done but she did not answer, she only pushed past me into the lobby. I heard the sound of her beaded curtains, and the crash of the tub hitting a wall. Now I stood awhile on the stairs, listening to the hotel sounds floating all around, the invisible footsteps and creakings, doors opening and closing, muffled laughter and talking, a baby crying. I noticed an unlit candle on the stairwell wall before me. I lit it, then blew out the match, propping this against the candle. Looking to the top of the stairs, I saw that my and Charlie's door was ajar; as I approached I was surprised to find him speaking, and speaking to me, though for all he knew I was not there. He was speaking aloud in the bathtub, a habit he had picked up in childhood. I snuck to the door and listened:

'But I *am* the lead man. Yes. Well, I am. You? You cannot lead your horse without assistance. Also you are sickly. Yes, you are. You invite sickness and worry. If you were not a blood relative I would have kept you back a long time ago. In fact the Commodore asked me to do just this, but I said no. He admired my faithfulness. It seems I cannot lose with him. "Faith will be repaid with faith," he said. He has faith in me. Yes, he does, brother. There you go, laugh. You laugh at everything. But I ask you this question, and it is a serious one. Who do you know that has faith in you?'

He paused to dunk and scrub his body. I knocked upon the door as I opened it, stamping my feet ridiculously and clearing my throat. 'Charlie,' I called out. 'I have your medicine with me.' I puffed myself up to make my voice sound natural but my tone reflected the hurt I had suffered by the unkind words of my brother. When I entered the bathroom he was leaning halfway out of the tub, his body bright red from the waist down as though he were wearing pants. He was retching into a spittoon and I watched his sides spasming as he pushed out his poison bile. Holding up a finger and gasping, he said, 'Don't go anywhere.' He continued his retching and I pulled up a chair to sit beside him. My knees were shaking and I wished, impossibly, I had never heard his speech. Finally I decided I could not stay in the room with him. I stood and laid the morphine on the chair, pointing to the door as though some pressing task awaited me on the other side. He did not notice my leaving, I do not think, preoccupied as he was with his vomiting and unwellness.

I had nowhere to go, and did not wish to be seen by anyone for fear they would recognize my sadness, and so for several minutes I simply stood in the hall, shifting my weight and breathing and attempting to clear my mind of every recognizable thought. I noticed the candle I had lit was once again out. I assumed a draft had snuffed the flame but on closer inspection I saw my match was gone; I repeated my previous action of lighting the wick and propping the spent match against the candle in its black metal holder. I had the sensation of conversing, with whom I did not know, likely the hotel woman. Might I leave her a secret note? But I had no paper or ink and at any rate what would I say to her? *Dear Miss, I wish you would wash your face and be nice to me. I have money. Do you want it? I never know what to do with it.*

I sat on the stairs for twenty more minutes before returning to the room. Charlie was sitting on his bed, wearing his new shirt but no pants. He held one of his new boots in his hands, patting and admiring it. He had drunk a third of the morphine and its powers had taken hold; his eyes were sagging at their edges and he looked pleased as a pig on holiday.

'Headache's gone, brother?'

'No, she's still there, but the medicine makes it so I don't mind her.' Flipping the boot to study its interior he said solemnly, 'The skill and patience involved with the making of this boot humbles me.'

I felt repulsed by Charlie then. 'You make for a pretty picture.'

His lids were rising and falling like a pair of blinds being lifted and dropped. He shrugged and said, 'Some days we are stronger . . . than others.'

'When do you want to get moving?'

Now he spoke with his eyes closed: 'I cannot travel in this state. Another day in town won't matter. The woman mentioned a duel in the morning. We will leave just after that.'

'Whatever you say.'

He opened his eyes to slits. 'What's the matter with you? You're acting differently.'

'I feel the same as before.'

'You were listening to me in the bathtub, weren't you?' I did not reply and his eyes fully opened: 'I thought I heard you out there. Here is the fate of the sneak and the eavesdropper.' Suddenly he doubled over, and a thin column of yellow bile poured from his mouth and onto the floor. His face was dripping when he raised it, his wet lips arched in a devilish smile. 'I *almost* vomited in the boot! I was *just about* to vomit in the boot! Can you imagine how upset I would have been?'

'I will see you later on,' I told him.

'What?' he said. 'No, stay here with me. I am not feeling well. I'm sorry if I made you feel badly before. They were just some thoughtless words.'

'No, I would like to be alone. You drink your morphine and go to sleep.'

I turned for the door but he, either not noticing this or pretending it was not happening, continued to speak to me. 'There was some type of poison in that brandy, I think.' He retched in his own mouth. 'This is the worst I've ever felt from alcohol.'

'I drank the same brandy and I am not poisoned.'

'You did not drink as much as I did.'

'There's no percentage in arguing with a drunkard as per whom should be blamed.'

'So I'm a drunkard, now.'

'I'm through with you for the day. I must attend to my stitches and wounds. I will see you later on, brother. I advise you to stay away from the saloon in the meantime.'

'I don't know if I'll be able, being so depraved a drunkard as I am.'

He only wished to fight and cultivate an anger toward me, thus alleviating his guilt, but I would not abet him in this. I returned to the lobby (the candle, I noticed on my way down, had remained lit, the match untouched), where I found the woman behind her desk, reading a letter and smiling. Apparently this note brought welcome news, for she was in better spirits because of it and she greeted me, if not warmly, then not nearly as coldly as before. I asked to borrow a pair of scissors and a looking glass and she did not answer but offered to cut my hair for fifty cents, assuming this was my reason for needing the tools. I declined with thanks, explaining about my stitches; she asked if she might follow to my room and witness the gory procedure. When I told her I had hoped to spend some time apart from my brother she said, 'That I can understand.' Then she asked where I was planning to perform my minor surgery; when I admitted I had not thought about this, she invited me into her quarters.

'Haven't you some other pressing business?' I asked. 'You hadn't a moment to spare, earlier this morning.'

Her cheek flushed, and she explained, 'I'm sorry if I was short with you. My help disappeared last week and I've been losing sleep hoping to keep up. Also there has been a sickness in my family that I have been anxious to know about.' She tapped the letter and nodded.

'All is well then?'

'Not all but most.' With this, she invited me behind her sacred counter and I followed her through the beaded curtain and into her private world. The beads felt lovely and tickling on my face, and I experienced a shudder of happiness at this. It is true, I thought. I am living a life.

Her room was not the room I would have imagined, if
I had had time to imagine her room, which I did not. But there
were no flowers and niceties, no silk or perfume, no lady things
hung with a lady's decorative hand; there were no volumes of
poetry, no vanity and brush set; there were no lace-edged pil-
lows featuring heartening proverbs meant to calm the spirit in
times of distress or else lead us through the monotony of end-
lessly redundant days with their succoring words and tones. No,
her room was a low-ceilinged bunker, without any windows or
natural light, and as it was located just next to the kitchen and
laundry it smelled of grease and brown water and moldy soap
flakes. She must have noticed my dismayed expression, for she
became shy, and said quietly that she did not suppose I was im-

pressed with her quarters; this naturally sent me falling over myself to praise the room, which I told her gave one the feeling of safety by way of impenetrability and also that it was perfectly private. She said my words were kindly spoken but not necessary. The room was lacking, she knew this, but she would have to put up with it for only a short while longer, for owing to the constant stream of prospectors she was doing a remarkable business. 'Six more months, then I will move into the finest room in this hotel.' The way she spoke this last sentence informed me it was a significant ambition for her.

'Six months is a long time,' I said.

'I have waited longer for less.'

'I wish there was some way I could hurry it along for you.'

She puzzled over this. 'What a strange thing to tell a stranger,' she said.

Now she guided me to a small pine table, propping a looking glass before me. My overlarge face leapt into view, which I studied with my usual mixture of curiosity and pity. She fetched me a pair of scissors and I took them up, holding the blades between my palms to warm them. Tilting the glass so that I could watch myself working, I snipped at the knotted stitching and began pulling away the black string from my mouth. It did not hurt but vaguely burned, as when a rope is run through your hands. It was too early to have removed the stitches and the string was coated in blood. I stacked the pieces in a pile at my feet and afterward burned these, as their smell was ungodly. Once this was finished I elected to show the woman my new toothbrush and powder, which I had in my vest pocket. She became excited by the suggestion, for she was also a recent convert to this method, and she hurried to fetch her equipment that we might brush simultaneously. So it was that we stood side by side at the wash basin, our mouths filling with foam, smiling as we worked. After we finished there was an awkward moment where neither of us knew what to say; and when I sat upon her bed she began looking at the door as if wishing to leave.

'Come sit beside me,' I said. 'I would like to talk to you.'

'I should be getting back to my work.'

'Am I not a guest here? You must entertain me, or I will write reproachful letters to the chamber of commerce.'

'Oh, all right.' Gathering her dress in her hands as she sat, she asked, 'What would you like to talk about?'

'Anything in the world. What about the letter, the one that made you smile? Who in your family was sick?'

'My brother, Pete. He was kicked in the chest by a mule but they tell me he's healing nicely. Mother says you can make out the hoof shape quite clearly.'

'He is lucky. That would have been a most undignified death.'

'Death is death.'

'You are wrong. There are many kinds of death.' I counted them off on my fingers: 'Quick death, slow death. Early death, late death. Brave death, cowardly death.'

'Anyway, he's weakened. I will send a letter inviting him to work with me.'

'You are close with your brother?' I said.

'We are twins,' she answered. 'We have always had a strong connection. I think of him sometimes and it is just as though he is in the room with me. The night he was kicked I awoke with a red mark over my breast. I suppose that sounds odd.'

'Yes, it does.'

'I believe I must have hit myself in my sleep,' she explained.

'Oh.'

'Is that man upstairs really your brother?'

'Yes.'

She said, 'You two are very different, aren't you? He is not bad, I don't think. Perhaps he is simply too lazy to be good.'

'Neither of us is good, but he is lazy, it's true. When he was a boy he would not wash until my mother actually wept.'

'What is your mother like?'

'She was very smart, and very sad.'

'When did she die?'

'She did not die.'

'But you said she *was* very smart.'

'I guess I only meant—well, she won't see us, if you want to know the truth. She is not happy with our work, and says she will not speak with us until we have found some other form of employment.'

'And what is it you two do?'

'We are Eli and Charlie Sisters.'

'Oh,' she said. 'Oh, my.'

'My father is dead. He was killed, and deserved to be killed.'

'All right,' she said, standing.

I gripped her hand. 'What is your name? I suppose you have a man already? Yes or no?' But she was edging toward the door and said she had not a minute longer to spare. I stood and moved in close to her, asking if I might steal a kiss, but she claimed once again to be hurried. I pressed her for details in respect to her feelings for me, if in fact she had any; she answered that she did not know me well enough to say, and admitted a preference for slight men, or at least men not quite as heavyset as me. She was not saying it to be cruel but the effects of her words stung me, and after she stole away I stood a long while before her looking glass, studying my profile, the line I cut in this world of men and ladies.

I avoided Charlie all that afternoon and evening. I returned to our room after dinner and found him sleeping, the morphine bottle toppled and empty on the floor. In the morning we ate breakfast together in our room, or he ate breakfast, as I had resolved to cease filling myself so gluttonously, that I might trim my middle down to a more suitable shape and weight. Charlie was groggy but glad, and wanted to make friends with me. Pointing his knife at my face he asked, 'Remember how you got your freckles?'

I shook my head. I was not ready to make friends. I said, 'Do you know the specifics of this duel?'

He nodded. 'One man is a lawyer, and by all accounts out of his element in such a fight. Williams is his name. He is going up against a ranch hand with an evil history, a man called Stamm. They say Stamm will kill Williams dead, no way around it.'

'But what are the specifics of their quarrel?'

'Stamm hired Williams to chase down some wages owed him by a local rancher. The matter went to court and Williams lost. The moment the verdict came in, Stamm challenged Williams to pistols.'

'And the lawyer has no history of shooting?'

'You hear talk of gentlemen gunfighters, but I've yet to meet one.'

'It doesn't sound like much of a pairing. I would just as soon move on.'

'If that's what you wish to do.' Charlie pulled a watch from his pocket. I recognized it as the watch of the prospector he had killed. 'It is just past nine o'clock, now. You can go ahead on Tub, and I'll catch up after the duel, in an hour's time.'

'I believe I will,' I said.

The hotel woman knocked and entered to collect our plates and cups. I bid her a good morning and she responded kindly, laying a hand on my back as she passed. Charlie also greeted her, but she pretended not to have heard. When she commented on my untouched plate, I patted my stomach and said I was hoping to slim down for reasons of the heart.

'Is that so,' she said.

'What are you talking about?' asked Charlie.

The woman's stained smock was nowhere in sight, replaced by a red linen blouse, cut low to reveal her throat and collarbone. Charlie asked if she would attend the gunfight and she answered in the affirmative, telling us, 'You men would do well to hurry up and find yourselves a place to watch. The streets fill up quickly here, and people are loath to give up their positions.'

'Perhaps I will stay on,' I said.

'Oh?' asked Charlie.

We three walked out to the dueling grounds together. As I pushed through the crowd I was pleased to notice the woman's arm on mine. I was feeling very grand and chivalrous; Charlie brought up the rear, whistling a conspicuously innocent melody. We found our place in the crowd and it was as the woman predicted, the competition for choice locations was fierce. I threatened a man who pushed against her, and Charlie called out, 'Beware the Rabid Gentleman, you faithful natives.' As the duelists arrived a body at my back bumped into me once, and then again. I turned to complain and saw it was a man with a child of seven or eight resting upon his shoulders—the child had been hitting me with his boot. 'I would appreciate your boy not kicking my back,' I said.

'Was he kicking you?' asked the man. 'I don't think he was.'

'He was, and if it happens again I will lay blame with you alone.'

'Is that a fact?' he said, making an expression that imparted his belief I was being unreasonable or overly dramatic. I tried to match his eyes then, that I might inform him of the peril his attitude was leading him toward, but he would not look at me, he only peered over my shoulder at the dueling grounds. I turned away to stew, the woman clutching my forearm to soothe me, but my temper was up now, and I spun around to readdress the man: 'Anyway, I don't understand why you would show the lad such violence at his age.'

'I've seen a killing before,' the boy told me. 'I saw an Indian cut through with a dagger blade, his guts running out of him like a fat red snake. I also saw a man hanging from a tree outside of town. His tongue was swelled up in his head, like this.' The child made an ugly face.

'I still don't think it's correct,' I told the man, who said nothing. The child continued to make his face and I turned back to watch the men taking their places in the street. They were easy enough to identify: The hand, Stamm, was in leather and well-worn cotton, his face weathered and unshaven. He stood alone, without a second to assist him, looking out at the crowd with a dead expression in his eyes, his arms hanging slack at his sides. The lawyer Williams wore a gray tailored suit, his hair center-parted, his mustache waxed and trimmed. His second, similarly dandified, removed Williams's coat, and the crowd watched the lawyer performing a series of knee-bending exercises. Now he leveled a phantom gun at Stamm and imitated its recoil. These pantomimes were the cause of some stifled chuckling in the crowd, but Williams's face was perfectly serious and solemn. I thought Stamm was drunk or had recently been drunk.

'Who are you hoping for?' I asked the hotel woman.

'Stamm is a bastard. I don't know Williams but he looks like a bastard, also.'

The man with the child on his shoulders overheard this and said, 'Mister Williams is not a bastard. Mister Williams is a gentleman.'

I turned slowly. 'He is a friend of yours?'

'I am proud to say he is.'

'I hope you have said your good-byes. He will be dead within the minute.'

The man shook his head. 'He is not afraid.'

It was such a stupid thing to say, I actually laughed. 'So what if he isn't?'

The man dismissed me with a wave. The child, anyway, had heard me; he regarded me with a knowing fear. I told him, 'Your father wants you to see violence, and today you will.' The man stood a moment, then cursed under his breath and moved away, pushing through the throng to watch the duel from another location.

Now I heard Williams's second call out to Stamm: 'Where is your second, sir?'

'I don't know, and I don't care,' Stamm replied.

Williams and his second had a private word. The second nodded and asked Stamm if he might inspect his pistol. Stamm repeated that he did not care, and the second took up the weapon to check it. Nodding his approval, he asked if Stamm wished to check Williams's pistol, and Stamm said he did not. Now Williams approached, and he and Stamm stood facing each other. Despite the show of bravery, it did not seem that Williams's heart was in the fight; sure enough, he whispered into his second's ear and the second said to Stamm, 'If you wish to make an apology, that would satisfy Mr. Williams.'

'I don't,' said Stamm.

'Very well,' said the second. He stood the men back-to-back and called it at twenty paces. He began to count it out and the duelists took their steps in time. Williams's forehead was shining with perspiration, and his pistol was trembling, while Stamm might have been walking to an outhouse, for all the concern he displayed. At the count of twenty they swiveled and fired. Williams missed but Stamm's bullet struck Williams in the center of his chest. The lawyer's face transformed to a ridiculous mask of agony and surprise and, I thought, a degree of insult. Staggering this way and that, he pulled his trigger and fired into the body of onlookers. A series of shrieks, then—the bullet had struck a young woman in the shin and she lay in the dirt writhing and clutching her leg. I do not know if Williams noticed his shameful error or not; by the time I looked back at him he was dead on the ground. Stamm was walking away in the direction of a saloon, pistol holstered, his arms once more at his sides. The second stood alone on the dueling ground, looking impotently to his left and right. I scanned the crowd for the man with the boy on his shoulders, that I might make a scornful face at him, but they were nowhere to be found.

The woman had some work to attend to, and excused herself while I packed my bags to leave. I searched the hotel to say good-bye but could not find her, so I made her a present of five dollars, hiding the coin beneath the sheets, that she might associate her thoughts of me with the notion of a marriage bed, or anyway a bed. Charlie caught me doing this and said he admired the gesture but that my plan was flawed in that the sheets were dirty and would continue to accumulate dirt because the woman had no interest in keeping a tidy business. 'You are only giving away that money to the next man who sleeps in this room.'

'She may find it,' I said.

'She will not, and besides that, five dollars is too much. Leave her a dollar at the front desk. She could have her smock cleaned, with enough left over to drink herself into a stupor.'

'You are only jealous because you don't have a girl.'

'Is that hard scrubber your girl? My congratulations. It's a shame we couldn't take her to Mother. She would be so glad to meet the delicate flower.'

'If it's a question of talking with a fool or not at all, I will choose the second.'

'Spitting into the dirt, wiping her nose on her sleeve. A very special lady indeed.'

'Not talking at all,' I said, and I left him to gather his things. Stepping into the road to meet Tub, I greeted him and asked how he was feeling. He appeared more alert than the day previous, though his eye was so much the worse, and I found myself sympathetic to the animal. He was resilient, if nothing else. I moved to stroke him but when my hand landed on his face he started, and I experienced shame at this, that he was so unused to a gentle touch. I decided to try to show him a better time, and made a private promise to this effect. Now Charlie exited the hotel, chuckling at the tender scene. 'Witness here the lover of all living things,' he called. 'Will he leave his faulty beast cash in its feedbag? I would not put it past him, friends.' He approached and snapped his fingers on either side of Tub's head. Tub's ears twitched and Charlie, satisfied with the test, moved to attend to Nimble. 'We will be out of doors for the rest of the trip,' he said. 'No more lazing about in hotel rooms for us.'

'It makes no difference to me,' I told him.

He paused. 'I only mean, if you suffer another of your spells or illnesses, I will have to carry on without you.'

'Spells or illnesses? That's fine, coming from you. Two times now you've slowed our progress with your drinking.'

'All right then, let's just say that we've had some bad luck, and set a poor example for ourselves. What's passed is passed, but that's the last of it, are we agreed?'

'Let's not hear anymore of my spells or illnesses.'

'Fair enough, brother.' He mounted Nimble and looked down the road, beyond the storefronts and toward the wilderness. I heard the tapping of metal on glass and saw the hotel woman standing in mine and Charlie's room on the second story, the five dollars gripped between her fingers as she rapped it across the pane. Now she kissed the coin and held her palm to the window, and I crossed my arms at Charlie, whose face was cold and thoughtless; he kicked Nimble in the ribs and rode away. I raised a hand to the woman and she mouthed some words that I could not decipher but assumed were an expression of thanks. I turned to follow Charlie, thinking of her voice in the empty room where she worked and worried, and I was glad to have left her the money and hoped it would make her happy, if only for a little while. I resolved to lose twenty-five pounds of fat and to write her a letter of love and praises, that I might improve her time on the earth with the devotion of another human being.

There was a storm at our backs, the last true storm of
the winter, but we managed to keep ahead of it and made good
time through the afternoon and into the night. We set up camp
in a large cave, its roof blackened with the soot of other men's
fires. Charlie made us a dinner of beans and pork and biscuits
but I only ate the beans, secretly feeding the rest to Tub. I went
to sleep hungry and woke up in the middle of the night to find a
riderless horse standing at the mouth of the cave, breathing and
rocking on its feet. It was black in coloring and slick with sweat;
when he began to shiver, I approached him and tossed my blanket over his back.

'What's the matter?' asked Charlie, leaning up on his elbow
beside the fire.

'A horse.'

'Where is the rider?'

'There is no rider that I can see.'

'If the rider appears, you may wake me.' He turned and fell back asleep.

The horse was seventeen hands tall and all muscle. He had no brand or saddle or shoes but his mane was clean and he did not shy from my hand. I brought him a biscuit but he was not hungry and only nibbled at it. 'Where are you headed to, running through the night like that?' I asked him. I tried to guide him toward Nimble and Tub, to share in their huddled heat, but he pulled away and returned to the mouth, where I had found him. 'You mean to leave me without a blanket, is that it?' I reentered the cave to stoke the fire, curling up beside it for warmth, but I could not sleep without proper covering and instead spent the rest of the night rewriting lost arguments from my past, altering history so that I emerged victorious. By the time the sun rose in the morning I had decided to keep this horse for my own. I told my plan to Charlie as I handed him his coffee and he nodded. 'You can have him shoed in Jacksonville. And we might get a fair price for Tub, though I doubt it—they'll probably only slaughter him. Well, you can keep whatever money you get. You've had a tough time with Tub, I'll not deny it. A happy coincidence, this horse just walking up to meet you. What will you call him? What about, Son of Tub.'

I said, 'I should think some farmer would be happy to pay for Tub's services. He has a few good years left yet.'

'I wouldn't get his hopes up.' He turned to Tub and said, 'Stew meat? Or pretty pasture, with the farmer's soft-bottomed daughter?' To me he whispered, 'Stew meat.'

The black horse accepted the bit and saddle without incident.

Tub hung his head when I slung a rope around his neck and I could not meet his eyes. We were two miles out when we found the dead Indian on the ground. 'This will be the previous owner,' Charlie said. We rolled him over to get a look. His body was stiff and distorted, his neck snapped back and his mouth open wide in an expression of absolute suffering.

'Strange, though, that an Indian horse would take a bit and saddle,' I said.

'Must've been that he stole it from a white man,' said Charlie.

'But the horse has no shoes or brand?'

'It's a conundrum,' he admitted. Pointing to the Indian, he said, 'Ask him.'

The Indian had no wounds to explain his death but was extremely heavyset and we thought perhaps he had suffered an attack of organ failure, then fell from the horse and broke his neck. 'Horse just kept on going,' Charlie said. 'Likely they were headed to the cave. I wonder what he'd have done, the two of us sleeping in his spot like that.' The black horse lowered his head to the Indian, smelling and nudging him. At this same time I could feel Tub looking at me. I decided to return to our travels. At first the black horse didn't want to leave but once we were clear he ran very nicely despite the rough terrain, and having Tub in tow behind us. A heavy rain began to fall but the chill was gone from the air; I was sweating, as was the new horse, and his smell and warmth were agreeable to me. His every move was sharp and graceful and I found him to be an altogether gifted runner, and though it did not feel good to think of it, I knew it would be a great relief to be free of Tub. I looked back at him and watched as he did his best to keep up. His eye was watering and bloodshot and he held his head up and to the side, as if to avoid drowning.

When we arrived in Jacksonville, I wondered if Charlie would honor his vow to sleep out of doors; I knew he would not when I saw his face look searchingly into the glowing windows of the first saloon we passed. We stabled the horses for the night. I told the hand to shoe the black horse and asked him for a price on Tub. The man held his lantern next to Tub's injured eye and said he would tell me in the morning, when he might get a better look at him. Charlie and I parted ways in the center of town. He wished to drink and I to eat. He pointed to a hotel as our eventual meeting place, and I nodded.

The rainstorm had passed; now the moon was full and low and the stars were bright. I entered a modest restaurant and took a seat by the window, watching my hands on the bare table. They were still and ivory looking in the light of the planets, and I felt no particular personal attachment to them. A boy came by and placed a candle on the table, ruining the effect, and I studied the bill of fare posted on the wall. I had eaten little at breakfast, despite having gone to sleep with an empty stomach, and my insides were squirming with hunger. But I found the food to be of the most fattening sort, and when the waiter arrived at my side, half bowing with a pencil at the ready, I asked him if he had anything to offer that was not quite so rich.

'Not hungry tonight, sir?'

'I am weak with hunger,' I told him. 'But I am looking for something less filling than beer, beef, and buttered spuds.'

The waiter tapped his pencil on his pad. 'You want to eat but you don't want to become full?'

'I want to be *unhungry*,' I said.

'And what is the difference?'

'I want to eat, only I don't want to eat such heavy foods, don't you see?'

He said, 'To me, the whole point of eating *is* to get full.'

'Are you telling me there are no options other than what's listed?'

The waiter was baffled. He excused himself to fetch the cook from the kitchen; she was overworked and annoyed at the inconvenience.

'What's the problem, sir?' she asked, wiping her hands on her sleeves.

'I never said there was a problem. I only wonder if there's a lighter option than the meals listed on the bill of fare.'

The cook looked at the waiter and back to me. 'Aren't you hungry?'

'We could give you a half portion, if you're not hungry,' said the waiter.

'I've already told you I'm hungry. I'm famished. But I'm looking for something that isn't so filling, do you see?'

'When I eat a meal, I *want* to get full,' said the cook.

'That's the object of eating!' said the waiter.

'And then, when you finish, you pat your belly and say, "I'm full."'

'Everybody does that.'

'Look,' I said. 'I'll take a half portion of beef, no spuds, with wine. Do you have any vegetables? Any greens?'

I thought the cook would laugh in my face. 'I believe there are some carrots out by the hutches.'

'Bring me a handful of carrots, opposite the beef, peeled and boiled. You can charge me the price of a full plate for the trouble, is that all right?'

'Whatever you say,' said the cook.

'I'll bring the wine out now,' said the waiter.

When they brought me my plate it was heaped with limp, hot carrots. The cook had skinned the stalks but left the green tops attached, a malicious oversight, I felt. I choked down half a dozen of these but it was as though they disappeared before arriving in my stomach, and I began somewhat despairingly to root for the beef. I found this at the bottom of the pile and savored every bite, but it was gone far too quickly, and I became depressed. I blew out the candle and stared once more at my ghostly hands. When they began to tingle, I wondered about the curse from the gypsy-witch's shack. When would it come to bloom, if ever? What form would it take? The waiter returned to clear the table and pointed at the remaining carrots. 'Didn't you care for the vegetables?' he asked naively.

'All right,' I said. 'Take it away.'

'More wine?'

'One more glass.'

'Would you like any dessert?'

'No! Goddamnit!'

The tormented waiter hurried away from me.

In the morning I checked on Charlie and was unsurprised to find him sick and disinclined to travel. I started in with my halfhearted reprimand, but it was not necessary; he knew as well as I we could not pass another day without hard riding and he promised to be ready in one hour. I did not know what magic he thought to conjure that might bring his suffering to an end in so short a time but I did not engage him on this topic, leaving him instead to his vapors and pains and returning to the restaurant from the night previous for my much needed breakfast. The waiter was not there but in his place was a lad who resembled him and whom I assumed was his son; however, when I asked, 'Where is your father?' the boy gripped his hands and said, 'Heaven.' I ate a small portion of eggs and beans and was still very hungry when I was finished. I sat looking at the greasy plate, wishing, frankly, to lick it, but decorum kept me from doing so. When the lad came by and picked the plate up I watched it hovering across the dining room and into the kitchen, out of my field of vision. The boy returned and asked if I wanted anything more before paying up. 'Fresh pie this morning,' he said.

'What kind of pie?' I demanded. I thought, Don't let it be cherry.

'Cherry,' said the boy. 'Just out of the oven. They go fast around here. Kind of famous, really.' I must have been making a face, for he asked me, 'You okay, mister? You look hurt.'

Beads of sweat grew from my forehead, and my hands were trembling. My very blood wanted that cherry pie. Dabbing my face with the napkin, I told the lad I was fine, only tired.

'Pie or no pie?' he asked.

'No pie!' I said. He laid down the bill and returned to the kitchen. After paying up I set out to replenish my and Charlie's stock of food, humming my tune of virtue. A rooster stood before me in the road, looking for a fight; I tipped my hat to him and he scooted away over the puddles, all brawn and feathers and brainlessness.

With my tooth powder dwindling, I asked the proprietor at the trading post if he carried any and he pointed to a short row of boxes, each of these advertising a different scent or flavor: Sage, pine, mint, and fennel. When he asked which flavor I was after I told him I might stick to mint, as I had been happy with its taste up to then, but the man, a pigeon-in-a-vest type, insisted I sample the others. 'The spice of life,' he said, and though I did not care for his satisfied attitude, I was curious about these others and carried them to a washbasin in the back room, careful not to bend or damage the boxes lest I be forced to purchase one I did not care for. I sampled them one after the other. Returning to the front room I told the proprietor, 'The pine is all right. It offers a fine, clean feeling on the tongue. The sage burns my throat; I did not like it much. The fennel is downright foul. I will take this mint one, as I said before.'

'It is always better to know for sure,' he said, an obvious, somewhat idiotic statement to which I did not respond. In addition to the powder I purchased a pound of flour, a pound of coffee, a half pound of sugar, two pounds of beans, two pounds of salted pork, and two pounds of dried fruit, my stomach now actively groaning. I drank a large cup of water and walked to the stable, my insides sloshing with each step.

The stable hand had just finished shoeing the black horse when I entered. 'I will give you six dollars for the low-backed animal,' he said. 'We will call it a dollar for the shoes, so let's say five dollars.' I approached Tub and placed a hand on his muzzle. 'Good morning,' I told him. I felt he recognized me; he looked at me honestly, and without fear or malice. The stable hand stood at my back. 'He'll very probably lose that eye,' he told me. 'Will he even pull a cart? I will give you four dollars.'

'I have decided not to sell him,' I said.

'I will give you six dollars, including the shoes.'

'No, I have changed my mind. Let us discuss the black horse.'

'Seven dollars is my final offer for the low-backed animal.'

'What will you give me for the black horse?'

'I cannot afford the black horse. I will give you eight dollars for the other.'

'Make me an offer on the black horse,' I said.

'Twenty-five dollars.'

'He is worth fifty dollars.'

'Thirty dollars with the saddle.'

'Don't be ignorant. I will take forty, without the saddle.'

'I will give you thirty-five dollars.'

'Thirty-five dollars without the saddle?'

'Thirty-five, without the saddle, minus a dollar for the shoes.'

'You expect me to pay for shoes on a horse I'm not keeping?'

'You asked me to shoe him. Now, you must pay for the service.'

'You would have shoed him anyway.'

'That is neither up nor down.'

'Thirty-four dollars,' I said.

The hand disappeared into his quarters to fetch his money. I could hear him arguing with a woman about it. He spoke in a hiss, and though I could not grasp the words, I understood the sentiment: *Shut up! The man out there is a fool!* Charlie entered the stable then, green at the neck but hoping to hide it. When the hand came out with the money, he also brought a bottle of whiskey to toast the deal in good faith. I offered a drink to my brother and he swooned. He was so distracted by his own suffering he did not notice my business dealings until we were ten miles out of town.

'Where is the black horse? Why are you still riding Tub?'

'I had a change of heart and have decided to keep him.'

'I don't understand you, brother.'

'He has been a faithful animal to me.'

'I don't understand you. That black horse was one in a million.'

I said, 'It was a few days ago you were holding me back from selling Tub. You were only converted to my way of thinking when a suitable replacement showed up on the wind, free of charge.'

'You are always harkening back in arguments, but another time is another time and thus irrelevant. Providence brought you that black horse. And what will become of the man who shuns Providence?'

'Providence has no place in this discussion. An Indian ate too much and died, that was the source of my good fortune. The point of my argument is that you were only keen on Tub's departure when it suited you financially.'

'So I am a drunkard *and* a miser?'

'Who is harkening back now?'

'A drunken miser. There is my sorry fate.'

'You are a contrarian.'

He lurched, as if hit by a bullet. 'A drunken, miserly contrarian! The heat of his vicious words!' He chuckled to himself. In a moment he grew thoughtful and asked, 'What did we make on the black horse, anyway?'

'We?' I said, and I laughed at him.

We quickened the pace of our animals. Charlie's sickness was stubborn and twice I watched him spit out mouthfuls of bile midstride. Was there any greater agony than riding a horse while brandy-sick? I had to admit my brother took his punishments without complaint, but I knew he could not keep up the pace for longer than a couple of hours, and I believe he was about to call for a rest when we spied a grouping of wagons at the base of a pass in the distance. He headed in their direction, riding purposefully, with an air of dutiful seriousness, but I knew he was only counting the seconds until he could dismount and rest his tortured innards.

We rode around the three wagons but saw no sign of life save for the small fire at its center. Charlie called out a greeting but received no response. He dismounted and moved to enter the circle by climbing over the hitches of two adjoining wagons when the barrel of a bulky rifle emerged silently, viperlike from one of the canopies. Charlie stared up at the gun, his eyes slightly crossing. 'Okay,' he said. The barrel rose to his forehead, and a boy of fifteen years or less looked upon us. His face was dirt caked, blistered at the nostrils and mouth, his expression a permanent sneer; his hands were steady and his posture was at ease with the weapon—I believed he was well acquainted with it. His eyes were full of mistrust and dislike and he was in short a most unfriendly young man, and I was concerned he would murder my brother if we did not communicate ourselves, and quickly. 'We don't mean you any mischief, son,' I said.

'That's what the last ones told me,' said the boy. 'Then they hit me on the head and took all my potato cakes.'

'We don't want any potato cakes,' Charlie said.

'We're a good match then, because I haven't got any.'

I could see the boy was near starved, and told him he was welcome to our pork if he was hungry. 'I bought it just this morning, in town,' I said. 'And flour, too. Would you like that, boy? A feast of pork and biscuits?'

'You are a liar,' he said. 'There's no town near here. My daddy went searching for food a week ago.'

Charlie looked over at me. 'I wonder if that is the man we met on the trail yesterday. He was in a hurry to get back and feed his son, remember?'

'That's right. And he was heading this way, too.'

'Was he riding a gray mare?' asked the boy, his expression transformed to one of pitiful hopefulness.

Charlie nodded. 'A gray mare, yes he was. He told us what a fine boy you were, how proud he was of you. He was worried sick, he said. Couldn't hardly wait to see you.'

'Daddy said that?' the boy asked doubtfully. 'Did he really?'

'Yes, he was mighty glad to be heading back. It's a shame we had to kill him.'

'W-what?' Before the boy could recover Charlie snatched the rifle away and jammed him hard on the head with the stock. The boy fell back into the canopied wagon and was silent. 'Let's get some coffee on that fire,' Charlie said, jumping over the hitches.

Charlie had been invigorated by this latest adventure

—the blood rush had banished his sickness he said—and he fell to preparing our lunch with an uncommon enthusiasm. He agreed to make enough for the boy, but not until I checked his condition, because for all we knew the blow had killed him. I put my head in the canopy and saw he was alive, sitting up now, and turned away from me. 'We're cooking some food out here,' I told him. 'You don't have to eat with us if you don't want to but my brother's making you a plateful.'

'Bastards killed my daddy,' said the boy, choking on his tears.

'Oh, that was just a ruse to get clear of your rifle.'

He turned and looked at me. The blow had split his forehead

and a trickle of blood was thickening over his eyebrow. 'You mean it?' he asked. 'You put it on God?'

'That wouldn't mean anything to me, so I won't bother with it. I'll put in on my horse, though, how about that?'

'You never saw a man on a gray mare?'

'We never saw him.'

The boy collected himself and began climbing toward me over the wagon benches. I took his arm to help him down; his legs were weak as I walked him to the fire. 'Look who's back from the brink of lonely death,' Charlie said cheerfully.

'I want my rifle,' said the boy.

'Best to brace yourself for disappointment then.'

'We'll give it back on our way out,' I told the boy. I handed him a plate of pork and beans and biscuits but he did not eat, he only stared mournfully at the food, as though the meal itself was somehow melancholy to him. 'What's the matter?' I asked.

'I'm tired of this,' he said. 'Everybody's always hitting me on the head.'

'You're lucky I didn't take yours off with a bullet,' said Charlie.

'We won't hit you again,' I told him, 'as long as you don't try anything smart. Now, eat your pork before it gets cold.'

The boy cleaned his plate but quickly vomited it back up. He had gone too long without solid food and his stomach could not accept so much out of the blue. He sat there looking at his half-digested lunch on the ground, wondering I suppose if he should scoop it up and try again. 'Kid,' Charlie said, 'you so much as touch it and I'll shoot you dead.' I gave the boy the bulk of my plateful and instructed him to eat slowly, and afterward to lay back and breathe in plenty of fresh air. He did this and fifteen minutes passed without incident, though his stomach was loudly squirming. The boy sat up and asked, 'Aren't you going to be hungry now?'

'My brother is fasting in the name of love,' said Charlie.

I blushed and said nothing. I had not known my brother was aware of my diet; I could not match his playful gaze.

The boy was looking at me for an explanation. 'You got a yourself a girl?' Still I said nothing. 'I got one too,' he told me. 'At least she was my girl when Daddy and I left Tennessee.'

Charlie said, 'How it is that you've found yourself alone with three wagons, no animals, and no food?'

He said, 'There was a group of us heading out to work the California rivers. Me and my daddy and his two brothers, Jimmy and Tom, and one of Tom's friends and then Tom's friend's wife. She was the first to die. Couldn't keep any food in her. Daddy said it was wrong to've brought her, and I guess it was, too. We buried her and kept on, then Tom's friend turned home, said we could keep his wagon and gear because his heart was broken and he wanted to get back to start his grieving. Uncle Tom took a shot at him once he was about a quarter mile out.'

'Just after the man's wife died?' I asked.

'It was a couple days after she died. Tom wasn't trying to hit him, just scare him. A bit of fun, he called it.'

'That's not very kind of him.'

'No, Uncle Tom never did anything kind in his life. He died next, in a saloon fight. Took a knife in the belly and the blood pooled out like a rug underneath him. We were all pretty glad he was gone, to tell you the truth. Tom was hard to be around. He hit me on the head more than anybody else. Didn't even need a reason, just passing time.'

'Didn't your daddy tell him to stop?'

'Daddy was never much for talking? He's what you might call the private type.'

'Carry on with the story,' said Charlie.

'Right,' said the boy. 'So Tom's dead, and we sold his horse and tried to sell his wagon, but nobody wanted it because it was so poorly outfitted. Now, we got two oxen pulling three carts, and what do you think happens next? The oxen die, starved and thirsty, with whipping wounds on their backs, and now it's me and Daddy and Uncle Jimmy, and the horses are pulling the carts, and the money's going quick and so's the food, and we're looking at one another and we're all thinking the same thing: Dang.'

'Was Uncle Jimmy nasty, too?' I asked.

'I liked Uncle Jimmy right up until he took all the money and ran out on us. That was two weeks ago. I don't know if he went east or west or north or south. Daddy and I've been stuck here, sitting and thinking what to do. He left, like I said, a week ago. I expect he will be back soon. I don't know what could have taken him so long as this. I'm obliged to you for sharing this food with me. I nearly killed a rabbit yesterday but they're hard to lay a bead on, and my ammunition's not very well stocked.'

'Where is your mother?' Charlie asked.

'Dead.'

'I'm sorry to hear that.'

'Thank you. But she was always dead.'

'Tell us about your girl,' I said.

'Her name is Anna, and her hair is the color of honey. It is the cleanest hair I have ever seen and runs halfway down to the ground. I am in love with her.'

'Are your feelings reciprocated?'

'I don't know what that word means.'

'Does she love you too?'

'I don't think she does, no. I have tried to kiss and hold her but she pushes me away. Last time, she said she would have her father and brothers beat me if I did it again. But she'll change her tune when she sees my pocketful of riches. There is gold tumbling down those California rivers like hop-frogs, and all you have to do is stand still and catch them in your pan.'

'Is that what you believe?' asked Charlie.

'It said as much in the newspaper.'

'You are in for a rude awakening, I fear.'

'I just want to get there already. I'm tired of sitting here with nothing to do.'

'You're not far now,' I told him. 'That's California just over the pass, there.'

'That's the direction Daddy went.'

Charlie laughed.

'What's so funny?' asked the boy.

'Nothing,' Charlie answered. 'He probably just dashed over to catch a few pounds of tumbling gold. He'll be back with some ready cash by suppertime, I am sure of it.'

'You don't know my daddy.'

'Don't I?'

The boy sniffed and turned to me. 'You never told me about your girl. What color is her hair?'

'Chestnut brown.'

'Mud brown,' said Charlie.

'Why do you say that?' I asked. I watched him, but he did not answer.

'What's her name?' asked the boy.

I said, 'That is all to be worked out.'

The boy drew in the dirt with a stick. 'You don't know her name?'

'Her name is Sally,' Charlie said. 'And if you're curious how I know that and my brother doesn't, so should he be.'

'What's that mean?' I asked sharply. He still did not answer. I stood and looked down over him. 'What the hell does it mean?'

'I only say it to put you on the proper path,' said Charlie.

'Only say what?'

'That I got for free what you paid five dollars for and still did not get.'

I started to speak but trailed off. I remembered meeting the woman on the stairs of the hotel. She had been in Charlie's room, filling his bathtub, and she was upset. 'What did you do to her?'

'She laid it out for me. I wasn't even thinking of it. Fifty cents for hand work, dollar for the mouth, fifty cents more for the whole thing. I took the whole thing.'

My head was thumping hard. I found myself reaching for a biscuit. 'What was she so upset about?'

'If you want the truth, I found the service lacking. My payment reflected this, or should I say my nonpayment, and she took offense. You have to know, I wouldn't have touched the girl if I'd known how you felt. But I was sick, you'll remember, and in need of comfort. I'm sorry, Eli, but at that time, far as I knew she was up for grabs.'

I ate the biscuit in two bites and reached for another. 'Where's the pork fat?' The boy handed me the tin and I dipped the biscuit whole.

'I let your five dollars slide,' Charlie continued, 'but I didn't want to see you starve yourself for no reason.' My blood was pulsing ebulliently in celebration of the arrival of the heavy food, while my heart was struck dumb from this news of the hotel woman's character. I sat back down, chewing and thinking and brooding. 'I could make some more pork,' Charlie offered peaceably.

'Make more of everything,' I said.

The boy pulled a harmonica from his shirt pocket and tapped it on his palm.

'I will play an eating song.'

two

CALIFORNIA

The boy said he had a horse hidden in a nearby cluster
of timber, and asked if he could ride along with us to the California border. Charlie was against it but I could not see the harm and
told the boy he had five minutes to gather his effects. He left and
returned with his horse, a small and sickly thing with no saddle or
accoutrements, and with patches of its hair fallen away, exposing
raw flesh and rib bones. In response to our concerned expressions
the boy replied, 'I know he doesn't look like much, but Lucky Paul
can climb these steep hills like a spider climbs a wall.'

Charlie asked me, 'Will you speak to him, or shall I?'

I said that I would and Charlie stepped away. I was not sure
where to begin but decided to address the problem from the
practical standpoint.

'Where is your saddle, boy?'

'I have a blanket, and my own personal padding.' He tapped his backside.

'No bit? No reins?'

'Uncle Jimmy took those with him. Who knows why. But it doesn't matter. Lucky Paul knows which way to go.'

'We will not wait for you,' I told him.

He was feeding the horse a biscuit. 'You do not understand, but you will. He is fed and rested and ready to cover some ground.'

His confidence was true, and I had a hope Lucky Paul was just the type of runner the boy claimed him to be, but this was not the case, and we lost them instantaneously. The horse had no interest in climbing the long pass; looking back I saw the boy pummeling him about his skull and neck. Charlie nearly fell off Nimble from laughing, and neither was the humor of the episode lost on me, but this diversion quickly lost its appeal and we settled into some serious riding, so that we hit the snowy summit in a matter of four hours. Despite Tub's eye wound he never so much as stumbled, and I felt for the first time that we knew and understood each other; I sensed in him a desire to improve himself, which perhaps was whimsy or wishful thinking on my part, but such are the musings of the traveling man.

The far side of the pass presented us with more favorable terrain, and by dusk we had crossed beneath the snow line, where we set up for the night. In the morning we slept late and rode at a moderate pace into California. We entered a dense and tall forest of pines late in the afternoon and happened on a small, winding stream, the sight of which gave us pause. Here before us was the very thing that had induced thousands of previously intelligent men and women to abandon their families and homes forever. The both of us stared at it, saying nothing. Finally Charlie could not help himself; he dismounted and squatted beside the stream, pulling up a handful of wet sand and rooting through it with his finger.

I spied a tent on the far side of the water, a quarter mile to the north. A lone face, bearded and extremely dirty, peered out from behind it. I held up my hand in greeting and the face darted back. 'I believe we have us a real live prospector,' I said.

'Pretty far out to be working, don't you think?'

'For all we know. Shall we pay him a visit and see how he is doing?'

Charlie threw the sand back. 'There is nothing in this river, brother.'

'But you're not curious to know?'

'If you want to check in with him, you go ahead while I make my toilet. But I cannot invest my own time with every curiosity.'

He walked into the forest and I rode Tub upstream, calling my greeting from across the water, but there was no sign of the bearded man. I saw a pair of boots in front of his tent and a small fire in a pit; there was a saddle on the ground, but no horse that I could see. I called out once again, and again I heard nothing. Had the man run barefoot into the woods rather than share news of unknown riches? But no, the sight of the blighted camp told me the prospector was not having any successes. Here was a man greedy for gold but not hearty enough to brave the wasps' nest that was California proper. He would find nothing, he would starve, he would rave and expire—I could see his naked body picked over by blackbirds. 'One of these cold mornings,' I said.

There came the sound of a rifle being cocked behind me. 'Cold mornings what?' said a voice. I raised my hands and the prospector began laughing, relishing his position.

'Tunnel under the river,' he said. 'Weren't thinking of that, were you?' He jabbed my thigh painfully with his gun muzzle and I began to turn. 'Look at me, I'll shoot your face off, bastard,' he hissed.

'There's no need for this,' I said. 'I don't mean you any harm.'

He jabbed my leg again. 'Maybe I do you, think of that?' His laughter was high pitched and wistful and I thought he had likely gone crazy or was going crazy. I realized with annoyance that Charlie had been correct to leave the man alone. 'You're a hunter, that it?' he asked. 'You looking for the red-haired she-bear?'

'I don't know about a red-haired she-bear,' I said.

'There's a red-haired she-bear near here. Mayfield put the price of a hundred dollars on her and now the hunters are going mad for the pelt. I saw her two miles north of camp yesterday morning. Took a shot but couldn't get in close enough.'

'I'm not interested in it one way or the other, and I don't know anyone called Mayfield.'

He jabbed my leg again. 'Wasn't you just with him, you son of a bitch? And him checking the sand in my riverbed?'

'You're talking about my brother, Charlie. We're heading south from Oregon Territory. We've never been through this way and don't know anyone in these parts.'

'Mayfield's big boss around here. Sends men over to upset my camp when I'm in town fetching supplies. Sure that wasn't him a minute ago? I thought I saw his stupid, laughing face.'

'That's only Charlie. He's ducked into the woods to make his toilet. We're on our way south to work the rivers.'

I heard him step around to Tub's far side, and then back. 'Where's your gear?' he asked. 'You say you're going to work the rivers but you got no gear?'

'We will buy our gear in Sacramento.'

'Right off the top then, you're losing money. Only a fool buys his gear in town.'

I had nothing to say to this. He jabbed my thigh and said, 'I'm talking to you.' I said nothing and he jabbed me.

'Stop jabbing me like that.'

He jabbed me. 'Don't like it, do you?' He jabbed me.

'I want you to stop.'

'Think I care what you want!' He jabbed me and held the gun against my smarting leg. A twig snapped in the distance and I felt the gun go slack as the prospector turned to look. I grabbed the rifle barrel and yanked it away. The prospector lit out for the woods and I turned and pulled the trigger but the rifle was not loaded. I was reaching for my pistol when Charlie stepped from behind a tree and casually shot the prospector as he ran past. It was a head shot, which took the back off his skull like a cap in the wind. I dismounted and limped over to the twitching body. My leg was stinging terribly and I was possessed with a rage. The man's brain was painted in purple blood, bubbling foam emerging from its folds; I raised up my boot and dropped my heel into the hole with all my weight behind it, caving in what was left of the skull and flattening it in general so that it was no longer recognizable as the head of a man. When I removed my boot it was as though I were pulling it from wet mud. Now I walked away from the body, without purpose and for no reason besides needing to escape my own anger. Charlie called my name but did not pursue me, knowing to leave me alone when I am like this. I walked a half mile and sat beneath a broad pine, tensing and untensing my body with my knees against my chest. I thought I would break my own jaw from clenching, and stuck my knife's leather sheath between my teeth.

Rising to my knees, I pulled down my pants to check the state of my leg. The skin was inflamed and I could make out the perfect circular shape of the barrel, or series of barrels, a half-dozen red zeros—the sight of these made me frustrated all over again and I wished the prospector might come back to life so I could kill him myself, but slowly. I stood, thinking I would return to mutilate his body further, to unload my pistol in his stomach, but after a moment I decided against it, thankfully. My pants were still down and after collecting my emotions I took up my organ to compromise myself. As a young man, when my temper was proving problematic, my mother instructed me to do this as a means of achieving calm, and I have found it a useful practice ever since. Once accomplished I headed back to the river, feeling empty and cold inside but no longer angry. I cannot understand the motivation of a bully, is what it is; this is the one thing that makes me unreasonable.

I located the dead prospector's tunnel, so-called. I had imagined a head-high underground pathway with wooden supports and hanging lanterns, but it was barely large enough around to crawl through, and as it was located at the stream's thinnest point, only a few feet across. We dragged the prospector over and pushed him into the hole. I rode Tub over top of this, marching from one side of the stream to the other to cave it in. We had found little on his person, a pocketknife, a pipe, and a letter, which we buried with him, and which read:

Dear Mother,

I am lonely and the days are long here. My horse has passed and he was a close friend to me. I think of your cooking and wonder what I am doing. I believe I will come home soon. I have near two hundred dollars in gold dust.

It is not the pile I had hoped for, but good enough for now. How is Sis? I do not miss her so much. Did she marry that Fat man? I hope he took her far away! The smell of smoke is in my nostrils always and I haven't had a laugh in such a long, long while. Mother! I think I will leave here very soon.

Loveingly,

Your Own Son.

Thinking of it now I suppose it would have been best if I had posted the letter. But as I said, when my temper is up everything goes black and narrow for me, and such notions were not in my mind. It is lonesome to think of a headless skeleton under that cold, running water. I do not regret that the man is dead but wish I had kept better hold of my emotions. The loss of control does not frighten me so much as embarrass me.

Once the prospector was out of sight, Charlie and I began rooting around in search of his gold. It was not difficult to find. He had set it away from the camp twenty yards, marked with a small crucifix fashioned from twigs. It did not look like two hundred dollars' worth but I had never dealt with the powder and chunky flakes, and so could not be sure. We divided it fifty-fifty and I emptied my share in an old tobacco pouch I found buried in my saddlebag.

Charlie spent the night in the shelter and I had tried to also but could not stomach the lingering smell, both the dead prospector's and the horse's, which had been butchered, its meat lying on a makeshift drying rack at the rear of the tent. I slept beside the fire pit rather than contend with these fumes, passing a night under the stars. It was cold, but the cold did not have what I have heard called 'winter weight'—it chilled your flesh, but not your muscle and bone. Charlie emerged from the shelter half an hour past the dawn, looking a decade older and a good bit dirtier, also. He slapped his chest to show the cloud of dust rise away from him; he decided a morning bath was in order, and pulled one of the prospector's pans to the water's edge to fill it, afterward placing this on the fire. He then located a deep spot in the stream, stripped down, and leapt in, shrieking loudly at its coldness. I sat on the bank and watched him splashing and singing; he had not had anything to drink the night before and there had been no other people around to upset his volatile nature, and I found myself becoming sentimental by this rare show of innocent happiness. Charlie had often been glad and singing as a younger man, before we took up with the Commodore, when he became guarded and hard, so it was sad in a way to watch him frolic in that shimmering river, with the tall snowy mountains walling us in. He was revisiting his earlier self but only briefly, and I knew he would return to his present incarnation soon enough. He rushed naked up the bank to stand near the fire. His genitals were shriveled and he made a joke about how swimming always brought him back to childhood. Lifting the pan from the fire, he poured the hot water over his head, which inspired another round of joyous screaming and bellowing.

After breakfast, I took advantage of his good humor, convincing him to try my toothbrush. 'That's it,' I said. 'Up and down. Now, give the tongue a good scrub.' Breathing in, he felt the mint on his tongue and was impressed with the sensation of it. Handing back the brush and powder he said, 'There is a *very* fine feeling.'

'That is what I've been telling you.'

'It is as though my entire head has been cleaned.'

'We might pick you up a brush of your own in San Francisco.'

'I think we may have to.'

We were preparing to leave when I saw the boy and Lucky Paul emerge from the forest on the opposite side of the stream. He had fresh blood all about his face and head and looked to be half dead. He saw me and raised his hand before dropping from his horse to the ground, where he lay still and unmoving. Lucky Paul took no notice of this but approached the river to drink.

We dunked the boy in the stream and he awoke with a start. He was happy to see us, amused as he sat up. 'I have never come to in running water before.' He clapped the surface with his palm. 'My *God*, it's cold.'

'What happened to you?' I asked.

'At the start of the woods I met a group of trappers on horse-back, four of them, said they were looking for a red-colored bear. When I told them I hadn't seen the bear they hit me on the head with a club. I dropped to the dirt and they rode off laughing. After I got my bearings I climbed back on old Paul and he led me here, to you all.'

'He led himself to water, is what he did,' said Charlie.

'No,' said the boy, patting and stroking Lucky Paul's face. 'His thoughts were with me, and he did what was needed.'

Charlie said, 'You sound like my brother and his horse, Tub.' He turned to me. 'You and this boy should come together and form a committee or association of some kind.'

'Which way did these men go?' I asked the boy.

'The Protectors of Moronic Beasts,' said Charlie.

The boy said, 'I heard them say they were heading back to Mayfield. Is that a town? I wonder if that's where my father is.'

'Mayfield is the boss man around here,' I explained, relaying to Charlie what the prospector had said about the hundred-dollar tariff for the elusive bear's pelt. Charlie said any man who would pay that much for a bear skin was a fool. The boy, washing the blood from his face and hair, said a hundred dollars would buy him all he needed in a lifetime. I pointed out the camp across the stream and told him he might make use of the fire and find temporary shelter there. At this, he appeared confused. 'I thought I would come along with you two.'

'Oh, no,' said Charlie. 'It was humorous the one time, but that's the end of that.'

'Now that we are clear of the pass, Lucky Paul will show you his stuff.'

'Last you said he was one for the hills.'

'He is slick as grease on the flats.'

'No and no again,' Charlie said.

The boy appealed to me with a sorrowful look but I told him he was on his own. He started crying and Charlie moved to strike him; I held my brother back and he broke off, returning to the camp to pack. I do not know what it was about that boy but just looking at him, even I wanted to clout him on the head.

It was a head that invited violence. Now he was weeping in earnest, with bubbles of mucus blooming from his nostrils, and no sooner had the right nostril's bubble exploded than another took shape in the left. I explained we were in no position to care for children, that our way was a swift and dangerous one, a speech likely made for nothing, the boy being so engrossed with his own sadness I do not think he heard my words. At last, fearful I might hurt him if he did not cease his mewling, I walked the boy across the stream to the prospector's camp and pulled the tobacco pouch from my saddlebag. Showing him the gold, I told him, 'This will get you back to your home, and your girl, if you can avoid having your skull knocked from your shoulders. There is horse meat in that shelter. I suggest you feed yourself and Lucky Paul and rest for the night. At first light I want you to backtrack, just the same way you came.' I handed him the pouch and he stood there staring at it in his palm. Charlie had seen the transaction out of the corner of his eye and he moved to stand beside us.

'What are you doing?' he asked me.

'You are giving me this?' said the boy.

'What do you think you're doing?' Charlie asked.

I told the boy, 'Return over the pass and keep to the north. When you arrive in Jacksonville, find the sheriff there and explain your situation. If you think him trustworthy, ask him to exchange your dust for hard cash.'

'Ho-ho!' said the boy, bouncing the pouch in his hand.

'I am against this,' Charlie said. 'You are throwing that money away.'

I said, 'That was money pulled from the ground, when neither one of us needs it.'

'Simply dug up from the ground, is that all? But I seem to recall some element of work involved outside of wholesomely burrowing in the soil.'

'Well, the boy has my share, if not yours.'

'When did my share enter into the conversation, even?'

'Never mind then.'

'Who ever said anything about it?'

'Never mind.' Refocusing on the boy, I said, 'Once the sheriff sets you right with the dust I want you to outfit yourself with some new clothes, ones that make you look older. I should think it wise to buy yourself the largest hat you can find, that it might cover up your head. Also you will need a new horse.'

'What about Lucky Paul?' asked the boy.

'You should sell him for whatever price you can get. If you cannot find a buyer I would advise abandoning him.'

The boy shook his head. 'I will never part with him.'

'Then you will never get home. He will hold you up until your money's gone and you're both starved. I am trying to help you, do you understand? If you don't listen to me I will take that gold dust back from you.'

The boy withdrew into silence. I threw some wood on the fire and instructed him to dry his clothes well before sunset. He stripped down but did not hang his clothing; it lay in a heap in the mud and sand and he stood before us, lumpily naked and full of petulance and defeat. He was an unattractive creature with his clothes on; in the nude I thought he looked something like a goat. He began once more to cry, which I took as my cue to sever our ties. As I climbed onto Tub I wished the boy safe travels, but these were empty words, for he was clearly doomed, and it was a mistake to have given him that gold but it was not as though I could take it back now. He stood there weeping and watching us go, while behind him Lucky Paul entered and collapsed the prospector's tent, and I thought, Here is another miserable mental image I will have to catalog and make room for.

We headed south. The banks were sandy but hard packed and we rode at an easy pace on opposite sides of the stream. The sun pushed through the tops of the trees and warmed our faces; the water was translucent and three-foot trout strolled upriver, or hung in the current, lazy and fat. Charlie called over to say he was impressed with California, that there was something in the air, a fortuitous energy, was the phrase he used. I did not feel this but understood what he meant. It was the thought that something as scenic as this running water might offer you not only aesthetic solace but also golden riches; the thought that the earth itself was taking care of you, was in favor of you. This perhaps was what lay at the very root of the hysteria surrounding what came to be known as the Gold Rush:

Men desiring a feeling of fortune; the unlucky masses hoping to skin or borrow the luck of others, or the luck of a destination. A seductive notion, and one I thought to be wary of. To me, luck was something you either earned or invented through strength of character. You had to come by it honestly; you could not trick or bluff your way into it.

But then, as if California wished to prove me wrong on this point, we had stopped for a drink of water when the red-haired she-bear emerged from the forest and walked across the stream not thirty yards in front of us. She was fully grown and her pelt, which I had imagined might be blond-ginger, was in fact apple red. She looked at us cursorily and lumbered away into the woods. Charlie checked his pistols and made to follow after her; when I stood by he asked what I was waiting for.

'We don't even know where this Mayfield lives,' I said.

'We know he lives downriver.'

'We have been riding downriver all morning. What if we passed him by? I don't like the idea of climbing hills and mountains with a dead bear tied to my horse.'

'Mayfield is only after the pelt.'

'And which of us will skin her?'

'Whoever shoots her, the other will skin her.' Now he stepped away from Nimble. 'You're really not coming with me?'

'There is no reason for it.'

'Best get your knife ready then,' he said, dashing away into the woods. I stood awhile, watching the passing trout and inspecting Tub's worsening eye and hoping against hope I would not hear the report from Charlie's gun. But he was a keen tracker and dead shot, and when his pistol sounded five minutes later I accepted my fate and moved toward the noise with my knife. I found Charlie sitting next to the fallen animal. He was panting and laughing, and he nudged the she-bear's belly with his boot.

'Do you know how much a hundred dollars is?' he asked. I said that I did not and he answered, 'It is a hundred dollars.'

I rolled the bear onto her back and plunged my knife in the center of her chest. I have always had a feeling that an animal's insides are unclean, more so than a man's, which I know does not make sense when you consider what poisons we put into our bodies, but the feeling was one I could not escape, and so I loathed and was resentful about having to skin the bear. After Charlie caught his breath he left to search out the boss-man Mayfield's encampment, saying he had seen a series of trails some miles back, these leading away from the stream and to the west. Three-quarters of an hour later I was washing the she-bear's fur and sticky blood from my hands and forearms, and the black-eyed pelt was lain out over some fern plants. The carcass lay on its side before me, no longer male or female, only a pile of rib-boned meat, alive with an ecstatic and ever-growing community of fat-bottomed flies. Their number grew so that I could hardly see the bear's flesh, and I could not hear myself thinking, so clamorous was their buzzing. Why and how do flies make this noise? Does it not sound like shouting to them? When the buzzing suddenly and completely ceased I looked up from my washing, expecting to find the flies gone and some larger predator close by, but the insects had remained atop the she-bear, all of them quiet and still save for their wings, which folded and unfolded as they pleased. What caused this uniform silence? I will never know. Their buzzing had returned in full when Charlie, back from his patrol, let out a shrill whistle. At this, the flies rose away from the bear in a black mass. Upon seeing the carcass my brother called out his happy greeting: 'God's little butcher. God's own knife and conscience, too.'

I had never before seen so many pelts and heads and cotton-stuffed hawks and owls in one place as in Mister May-field's well-equipped parlor, located in the town of Mayfield's one hotel, which I was unsurprised to learn was named: May-field's. The man himself sat at a desk, behind a curtain of cigar smoke. Not knowing our business, neither who we were nor why we had come, he did not rise to shake our hands or greet us verbally. Four trappers matching the description given by the hit-on-the-head boy stood two on either side of him. These enormous men looked down on us with full confidence and no trace of concern. They struck me as fearless but mindless, and their outfits were exaggerated to the point of ridiculousness, being so heavily covered in furs and leather and straps and pistols and knives that I wondered how they stood upright to carry these burdens. Their hair was long and stringy and their hats were each matching but of a kind I had not seen before: Wide, floppy brims, with tall, pointy tops. How is it, I wondered, that they all look so similar to one another when the dress is so eccentric? Surely there was one among them who had been first to outfit himself in such a way. Had this man been pleased when the others imitated him, or annoyed, his individual sense of flair devalued by their emulation?

Mayfield's desktop was the base segment of a moderately sized pine tree, perhaps five feet across and four or five inches thick, with the bark intact. When I reached up to touch the chunky outer ring Mayfield spoke his first words: 'Don't pick at it, son.' At this I jerked my hand back, and experienced a flash of shame at succumbing to the reprimand. To Charlie, he explained, 'People love to pick the bark. Drives me crazy.'

'I wasn't going to pick it, just touch it,' I said, a statement that effectively doubled my discomfort with its wounded tone. I decided the table was the stupidest piece of furniture I had ever laid eyes on.

Charlie handed over the she-bear's pelt and Mayfield's face transformed from its expression of apparent indigestion to that of a lad gazing upon his first set of naked breasts. 'Ah!' he cried. 'Aha!' There were three brass handbells on his desk, identical save for their sizes, small, medium, and large; he rang the smallest bell, which summoned an old hotel crone. She was told the pelt should be hung on the wall behind him and she unfurled it with a snap. But as I had failed to scrape the skin, this sent red globules of fat and blood flying across the room. These clung to the windowpane and Mayfield, scowling distastefully, called for the pelt to be cleaned. The woman re-rolled it and left, her eyes on the ground as she walked.

The trappers, meanwhile, were unhappy we had usurped their glory with the she-bear and were, I felt, preparing to exhibit rudeness. To thwart this I introduced Charlie and myself, our full names, which silenced them. Now they will hate us ever more virulently, but secretly, I thought. Charlie found these men amusing, and could not help but make a comment. 'It seems you four are involved in a kind of contest to become totally circular, is that it?'

Mayfield laughed about this. The trappers looked at one another uneasily. The largest one of the group said, 'You do not know the customs here.'

'If I were to linger, do you suppose I too would take on the physical proportions of the buffalo?'

'Do you plan to linger?'

'We are only passing through, for now. But I am for getting to know a place intimately, so do not be surprised if you see me on my return trip.'

'Nothing in this world could surprise me,' said the trapper.

'Nothing?' Charlie wondered, and he winked at me.

Mayfield sent these men away. As the evening came upon us, he called for the room to be lit. This was accomplished by ringing the medium-sized bell, which produced a different tone and thus summoned a different human, a Chinese boy of eleven or twelve; we watched as he flitted from candle to candle with admirable precision and not a half second wasted. Charlie said, 'He moves like his life depends on it.'

'It's not his life, it's his family's,' said Mayfield. 'He's saving to bring them over from China. Sister and mother and father—a cripple, from what I gather, though to tell you the truth I don't know what he's talking about half the time. Little bastard might see his mission through, though, the way he hops to.' When the young fellow had finished, the room was bathed in light, and he stood before Mayfield, removing his silken hat and bowing. Mayfield clapped and said, 'Now, you dance, chink!' With these words the boy began dancing wildly and without grace, looking much like someone forced to stand barefoot over hot coals. It was an ugly thing to witness, and if I had not before this point made my decision about Mayfield, the matter was now settled in my mind. When he clapped a second time the boy dropped to his hands and knees, panting and spent. A handful of coins were tossed to the ground and the boy scooped these into his hat. He stood and bowed, and as he left his footsteps made no noise whatsoever.

The crone soon returned with the red pelt, now scraped and set on a kind of display to stretch it taut, something like a large drum lain on edge. She pulled this cumbersome apparatus across the threshold; I stood to assist her and Mayfield ordered me, a little too curtly I felt, to sit. 'Let her do it,' he said. She dragged the display to a far corner where we all might study the strange coloring of the she-bear. The crone wiped her brow and walked heavily from the room.

I said, 'The woman is too old for such tasks.'

Mayfield shook his head. 'She is a dynamo. I have tried to assign her simpler, lighter work, but she won't hear of it. She enjoys industry, is the long and short of it.'

'I could not see the joy. But perhaps it is the inward kind that strangers can never read.'

'My advice is to not bother yourself about it any longer.'

'I would not say I am bothered, exactly.'

'You are bothering me.'

Charlie said, 'About our payment for this pelt.'

Mayfield watched me a moment, then turned to Charlie. He tossed five double eagles across the table and Charlie dragged them into his palm. He handed me two coins and I took them. I decided I would spend the money even more carelessly than usual. What would the world be, I thought, without money hung around our necks, hung around our very souls?

Mayfield hefted and rang the third, largest bell. Presently we heard hurried footsteps in the hall and I was half prepared for the trappers to barge through and set upon us. Instead of this, the room filled with painted whores, seven in number, each of them in frills and lace, each of them already drunk. They fell to putting on their playful shows for us, re-creating themselves as curious, doting, loving, lusty. One of them thought it prudent to speak like a baby. I found their presence depressing but Charlie was in highest spirits, and I could see his interest in Mayfield growing before my eyes. I realized that by looking at this boss man I was witnessing the earthly personification of Charlie's future, or proposed future, for ours was so often in jeopardy; and it was true, just as the dead prospector had said, that Charlie and Mayfield bore a resemblance to each other, though the latter was older and heavier and doubly pickled from alcohol. But yes, just as I longed for the organized solitude of the shopkeeper, so did Charlie wish for the days of continued excitement and violence, except he would no longer engage personally but dictate from behind a wall of well-armed soldiers, while he remained in perfumed rooms where fleshy women poured his drinks and crawled on the ground like hysterical infants, their backsides in the air, shivering with laughter and brandy and deviousness. Mayfield must have thought I was acting without sufficient enthusiasm, for he asked me, in put-upon tone, 'You don't like the women?'

'The women are fine, thank you.'

'Maybe it is the brandy that makes you curl your lips when you speak?'

'The brandy is also fine.'

'It is too smoky in here, is that it? Shall I open a window? Would you like a fan?'

'Everything is fine.'

'Perhaps it is the custom where you come from, to squint and glare at your host.' Turning to Charlie, he said, 'I must admit I did not care for Oregon City, the one time I visited there.'

'What was your business in Oregon City?' Charlie asked.

'You know, I cannot exactly remember. In those younger days, I followed one mad idea after the other, and my purpose was often blurred. But Oregon City was a dead loss. I was robbed by a man with a limp. Neither of you has a limp, do you?'

'You saw us come in yourself,' I said.

'I was not paying attention then.' Half seriously he asked, 'Would you two object to standing and clicking your heels for me?'

'I would object to that strongly,' I told him.

'We are both healthy in our legs,' Charlie said assuredly.

'But you would not do it?' he asked me.

'I would sooner die than click my heels for you.'

'He is the unfriendly one,' Mayfield said to Charlie.

'We take turns,' Charlie said.

'Anyway, I prefer you to him.'

'What did this limping man get away with?' Charlie asked.

'He took a purseful of gold worth twenty-five dollars, and an ivory-handled Paterson Colt revolver that I could not put a price on. The name of the saloon was the Pig-King. Are you boys familiar with it? I would not be surprised if it wasn't there anymore, the way these towns jump up and down.'

'It is still there,' Charlie said.

'The man who robbed me had a knife with a hooked blade, like a small scythe.'

'Oh, you are talking about Robinson,' said Charlie.

Mayfield sat up. 'What? You know the man? Are you sure?'

'James Robinson.' He nodded.

'What are you doing?' I asked. Charlie reached over and pinched my thigh. Mayfield, fumbling with his ink pot, was scribbling the name down.

'Does he still live in Oregon City?' he asked breathlessly.

'Yes, he does. And he still carries the same curved blade he used to rob you. His limp was only a temporary injury that has since healed over, but you will find him sitting at the King, just as before, making jokes that no one enjoys and that in fact almost never make sense.'

'I've thought of the man many times, these last years,' Mayfield said. Returning his pen to its holder, he told us, 'I will have him gutted with that scythe. I will hang him by his own intestines.' At this piece of dramatic exposition, I could not help but roll my eyes. A length of intestines would not carry the weight of a child, much less a full grown man. Mayfield excused himself to make water; in the thirty seconds he was away my brother and I had this quickly spoken, whispered discussion:

'What do you mean, giving Robinson away like that?'

'Robinson died of typhus half a year ago.'

'What? You sure?'

'Sure I'm sure. I visited his widow last time we were in town. Did you know she had false teeth? I nearly gagged when she plopped them in her water glass.' A whore passed him by, tickling his chin; he smiled at her and asked me distractedly, 'What do you think about staying the night?'

'I'm for moving on. You'll just be sick in the morning and we'll miss another day of travel. Plus, there'll be trouble with Mayfield.'

'If there's trouble, it'll be trouble for him, not us.'

'Trouble's trouble. I'm for moving on.'

He shook his head. 'Sorry, brother, but the pipsqueak's going to war tonight.'

Mayfield emerged from the water closet, buttoning up his pants. 'What's this? I would never have pegged the famous Sisters brothers as secret tellers.'

With the whores like cats, circling the room behind us.

Charlie had drunk three glasses of brandy and his face was turning the familiar scarlet color that indicated the onset of sloven drunkenness. He began asking Mayfield questions about his business and successes, these put to the man in a deferential tone in which I did not like to hear my brother speak. Mayfield responded to the queries vaguely but I deduced he had hit a lucky strike and was now spending his golden winnings as fast as he was able. I grew tired of their strained banter and became quietly drunk. The women continued to visit and tease me, sitting on my lap until my organ became engorged, then laughing at me or it and moving on to my brother or Mayfield. I recall standing to correct and retuck the bloated appendage and noticing that both my brother and Mayfield were likewise engorged. Just your everyday grouping of civilized gentlemen, sitting in a round robin to discuss the events of the day with quivering erections. As the brandy took hold of my mind, I could not seem to place one particular girl; their cackles and perfumes blurred together in a garish bouquet that I found at once enticing and stomach turning. Mayfield and Charlie were ostensibly involved in a conversation, but really they were speaking to themselves and wished only to hear their own words and voices: Charlie made fun of my toothbrush; Mayfield debunked the myth of the divining rod. On and on like this until I despised them both. I thought, When a man is properly drunk it is as though he is in a room by himself—there is a physical, impenetrable separation between him and his fellows.

Another brandy, then another, when I noticed a new woman in the far corner of the parlor standing by herself at a window. She was paler and not so meaty as the others, her eyes ringed with worry or lack of sleep. Despite her sickliness, she was a true beauty, with jade-colored eyes and golden hair running to the small of her back. Emboldened with brandy and its attendant stupidity, I watched her alone until she could not help but return my attentions, when she offered me a pitying smile. I winked at her and her pity doubled. Now she crossed the parlor to leave, but with every step her eyes remained fixed upon me. She exited the room and I stared awhile at the door, which she had left ajar.

'Who was that?' I asked Mayfield.

'Who was who?' he said.

'Who-be-do?' said Charlie, and the whores all laughed.

I left the parlor and found the woman smoking a cigarette in the hall. She was not surprised I had followed her out, which is not to say she was happy about it. It was likely that each time she left a room, some man or another followed after her, and over time she had become accustomed to it. I reached up to remove my hat but it was not on my head. I told her, 'I don't know about you, but I've had enough of that room.' She said nothing. 'My brother and I sold Mayfield a pelt. Now we are obliged to sit and listen to his boasts and lies.' She continued only to stare, smoke draining from her mouth, a smile lingering on her lips, and I could not decipher her thoughts. 'What is your business here?' I asked.

'I live here. I'm Mr. Mayfield's bookkeeper.'

'Are your quarters a hotel room, or somehow different?' I thought, Here is precisely the wrong kind of question to ask, and I am asking it because of the brandy. I thought, Stop drinking brandy! Happily, the woman was not small about it. 'My room's a regular hotel room. But sometimes I'll sleep in a vacant room, just for the fun of it.'

'How is it fun?' I asked. 'Aren't they all the same?'

'They are the same on the surface. But the differences in actuality are significant.'

I did not know what to say in response but the brandy implored me to blather on, and I was opening my jaws to do just this when some deeper reasoning took hold and I closed my mouth, maintaining my silence. I was congratulating myself inwardly when the woman began casting around for somewhere to put her cigarette. I volunteered to dispose of it and she dropped the smoldering lump into my outstretched palm. I pinched its light shut between my fingers while staring coolly at the woman, hoping, I suppose, to display my threshold for pain, which has always been abnormally high: Stop drinking brandy! I put the ash and charred paper into my pocket. The woman's attentions remained foreign, separate. I said, 'I can't tell about you, ma'am.'

'What does that mean?'

'I can't tell if you're happy or sad or mad or what you are.'

'I am sick.'

'How are you sick?'

She produced from her dress pocket a handkerchief with dried bloodstains on it, flaunting this with a ghoulish amusement. But I did not take it lightly, and in fact was outraged by the sight of the stains. Mindlessly then, I asked if she was dying. Her expression was downcast and I sputtered my apologies: 'Don't answer that. I have had too much to drink. Will you forgive me? Please, say you will.'

She did not, but neither did she appear to be holding a grudge, and I decided to carry on just as if I had not made the blunder. As casually as I could manage, I said, 'Where are you going now, can I ask?'

'I have no place in mind. There is no other place than this hotel, at night.'

'Well,' I said, clucking my tongue, 'it seems that you were waiting for me out here.'

'I was not.'

'You left the door open, that I might follow after you.'

'I did not.'

'I think you probably did.'

I heard a creaking down the hall; the woman and I turned to find one of the trappers standing at the top of the stairway. He had been eavesdropping, and his face was unsmiling. 'You should get to your room now,' he said to her.

'How is that your concern?' she asked.

'Don't I work for the man?'

'Don't I? I am speaking to a guest of his.'

'There will be problems if you keep it up.'

'Problems with whom?'

'You know. Him.'

'You,' I said to the trapper.

'What?'

'Go right away from here.'

The man paused, then plunged a hand in his blue-black beard, itching at his cheek and jaw. He turned and walked back down the stairs and the woman told me, 'He follows me around the hotel. I have to keep my door locked at night.'

'Mayfield is your man, is that it?'

She pointed to the whore-filled parlor. 'He has no one woman.' At my sunken expression, for this answer was suspiciously incomplete, she added, 'But no, we are not connected. Once, perhaps, in a way.'

From behind the doors I could hear my brother's high-volume laughter. Charlie has an unintelligent-sounding laugh. It is braying, is what it is. 'This town is leaving a poor impression on me,' I said.

The woman took a step toward me. Was she leaning in for a kiss? But no, she only had a secret to tell me: 'I heard that trapper and the others talking about you and your brother. They have some plan against you. I couldn't understand, exactly, but every other night they are drinking, and tonight they are not. You should be careful.'

'I have had too much brandy to be careful.'

'Then you had better return to your party. To stay close to Mayfield would be best, I think.'

'No, I can't stay another minute in there. I only want to sleep.'

'Where has Mayfield put you?'

'He hasn't put me anywhere.'

'I will find you a safe place,' she said, and led me away to the far end of the hall, where she opened a door with a key from her pocket. She did this with care not to make a sound, and I found myself mimicking her cautious steps. We entered the darkened room and she closed the door behind us. She stood me against a wall and told me to stay still while she searched out a candle. I could not see her but listened to her movements—her footsteps, her hands rooting through drawers and over tabletops; I found this endearing, her nearness to me, her busyness, and my not knowing just what she was doing. I decided I liked her then; I was flattered she was devoting her time and concerns to me and I thought, I do not need much at all, to make me feel contented.

She lit a candle and drew open the curtains to let in the light of the moon. It was a hotel room just like any other, only there was a dust and staleness on the air, and she explained to me, 'This is always vacant because the key was misplaced, and Mayfield's too lazy to bring in a locksmith. Except the key wasn't misplaced, I took it. I come here sometimes, when I want to be alone.'

Nodding politely, I said, 'Yes, well, it is fairly obvious that you are in love with me!'

'No,' she said, coloring. 'Not that.'

'I can see it. Hopelessly in love, powerless to guard against it. You shouldn't feel too badly about it, it has happened before. It seems that every time I walk down the road there comes a woman in my direction, her eyes filled up with passion and longing.' I flopped onto the small bed, rolling around on the mattress. The woman was amused by me but not so much that she wished to stay any longer, and she returned to the door to leave. I jostled back and forth and the bed issued its plaintive squeaks and she told me, 'You should stop that rolling on the bed. The trappers' quarters are just beneath us.'

'Oh, stop talking about them already. I don't care about it, and there isn't anything they can do to me.'

'But they are killers,' she whispered.

'So am I!' I whispered back.

'What do you mean?'

There was something about the look on her face, her paleness and unsureness, it made me wild, and I was seized by a kind of cruelty or animal-mindedness. Standing, I shouted out: 'Death stalks all of us upon this earth!' These words came from I knew not where, and they inspired me terribly; I lurched away from the bed, taking up my pistol and firing a shot into the floorboards. The report was terrifically loud; it doubled off the walls and the room filled with smoke and the horrified woman spun on her heels and left me, locking the door with her key. I crossed over and unlocked it, opening it wide and sitting back on the tormented bed, my pistols drawn, cocked, and leveled. My heart was thudding and I was looking forward to an end-of-all-time fight, but after five minutes my eyes began growing heavy. After ten minutes I decided the trappers had not heard the shot. They were not in their room, or I had fired into a room that was not theirs. I gave up my adventure for dead. I brushed my teeth and went to sleep.

It was sunny in the morning, and the open window carried cool air over my face as I lay in the bed. I was fully clothed and the door was closed and bolted. Had the bookkeeper returned in the night to protect me? I heard a key in the lock and she entered, sitting on the edge of the mattress and smiling. I asked after Charlie and she said he was fine. She invited me to go walking with her, and though she still looked only half living she was a sweet-smelling, powdered beauty, and appeared not unhappy to be visiting. Pulling myself up from the bed, I stepped to the window and propped myself against its frame, looking down over the road beneath the hotel. Men and women passed this way and that, saying their good mornings, bowing and tipping their hats. The woman cleared her throat and said,

'Last night you said you couldn't tell about me. Now I find myself thinking the same thing about you.'

'What do you mean?'

'For one, why in the world did you shoot your pistol into the floor?'

'I am embarrassed by that,' I admitted. 'I'm sorry if I frightened you.'

'But why would you do it?'

'Sometimes, if I drink too much, and I'm feeling low, a part of me wants to die.' I thought, Who is showing whom their bloody rag now?

'Why were you feeling low?'

'Why does anyone? It creeps up on you from time to time.'

'But you were glad the one moment, then suddenly not.'

I shrugged. In the road I saw a man who was familiar to me, but I could not determine his position in my past. His carriage was heavy and dazed, his gait aimless, as though he did not have any one destination in mind. 'I know that person,' I said, pointing. The woman stood beside me to look but the man had moved out of sight. Straightening her dress, she asked, 'Will you come walking with me or not?'

I ate some tooth powder and she led me down the hall by my arm. As we passed the open door to Mayfield's parlor I saw the boss man sleeping facedown at his desk, head and arms resting amid the upset of bottles and cigar ash, the three toppled bells. There was a large whore, stark naked and flat on her back on the floor beside him. Her face was turned away and I paused to watch her dozing body, breasts and stomach rising and falling with her breath. Here was the picture of moral negligence, and I found myself startled by the sight of her genitals, the hair matted and stamped upon. I noticed my hat was hanging from the antler of a buck on the far wall and I crossed the great room to retrieve it. Achieving this, I was doubling back, dusting ash from the hat's brim when I tripped and fell onto the floor. I had been caught up on the fur stretching rack, which I now saw was without the red pelt. This had not been untied, but quickly and indelicately cut away. I looked back at the bookkeeper standing under the jamb; her eyes were closed and she was rolling her head in slow circles and I thought, She is stuck fast under the weight of her burdens.

The road had turned to mud and deep puddles, and to cross we were forced to hobble over a series of wooden planks. The woman enjoyed this and her laughter was clear and rich in the morning. Her laughter and this cold, fresh air, I thought. They are just the same welcome and cleansing thing to me. It is odd to think this struck me as an adventure, I who had had so many truly dangerous adventures already, but there I was, holding her hand and pointing the way along the rocking boards; nausea was ever looming but this only made the event that much more comical, and therefore merry. By the time we arrived on the far side of the road my boots were mud covered but hers had not a blemish upon them and for this she said the words, 'Thank you.' Safely installed on the dry wooden walkway, she held her grip on my arm for a half-dozen paces, then broke off to pat and refashion her hair. I do not think there was any precise need for her to have broken away, that it was done in the name of good taste and principles. I believe she enjoyed the feel of my arm and wished to grip it longer. This at any rate was my hopeful impression.

I asked, 'How is it working for Mayfield?'

'He pays me well enough, but he is hard to be around, always wanting to show he is the right one. He was a good man, before he hit his strike.'

'He looks to be spending it quickly enough. Perhaps he will change back to the first man once it's all gone.'

'He will change, but not back to the first man. He will become a third man, and I think the third will be even less pleasant than the second.' I remained quiet and she added, 'Yes, there isn't anything to say about it.' A moment passed and she reached up to grip my arm again. I felt proud, and my legs were sure and confident beneath me. I said, 'How is it that my door was locked this morning? Did you return later in the night to visit me?'

'You don't remember?' she asked.

'I am sorry to say I don't.'

'That makes me feel just wretched.'

'Will you explain what happened?'

She considered this, and said, 'If you really want to know, you will recall it by your own force of mind.' Thinking of something, she laughed once more, and the sound was bright and diamond shaped.

'Your laughter is like cool water to me,' I said. I felt my heart sob at these words, and it would not have been hard to summon tears: Strange.

'You are so serious all of a sudden,' she told me.

'I am not any one thing,' I said.

Reaching the edge of town, we crossed another line of planks and returned in the direction of the hotel. I thought of my room, of the bed I had slept in; I imagined my shape indented over the blankets. Remembering, then, I said, 'He is the weeping man!'

'Who is?' asked the woman. 'The what, now?'

'The person I saw from the window that I said was familiar to me? I met him in Oregon Territory some weeks ago. My brother and I were riding out of Oregon City and came across a lone man leading a horse on foot. He was in great distress but would not accept our help. His grief ran deep and made him unreasonable.'

'Had his luck changed at all, did you notice?'

'It did not appear to have, no.'

'Poor soul.'

'He makes good time for a hysterical man on foot.'

A pause, and she let go of my arm.

'Last night you spoke of some pressing business in San Francisco,' she said.

I nodded. 'We are after a man called Hermann Warm who is said to be living there.'

'What does that mean? After him?'

'He has done something incorrect and we have been hired to bring him to justice.'

'But you are not lawmen?'

'We are the opposite of lawmen.'

Her face became pensive. 'Is this Warm a very bad man?'

'I don't know. That is an unclear question. They say he is a thief.'

'What did he steal?'

'Whatever people normally steal. Money, probably.' This lying made me feel ugly, and I searched around for something to look at and find distraction in but could not locate anything suitable. 'Honestly, actually, he probably didn't steal a penny.' Her eyes dropped and I laughed a little. I said, 'It would not surprise me in the least if he was perfectly innocent.'

'And do you typically go after men you think are innocent?'

'There is nothing typical about my profession.' Suddenly I did not want to talk about it any longer. 'I don't want to talk about it any longer.'

Ignoring this statement, she asked, 'Do you enjoy this work?'

'Each job is different. Some I have seen as singular escapades. Others have been like a hell.' I shrugged. 'You put a wage behind something, it gives the act a sort of respectability. In a way, I suppose it feels significant to have something as large as a man's life entrusted to me.'

'A man's death,' she corrected.

I had not been certain she understood what my position consisted of. I was relieved to know she did—that I did not have to tell her precisely. 'However you wish to phrase it,' I said.

'Haven't you ever thought to stop?'

'I have wanted to,' I admitted.

She took up my arm again. 'What about after you deal with this man, Warm? What will you do then?'

I told her, 'I have a small home outside of Oregon City that I share with my brother. The land is pretty but the house is cramped and drafty. I would like to move but can't seem to find time to search out another spot. Charlie has many unsavory acquaintances. They have no respect for the traditional hours of sleep.' But the woman was made restless by my answer and I said, 'What is it that you are asking me?'

'My hope is that I will see you again.'

My chest swelled like an aching bruise and I thought, I am a perfect ass. 'Your hope will be fulfilled,' I promised.

'If you leave I don't think I will see you anymore.'

'I will be back, I give you my word.' The woman did not believe me, however, or she only partially believed me. Looking up at my face she asked me to take off my coat, which I did, and she pulled a length of bright blue silk from her layers. She tied the sash over my shoulder, fastening it with a snug knot and afterward stepping back to look at me. She was very sad, and beautiful, her eyes damp and heavy with their powders and ancient spells. I placed my hands on the material but could think of nothing to say about it.

She told me, 'You should always wear it just like that, and when you see it, you will remember me, and remember your promise to return here.' Stroking the fabric, she smiled. 'Will it make your brother very jealous?'

'I think he will want to know all about it.'

'Isn't it a fine piece, though?'

'It is very shiny.'

I buttoned my coat to cover it. She came forward and put her arms around me, resting the side of her face over my heart, listening to the organ's mad jumping. After this she said her good-byes, then turned and disappeared into the hotel, but not before I had slipped Mayfield's forty dollars in her petticoat pocket. I called out that I would see her on my return, but she did not respond and I stood alone, my thoughts dipping and shooting away, dipping and dying. I did not wish to be indoors, but to continue circulating in the open. I spied a row of houses off from the main road and walked in their direction.

INTERMISSION

I came upon a young girl of seven or eight years old, outfitted in the finest clothing from hat to shoe and standing stiffly before the fenced-in yard of a quaint, freshly painted house. She glared at the property with an intense dislike or malice—her brow was furrowed, her hands clenched, and she was crying, not forcefully, but calmly and without a sound. When I approached her and asked her what was the matter, she told me she had had a bad dream.

'Just now you had a bad dream?' I said, for the sun was high in the sky.

'In the night I had one. But I had forgotten about it until a moment ago, when that dog reminded me.' She pointed to a fat dog, asleep on the other side of the fence. I was startled when I spied what looked to be the dog's leg lying independently from the body, but upon closer inspection I saw it was the femur bone of a lamb or calf, this for the dog to chew on. It still had some meat and gristle attached, which gave it a fleshy appearance. I smiled at the girl.

'I thought it was the dog's leg,' I said.

The girl wiped the tears from her cheeks. 'But it *is* the dog's leg.'

I shook my head and pointed. 'The dog's leg is tucked under him, do you see?'

'You are wrong. Watch.' She whistled and the dog awoke and stood, and I discovered it truly was missing the leg closest to the bone on the ground, only the skin had long since healed over. It was a years-old wound, and though I was confused, I persevered: 'That there on the ground is the femur bone of a lamb, and not the dog's. Don't you see the animal suffered its loss some time ago and that he is not in pain?'

The statement angered the girl, and now she regarded me

with just the same malice with which she had been regarding the house. 'The dog *is* in pain,' she insisted. 'The dog is in no small amount of pain!'

The violence of her words and temper caught me by surprise; I found myself taking a step away from her. 'You are a peculiar girl,' I said.

'It's a peculiar lifetime on earth,' she countered. I did not know what to say to that. At any rate it was as truthful a statement as I had come across. The girl continued, her voice now honeyed and innocent: 'But you did not ask about my dream.'

'You said it was about this dog.'

'The dog was but a part of it. It was also about the fence, and the house, and you.'

'I was in your dream?'

'A man was in it. A man I did not know or care about.'

'Was he a good man or a bad man?'

She spoke in a whisper: 'He was a protected man.'

I thought at once of the gypsy-witch, of the doorway and necklace. 'How was he protected?' I asked. 'Protected from what?'

But she would not answer my question. She said, 'I was walking here to see this dog, which I hate. And as I slipped it its poison to kill it there appeared in this yard before me a fist-sized, swirling gray-and-black cloud. This grew bigger and was soon a foot across, then two feet, then ten—now it was big as the house. And I felt the wind from its spinning, a cold wind, so cold it burned my face.' She closed her eyes and tilted her head upward, as though recalling this sensation.

'What kind of poison did you slip the dog?' I asked, for I noticed her right hand had a grainy black residue over the knuckles.

'The cloud became bigger still,' the terrible girl continued, her volume and agitation increasing, 'soon lifting me into its center, where I hung in the air, tumbling lightly in circles. I think it might have been calming if the three-legged dog, now dead, was not also spinning within the orb beside me.'

'That is a distressing dream, girl.'

'The three-legged dog, now dead, spinning within the orb beside me!' She clapped once, turned abruptly around, and left me where I stood, dumbfounded and not a little unnerved. I thought, How I long for a reliable companion. The girl had rounded the corner before I looked back at the dog, which was once more lying prone on the ground, foam issuing from his mouth, ribs no longer rising to breathe, dead as dead could be. There was a shift of the curtains in the house and I turned and left just as hastily as the girl had but in the opposite direction, and I did not at any point look back. It was time to say good-bye and good riddance to Mayfield, for now.

END INTERMISSION

Passing Mayfield's parlor I peered in and saw both he and the naked woman were gone, and the pelt stand had been righted. Farther down the hall, one of the whores was standing with her head on the door of the room next to mine. Walking toward her, I asked if she had seen Charlie. 'He just escorted me out.' Her skin had a greenish tint to it; she was deathly brandy-sick. Belching, she covered her mouth with a balled fist. 'Oh, God,' she said. I opened the door to my room and asked her to tell Charlie to hurry along. 'I will not tell him a thing, sir. I am headed for my own bed to wait out these long hours in private.' I watched as she walked away, her fist on the wall, unsure in her footsteps. Charlie's door was locked and when I knocked he made a guttural sound communicating a desire for solitude.

When I called to him, he came to the door in the nude and waved me in.

'Where have you been?' he asked.

'I was walking with the girl from last night.'

'What girl from last night?'

'The pretty, thin one.'

'*Was* there a pretty, thin one?'

'You were too distracted with your guffawing to notice. Look at how red your head is.'

I could hear Mayfield's muffled, angry voice emanating from the parlor. I told Charlie about the missing pelt and he stiffened. 'What do you mean, missing?' he demanded.

'Missing. Not there. The stand was toppled and the pelt had been cut away.'

He studied this awhile, then began getting dressed. 'I will talk to Mayfield about it,' he said, groaning as he pulled on his pants. 'We got along very fine last night. Surely the responsible party was one of those filthy trappers he has on the payroll.'

He left and I sat heavily in a low wicker chair. I noticed Charlie's mattress had been pulled to the floor and shredded with a knife, its stuffing yanked out in shocks. I thought, Will his fondness for senseless carnage ever cease? He and Mayfield were having an argument but I could not understand the words. My body was burning with fatigue and I was halfway asleep when Charlie returned, his face tight, his fists clenched and white at the knuckle. 'There is a man who knows how to raise his voice,' he said. 'What a blusterer.'

'Does he think we took the pelt?'

'He most certainly does, and do you know why? One of his trappers claims to have seen you hurrying through the hall with it tucked under your arm. I asked Mayfield to upend our rooms and baggage but he said it was beneath him. He whispered to his whore, and she hurried away. She is searching the trappers out, I'd imagine.' He moved to the window, gazing down at the main road. 'It makes me angry to think of them playing such a trick on us. If I wasn't feeling so low I'd go right after them.' He looked over at me. 'What about you, brother? Are you up for a fight?'

'Hardly.'

Squinting, he asked, 'What's that under your coat?'

'A gift from the girl.'

'Is there to be a parade?'

'It's a simple bit of fabric to recall her by. A *bomboniere*, as Mother would say.'

He sucked his teeth. 'You should not wear it,' he said decisively.

'It's very expensive material, I think.'

'The girl has played a joke on you.'

'She is a serious person.'

'You look like the prize goose.'

I untied and removed the cloth, folding it into a tidy square. I decided I would keep it with me but regard it only in private. 'Now who has the red head?' said Charlie. Turning back to the window, he tapped the pane and said, 'Aha, here we go.'

I crossed over and saw the whore from the floor of the parlor speaking to the largest trapper. He stood listening, rolling a cigarette, and nodding; when she was through he shared with her some instruction or another, and she returned in the direction of the hotel. I watched her until she was out of sight, then looked again at the trapper, who had located us in the window and was staring from beneath his floppy-brimmed, pointed hat. 'Where do you even *get* a hat like that?' Charlie wondered. 'They must make them themselves.' The trapper lit his cigarette, exhaled a plume of smoke, and walked in the opposite direction of the hotel. Charlie slapped his leg and spit. 'I hate to admit it, but we're beat. Give me your double eagles, and I will hand mine in, also.'

'Returning the money is just the same as an admission of guilt.'

'It is our only option other than fighting or running, neither of which we are in any shape to do. Come on now, let's have it.' He approached and stood before me with his hand out. I went through the motions of patting my pockets, a sad pantomime that gave me away. Scratching his stubbly neck, he said, 'You left it for the woman, didn't you.'

'That was my own earned money. And what a man does with his earned money is no other man's business.' Remembering his whore's clutched hand as she had covered her mouth, I said, 'Didn't you give any of yours away?'

'You know, I hadn't thought of that.' He checked his purse and laughed bitterly. 'And Mayfield had said it was on the house, too.'

More shouting from the parlor. A bell was rung, a glass broken.

'I hope you don't propose to pay the man out of our own pockets,' I said.

'No, I am not *that* keen to make friends. Let me gather my things, then we'll fetch yours. We can exit out your window and hope for an unchecked departure. We will fight if we must but I would prefer to wait for another day, when we are feeling one hundred percent.' Bag in hand, then, he scanned the room and asked, 'Have we got everything? Yes? All right. Let us navigate the hall in pure silence.'

Pure silence, I thought as we crept along to my quarters. The words struck me as somehow poetical.

We climbed out the window of my room and snuck along the overhang that ran the length of the walkway. This proved handy to us, for Tub and Nimble were housed in a stable at the far end of Mayfield, and we covered that entire distance without a soul noticing our travels. At the halfway point, Charlie paused behind a tall sign to watch the largest trapper leaning against a hitching post below us. Now the other three joined him, and the group stood in a loose circle, speaking through their dirty beards. 'Doubtless they are infamous among the muskrat community hereabouts,' said Charlie. 'But these are not killers of men.' He pointed at the leader. 'He is the one who stole the pelt, I'm sure of it. If we come up against them, I will take care of him. Watch the rest take flight at the first shot fired.'

The men dispersed and we continued along the overhang to its limit, dropping off and sneaking into the stable, where I found the bucktoothed hand standing next to Tub and Nimble, staring at them dumbly. He jumped at our greeting and was loath to help us with the saddles, which I should have been made suspicious by but was too distracted with thoughts of escape to dissect properly. And so: Charlie and I were tying off our bags when the four trappers stepped noiselessly from the stall behind ours. We did not notice them until it was too late. They had us cold, the barrels of their pistols leveled at our hearts.

'You are ready to leave Mayfield?' asked the largest trapper.

'We are leaving,' said Charlie. I was not sure how he would play it, but he had a habit of cracking his index fingers with his thumbs just prior to drawing his guns and I kept my ear trained for the noise.

'You're not leaving without returning the money you owe Mr. Mayfield.'

'*Mr.* Mayfield,' said Charlie. 'The beloved employer. Tell us, do you make his bed down for him also? Do you warm his feet with your hands on the long winter nights?'

'One hundred dollars or I will kill you. I will probably kill you anyway. You think I am slow in my furs and leather, but you will find me faster than you had believed. And won't you be surprised to find my bullets in your body?'

Charlie said, 'I do think you are slow, trapper, but it is not your clothing that hinders your speed. Your mind is the culprit. For I believe you to be just as stupid as the animals you lurk in the mud and snow to catch.'

The trapper laughed, or pretended to laugh, an imitation of lightness and good nature. He said, 'I heard you getting drunk last night and thought, I will not drink a drop this evening. I will be rested and quick, just in case I have to kill this man in the morning. And now it is morning, and I ask you this only once more: Will you return the money, or the pelt?'

'All you will get from me is Death.' Charlie's words, spoken just as casual as a man describing the weather, brought the hair on my neck up and my hands began to pulse and throb. He is wonderful in situations like this, clear minded and without a trace of fear. He had always been this way, and though I had seen it many times, every time I did I felt an admiration for him.

'I am going to shoot you down,' said the trapper.

'My brother will count it out,' said Charlie. 'When he reaches three, we draw.'

The trapper nodded and returned his pistol to its holster. 'He can count to one hundred if it suits you,' he said, opening and closing his hand to stretch it.

Charlie made a sour face. 'What a stupid thing to say. Think of something else besides that. A man wants his last words to be respectable.'

'I will be speaking all through this day and into the night. I will tell my grandchildren of the time I killed the famous Sisters brothers.'

'That at least makes sense. Also it will serve as a humorous footnote.' To me, Charlie said, 'He's going to kill both of us, now, Eli.'

'I have been happy these days, riding and working with you,' I told him.

'But is it time for final good-byes?' he asked. 'If you look closely at the man you can see his heart is not in it. Notice how slick his flesh has become. Somewhere in his being there is a voice informing him of his mistake.'

'Count it out, goddamnit,' said the trapper.

'We will put *that* on your tombstone,' Charlie said, and he loudly cracked his fingers. 'Count three, brother. Slow and even.'

'You are both ready, now?' I asked.

'I am ready,' said the trapper.

'Ready,' Charlie said.

'One,' I said—and Charlie and I both let loose with our pistols, four bullets fired simultaneously, with each finding its target, skull shots every one. The trappers dropped to the ground from which none of them would rise again. It was an immaculate bit of killing, the slickest and most efficient I could recall, and no sooner had they fallen than Charlie began laughing, as did I, though more out of relief than anything, whereas Charlie I believe was genuinely tickled. It isn't enough to be lucky, I thought. A man has to be balanced in his mind, to remain calm, when your average man is anything but. The trapper with the blue-black beard was still gasping, and I crossed over to look upon him. He was confused, his eyes darting every which way.

'What was that noise?' he asked.

'That was a bullet going into you.'

'A bullet going into me where?'

'Into your head.'

'I can't feel it. And I can't hardly hear anything. Where's the others?'

'They're lying next to you. Their heads have bullets, also.'

'They do? Are they talking? I can't hear them.'

'No, they're dead.'

'But I'm not dead?'

'Not yet you're not.'

'*Ch,*' he said. His eyes closed and his head became still. I was stepping away when he shuddered and opened his eyes. 'Jim was the one who wanted to come after you two. I didn't want to.'

'Okay.'

'He thinks because he's big, he's got to do big things.'

'He's dead, now.'

'He was talking about it all night. They would write books about us, he said. He didn't like you all making fun of our clothes, was what it was.'

'It doesn't matter, now. Close your eyes.'

'Hello?' said the trapper. 'Hello?' He was looking at me but I do not think he could see me.

'Close your eyes. It's all right.'

'I didn't want to do this,' he complained. 'Jim thought he could lick you boys, and that he'd be able to tell everyone about it.'

'You should close your eyes and rest,' I said.

'*Ch. Ch, ch.*' Then the life hopped out of him and he died, and I returned to Tub, and the saddle. This 'counting to three' business was an old trick of ours. It was something we were neither ashamed nor proud of; suffice to say it was only employed in the direst situations, and it saved our lives more than once.

Charlie and I were set to leave when we heard a boot scrape in the loft above us. The hand had not left, but hidden away to witness the fight; sadly for him he had also witnessed our numbers trick, and we climbed the ladder to find him. This took some time as there were many tall towers of stacked hay bales in the loft, which made for excellent covering. 'Come out, boy,' I called. 'We are all through here, and we promise not to hurt you.' A pause, and we heard a scurrying in the far corner. I fired at the sound but the bales swallowed the bullet. Another pause, and more scurrying. Charlie said, 'Boy, come out here. We're going to kill you, and there is no chance for escape. Let's be sensible about it.'

'Boo-hoo-hoo,' said the hand.

'You are only wasting our time. And we have no more time to waste.'

'Boo-hoo-hoo.'

After we dispatched the hand we visited with May-field in his parlor. He was shocked when he found us knock-ing on his door, to the point that he could not speak or move for a time; I ushered him to his couch, where he sat awaiting his nameless fate. To Charlie I said, 'He is different from last night.'

'This is the true man,' Charlie told me. 'I knew it the mo-ment I saw him.' Addressing Mayfield, he said, 'As you may have guessed, we have cut down your help, all four of them, plus the stable boy, which was unfortunate, and unplanned. I am quick to point out that this is entirely your doing, as we brought you the red pelt in good faith and had nothing to do with its disappearance. Thusly, the deaths of your men and the boy should rest on your conscience alone, not ours. I do not ask that you agree with this necessarily, only that you recognize I have said as much. Are we understood?'

Mayfield did not answer. His eyes were pinpointed to a spot on the wall behind me. I turned to see what he was staring at and discovered it to be: Nothing. When I looked back at him he was rubbing his face with his palms, as though he were washing.

'All right,' Charlie continued. 'This next part you will not like, but here is the price to pay for the impositions you hefted upon my brother and myself. Are you listening to me, Mayfield? Yes, I want you to tell us, now. Where do you keep your safe?'

Mayfield was quiet for such a time I did not think he heard the question. Charlie was opening his mouth to repeat himself when Mayfield answered, in a voice scarcely above a whisper, 'I will not tell you.' Charlie walked over to him. 'Tell me where the safe is or I will hit you on the head with my pistol.' Mayfield said nothing and Charlie removed his gun from the holster, gripping it at the barrel. He paused, then clipped Mayfield on the very top of his skull with the walnut butt. Mayfield fell back onto the couch, covering his head and making restrained pain sounds, a kind of squealing through gritted teeth that I found most undignified. He began at once to bleed, and Charlie pressed a hanky into his fist as he sat the man up. Mayfield did not ball this into a bunch and hold it over his wound as anyone else might have, but laid the square of cotton flat over his head like a tablecloth; as he was bald on top, the blood fixed the hanky to his head quite handily. Whatever possessed him to do this? Was this a thoughtless inspiration, or something he had learned somewhere? Mayfield sat looking at us with a sulky expression on his face. He had only one boot on, and I noticed his bare foot was red and swollen at the toes. I pointed and said, 'Touch of chilblains, Mayfield?'

'What's chilblains?'

'It looks like that's what's wrong with your foot.'

'I don't know what's wrong with it.'

'I think it's chilblains,' I said.

Charlie snapped his fingers, both to quiet me and to regain Mayfield's attention. 'This time,' he said, 'if you do not answer me, I will hit you twice.'

'I won't let you have it all,' Mayfield said.

'Where is the safe?'

'I worked for that money. It is not yours to take.'

'Right.' He hit Mayfield twice with the butt and the man once again doubled over on the couch to wail and complain. Charlie had not removed the hanky to strike him and the blows were unpleasantly wet sounding. When he propped Mayfield upright, the man was tensing his jaws and panting and his entire head was slick with blood—the hanky itself was dripping. He stuck out his lower lip and was attempting a show of bravery, but he looked ridiculous, like something in a butcher's display, blood running down his chin and neck, soaking into his collar. Charlie said, 'Let's get something clear between us, now. Your money is gone. This is a simple truth, a point of fact, and if you struggle against it we will kill you, *then* we'll find your safe. I want you to ponder this: Why should you receive abuse and death for something that is already forfeit? Think on it. There is no sense in your attitude.'

'You are going to kill me one way or the other.'

'That is not necessarily the truth,' I said.

'It isn't,' said Charlie.

'Will you give me your word on it?' asked Mayfield.

Charlie looked at me, his eyes asking: *Should we let him live?* My eyes answered him: *I don't care.* He said, 'If you give us the money, we will leave you as we found you, living and breathing.'

'Swear on it.'

'I swear on it,' said Charlie.

Mayfield watched him, searching for some sign of devilishness. Satisfied, he looked over at me. 'You swear it also?'

'If my brother says it's so, then it's so. But if you want me to swear I won't kill you, then I swear it.'

He removed the heavy hanky and flung it to the ground; it clapped as it hit the floor and he regarded it with a measure of disgust. Now he straightened his vest and stood, teetering on his heels, then sitting back down, having nearly fainted from the effort. 'I need a drink, and something more to clean my head. I do not wish to walk through my hotel looking like this.' I fixed him a tall brandy that he drank in two long swallows. Charlie ducked into the water closet and emerged with a handful of towels, a bowl of water, and a hand mirror. These were placed on the low table before Mayfield, and we watched as he set to work cleaning himself. He was unemotional as he did this, and I felt an obscure admiration for him. He was losing all of his savings and gold, and yet he displayed as much concern as a man shaving his face. I was curious what he was thinking about, and asked him; when he said he was making plans I inquired as to what they might be. He lay the mirror facedown on the table and said, 'That depends entirely upon how much of my money you men will allow me to keep.'

'Keep?' said Charlie, eyebrows raised. He was rifling the drawers of Mayfield's desk. 'I thought it was understood you will keep none.'

Mayfield exhaled. 'None at all? Do you mean to say, absolutely none?'

Charlie looked at me. 'Was that not the plan?'

I said, 'The plan, if I'm not mistaken, was to kill him. Now that we have changed that part, we can at least talk about this new concern. I will admit it seems cruel, to leave him penniless.'

Charlie's eyes darkened, and he went into himself. Mayfield said, 'You asked what I was thinking. Well, I will tell you. I was thinking that a man like myself, after suffering such a blow as you men have struck on this day, has two distinct paths he might travel in his life. He might walk out into the world with a wounded heart, intent on sharing his mad hatred with every person he passes; or, he might start out anew with an empty heart, and he should take care to fill it up with only proud things from then on, so as to nourish his desolate mind-set and cultivate something positive anew.'

'Is he just inventing this as he goes?' Charlie asked.

'I am going to take the second route,' Mayfield continued. 'I am a man who needs to rebuild, and the first thing I will work on is my sense of purpose. I will remind myself of who I am, or was, for I fear my padded life here has made me lazy. I should say that your getting the better of me with such ease is proof of it.'

'He describes his inaction and cowardice as laziness,' Charlie said.

'And with five men dead,' I said, 'he describes our overtaking his riches as easy.'

'He has a describing problem,' said Charlie.

Mayfield said, 'My hope, I will put it to you men directly, is that you will see me through for trip expenses to your hometown of Oregon City, where I shall travel at once and lay waste to the mongrel with the scythe blade, James Robinson.'

He said this and immediately my brother and I had the same, evil thought.

'Tell me that it's not perfection,' said Charlie.

'But it is too tragic,' I said.

'You would protect this criminal acquaintance against what you have done to me?' Mayfield said indignantly. 'It is only just and proper that you men assist me in seeing this through. You have taken away all that I have earned, but you can redeem yourselves, at least partially, if you will only let me keep but a portion of my own fortune.'

This self-righteous speech sealed his fate, and we came to the agreement that Mayfield should be given one hundred dollars, just enough to get him to Oregon City, where he would be stuck, and where the first person he asked would inform him of Robinson's death, and he would know we had known and would recall our amusement in bitter, black blood. The money was paid out in stamped gold taken directly from his safe, which was located in the basement of the hotel. Staring into its open mouth, Mayfield said, 'That's the only time I've ever been lucky in my life. Filled up a safe with gold and papers. More than most can say, at any rate.' He nodded solemnly, but his show of bravado soon gave way to passionate emotion; his face dropped and tears began squirting from his eyes. 'But goddamnit, luck is a hard feeling to hold on to!' he said. Wiping his face, he cursed just as hotly and sincerely as he could, though quietly. 'I feel no luck in my body now, and that is a fact.' He cut a piteous silhouette with his little purse of money, pinching the strings the way one holds a dead mouse by its tail. We followed him outside and watched him tightening and refitting his clothing and saddlebags. He seemed to want to give a speech, but the words either did not come naturally or else he considered us unfit to receive them, and he remained silent. He mounted his horse, leaving with a curt nod and a look in his eyes that said: I do not like you people. We returned to the basement to count the safe's contents, splitting and pocketing the paper money, which amounted to eighteen hundred dollars. The gold proved to be too much to account for in our travels and so was hidden underneath a potbellied stove, resting on a pallet of hardwood in the far basement corner. This was a dirty job, as we had to dismantle the tin chimney to move the stove back and forth, and we were both rained down in black soot; but when we were finished I could not imagine a soul would ever find our treasure, for no one would think to look in so remote a spot. The rough estimate of these riches was set at fifteen thousand dollars; my take of this more than tripled my savings, and as we left the musty basement, heading up the stairs and into the light, I felt two things at once: A gladness at this turn of fortune, but also an emptiness that I did not feel *more* glad; or rather, a fear that my gladness was forced or false. I thought, Perhaps a man is never meant to be truly happy. Perhaps there is no such a thing in our world, after all.

As we walked the halls of the hotel the whores were abuzz with the news of Mayfield's head-wounded departure, and the disappearance of the trappers. I spied Charlie's whore, looking only slightly less green than before, and took her to the side, asking where the bookkeeper was.

'They ran her up to the doc's.'

'Is she all right?'

'I imagine. They're always running her up there.'

I pressed a hundred dollars into her hand. 'I want you to give this to her when she comes back.'

She stared at the money. 'Jesus Christ on a cloud.'

'I will return in two weeks' time. If I find she has not received it, there will be a price to pay, do you understand me?'

'Mister, I was just standing in the hall, here.'

I held up a double eagle. 'This is for you.'

She dropped the coin into her pocket. Peering down the hall in the direction Charlie had gone she asked, 'I don't suppose your brother'll be leaving *me* a hundred.'

'No, I don't suppose he will.'

'You got all the romantic blood, is that it?'

'Our blood is the same, we just use it differently.'

I turned and walked away. A half-dozen steps, and she asked. 'You want to tell me what she did for this?'

I stopped and thought. I told her, 'She was pretty, and kind to me.'

And the poor whore's face, she just did not know what to think about that. She went back into her room, slammed the door shut, and shrieked two times.

We rode out of town and followed the shallows of the river. We were days late for our meeting with Morris but neither of us was much concerned about this. I was reliving and cataloging the events of the previous thirty-six hours when Charlie began to chuckle. Tub and I were in the lead; without turning I called out, asking him what was so amusing.

'I was thinking of the day Father died.'

'What about it?'

'You and I were sitting in the field behind the house, eating our lunch when I heard he and Mother arguing. Do you remember what we were eating?'

'What are you telling me?' I asked.

'We were eating apples. Mother had wrapped them in a strip

of cloth and sent us outside. She had known they would argue, I believe.'

'The cloth was faded red,' I said.

'That's right. And the apples were green, and underripe. I remember you making a face about it, though you were so young I'm surprised you cared.'

'I can remember the apples being sour.' The vividness of the memory brought a pucker to my mouth, and saliva washed over my tongue.

Charlie said, 'It was the hottest day of a bona fide heat wave, and we were sitting there in the long grass, eating and listening to Mother and Father's screaming. Or I was listening to it. I don't know if you noticed.'

As he told the story, though, it was as if the scenario was coming into view. 'I think I noticed,' I said. Then I was sure I had. 'Did something break?'

'That's right,' he said. 'You really do remember.'

'Something broke, and she screamed.' My throat began to swell, and I found myself holding back tears.

'Father broke out the window with his fist and then hit her on the arm with an ax handle. He had gone crazy, I think. Before that he'd edged up next to craziness but when I entered the house to help Mother, I felt he had given over his whole being to it. He didn't recognize me when I came in with my rifle.'

'How is it that people go crazy?'

'It's just a thing that sometimes happens.'

'Can you go truly crazy and then come back?'

'Not truly crazy. No, I don't think so.'

'I've heard a father hands it down to the next.'

'I have never thought of it. Why, do you ever feel crazy?'

'Sometimes I feel a helplessness.'

'I don't think that is the same thing.'

'Let's hope.'

He said, 'Do you remember the first rifle of mine? The gun that Father called my pea shooter? He made no jokes about it when I began pulling that trigger.' Charlie paused. 'I shot him twice, one in the arm and another in the chest, and the chest shot brought him down. And he lay there, *spitting* at me, over and over—spitting and cursing and hating me. I have never seen hatred like that, never before or since. Our father, lying there, coughing up thick blood and spitting it at me. Mother was knocked out. Her arm was badly broken, and the pain made her faint. That's some kind of blessing, I guess, that she didn't have to see her son kill her husband. Well, Father laid his head down and died, and I dragged him out of the house and into the stable and by the time I came back, Mother'd woken up and was in a trance of pain or fright. She kept saying, "Whose blood's that? Whose blood's that on the floor?" I told her it was mine. I didn't know what else to say. I helped her up and out, walked her to the wagon. It was a long ride into town, with her screaming every time I hit a bump in the road. Her forearm was bent like a chevron. Like a shotgun opened for loading.'

'What happened next?' I asked, for this I could not recall.

'By the time I got some medicine in her, got her splinted up, it was late afternoon. And it wasn't until I was halfway back that I remembered about you at all.' He coughed. 'I hope that doesn't make you feel hurt, brother.'

'That does not hurt me.'

'I had been distracted. And you were always off in your private world of thoughts, quiet in the corners. But as I said, it was powerfully hot that day. And of course just as soon as I left you, you pulled your bonnet off. And there you sat, for four or five hours, with your fair hair and skin. Mother was sleeping in the wagon, drugged, and I left her there to rush out and see about you. I had not thought of you getting burned—my concern was that a coyote might have come along and picked you apart, or that you had walked down to the river and drowned. So I was very relieved to see you sitting there in one piece, and I ran down the hill to collect you. And you were just as red and burned as could be. The whites of your eyes turned red as blood. You were blind for two weeks and your skin peeled away in swaths like the skin of an onion. And that, Eli, is how you got your freckles.'

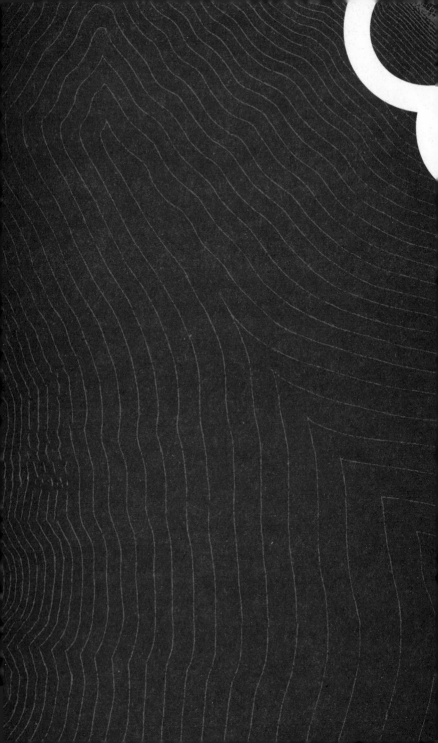

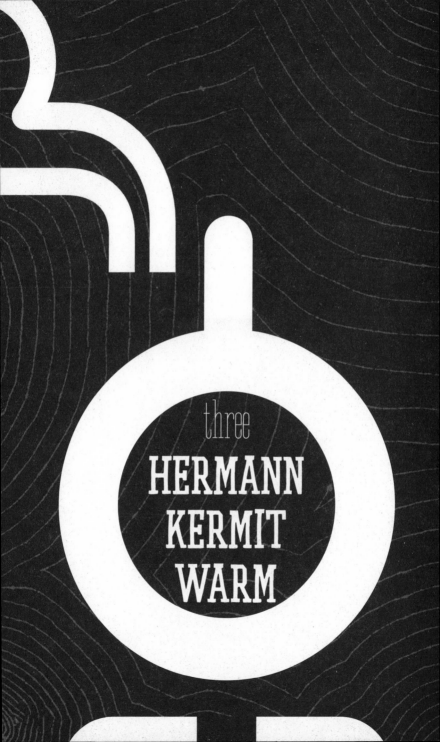

three

HERMANN KERMIT WARM

The harbor, at first sight, I did not understand it. There
were so many ships at anchor that their masts looked to be tangled impossibly; hundreds of them packed together so densely
as to give the appearance of a vast, limbless forest rolling on
the tides. Charlie and I threaded our way up the shoreline, and
all around us was chaos: Men of every race and age rushing,
shouting, pushing, fighting; cows and sheep were directed this
way and that; horse-led wagons carried lumber and bricks up
the mud-slick hill, and the sound of hammering and building
echoed from the city out to sea. There was laughter in the air,
though it did not give me the impression of gaiety, but something more maniacal and evil wishing. Tub was nervous, and
so was I. I had not seen anything remotely like it and I won-

dered how we might possibly find one man in these labyrinthine streets and alleyways, where all was queer and dark and hidden.

'Let us search out Morris,' I said.

'He has already waited weeks for us,' said Charlie. 'Another hour won't change anything.' Of course my brother *liked* the atmosphere, and was not the least bit uneasy.

I saw that many of the ships seemed to have been at anchor a long while, despite their still being loaded down with cargo, and I asked a man walking past about this. He was barefoot and held a chicken under his arm, which throughout our conversation he stroked lovingly on the head.

'Abandoned by their crews,' he told us. 'When the fever to dig is upon you, there is not a second to spare. Certainly one cannot be expected to unload crates of flour for a dollar a day with the rivers singing their song so nearby.' Blinking at the horizon, he said, 'I often look out at these boats and imagine their baffled investors, impotently raging in New York and Boston, and this pleases me. Can I ask, are you men just arriving in San Francisco? How are you finding it?'

'I can only say I am eager to know it better,' said Charlie.

The man said, 'My feelings about San Francisco rise and fall with my moods. Or is it that the town alters my moods, thus informing my opinions? Either way, one day it is my true friend, a few days after, my bitterest enemy.'

'What is your feeling this morning?' I asked.

'I am halfway between, just now. Altogether I am doing decently, thank you.'

Charlie said, 'How is it that these vessels have not been looted?'

'Oh, many have been. The ones that remain untouched are

either guarded by their stubborn captains or else are filled with nonvaluable cargo. No one has any concerns for free wheat or cotton, just now. Or should I say, almost no one.' He pointed to a lone man rowing a small boat in the bay, making his way between the tall ships. His skiff was ridiculously loaded down, and he dipped his oars with great caution so as to avoid tipping. 'That there is a fellow called Smith. I know him well enough. What will he do when he gets to shore? He will strap those heavy boxes to his sickly mule's neck and drag them up to Miller's General Store. Miller will skin Smith on the price and the money Smith receives for his backbreaking work will be lost in a single round of cards, or it will scarcely buy him a meal. I wonder if you two have had the pleasure of dining in our fair city? But no, I would know if you had, for your faces would be bloodless, and you would be muttering ceaseless insults to God in heaven.'

Charlie said, 'I paid twenty-five dollars for a whore in Mayfield.'

The man said, 'You will pay that same amount to simply sit at the bar with them in San Francisco. To lie down with one, expect to put up a minimum of a hundred dollars.'

'What man would pay that?' I asked.

'They are lining up to pay it. The whores are working fifteen-hour shifts and are said to make thousands of dollars per day. You must understand, gentlemen, that the tradition of thrift and sensible spending has vanished here. It simply does not exist anymore. For example, when I arrived this last time from working my claim I had a sizable sack of gold dust, and though I knew it was lunacy I decided to sit down and have a large dinner in the most expensive restaurant I could find. I had been living on the cold ground for three straight months, surviving on trout and pork fat and more trout. My spine was twisted from labor and I was utterly desperate for some type of warmth and pomp, a touch of velvet, and damn the cost. So it was that I ate a decent-sized, not particularly tasty meal of meat and spuds and ale and ice cream, and for this repast, which would have put me back perhaps half a dollar in my hometown, I paid the sum of thirty dollars in cash.'

Charlie was disgusted. 'Only a moron would pay that.'

'I agree,' said the man. 'One hundred percent I agree. And I am happy to welcome you to a town peopled in morons exclusively. Furthermore, I hope that *your* transformation to moron is not an unpleasant experience.'

Down the beach a half mile I noticed an enormous pulley system made of tall timbers and thick rope set back from the waterline; this was being used to run a steam-sailer ship aground. A man in a broad-brimmed black hat and tailored black suit was whipping a team of horses to turn the winch. I asked the chicken man about the purpose of this operation and he said, 'Here is someone with the same ambition as Smith, but with brains as well. That man in the hat has claimed the abandoned boat as his own, and is having it dragged to a sliver of land he had the foresight to buy some time ago. He will shore the boat upright and lease out its quarters to boarders or shopkeepers and make himself a speedy fortune. A lesson for you men: Perhaps the money is not to be made in the rivers themselves, but from the men working them. There are too many variables in removing gold from the earth. You need courage, and luck, and the work ethic of a pack mule. Why bother, with so many others already at it, piling into town one on top of the other and in a great hurry to spend every last granule?'

'Why do you not open a shop yourself?' I asked.

The question surprised him, and he took a moment to consider what the answer might be. When it came to him, a sadness appeared in his eyes and he shook his head. 'I'm afraid my role in all this is settled,' he said.

I was going to ask which role he was referring to when I heard a noise on the wind, a muffled crunching or cracking in the distance, followed by a whistling sound cutting through the thick ocean air. One of the pulley ropes had snapped, and I saw the man in the black suit standing over a horse lying on its side in the sand. That he was not whipping the horse informed me it was dying or dead.

'It is a wild time here, is it not?' I said to the man.

'It is wild. I fear it has ruined my character. It has certainly ruined the characters of others.' He nodded, as though answering himself. 'Yes, it has ruined me.'

'How are you ruined?' I asked.

'How am I not?' he wondered.

'Couldn't you return to your home to start over?'

He shook his head. 'Yesterday I saw a man leap from the roof of the Orient Hotel, laughing all the way to the ground, upon which he fairly exploded. He was drunk they say, but I had seen him sober shortly before this. There is a feeling here, which if it gets you, will envenom your very center. It is a madness of possibilities. That leaping man's final act was the embodiment of the collective mind of San Francisco. I understood it completely. I had a strong desire to applaud, if you want to know the truth.'

'I don't understand the purpose of this story,' I said.

'I could leave here and return to my hometown, but I would not return as the person I was when I left,' he explained. 'I would not recognize anyone. And no one would recognize me.' Turning to watch the town, he petted his fowl and chuckled. A single pistol shot was heard in the distance; hoofbeats; a woman's scream, which turned to cackling laughter. 'A great, greedy heart!' he said, and then walked toward it, disappearing into it. Down the beach, the man with the whip stood away from the dead horse, staring out at the bay and the numberless masts. He had removed his hat. He was unsure, and I did not envy him.

We knocked on Morris's door at the hotel but he did not answer. Charlie picked the lock and we entered, finding his many toilet items, his perfumes and waxes, stacked on the floor next to the entrance. But besides this there was no sign of the man, no clothing or baggage, and the bed was made, the windows all shut tight; I had the feeling Morris had been away several days. His absence struck Charlie and I as conspicuous bordering on unnerving, for while it was true we were tardy in arriving, Morris's instruction was to wait for us no matter the length of time, and it was out of character for him to stray from any prearrangement. When I suggested we might check to see if he had left word for us with the hotel proprietors, Charlie encouraged me to investigate. I was stepping toward the door when I noticed a large black horn emerging from the wall beside the bed. Hanging within was a polished brass bell. Below the horn there hung a sign that read: RING BELL TONGUE. SPEAK FOR SERVICE. I followed the instruction and the bell tone filled the room. This startled Charlie; he craned his neck to watch. 'What are you doing?'

'I have heard of this system in eastern hotels.'

'Heard of what system?'

'Just wait.' A moment passed and a woman's voice, shrunken and distant, emanated from the stomach of the building.

'Hello? Mr. Morris?'

Charlie turned all the way around. 'She is in the wall? Where is it coming from?'

'Hello?' the voice repeated. 'Did you ring for service?'

'Say something,' Charlie told me. But I felt inexplicably bashful, and motioned for him to speak. He called over, 'Can you hear me in there?'

'I can hear you faintly. Please speak into the horn directly.'

Charlie was enjoying this, and he stood up from the bed and approached the device, putting his face fully into the horn. 'How is that? Better?'

'That's better,' said the voice. 'What can I do for you today, Mr. Morris? I am relieved to have you back. We were worried when you went away with that strange little bearded man.' Charlie and I shared a look at this. Readdressing the horn, he said, 'This is not Morris, ma'am. I have come from the Oregon Territory to visit with him. He and I are employed by the same firm there.'

The voice paused. 'And where is Mr. Morris?'

'That I do not know.'

'We only just arrived,' I said, impelled to take part.

'Who was that?' said the voice.

'That is my brother,' said Charlie.

'So there are two of you, now.'

'There was always two of us,' I told her. 'Since the day I was born there was.' Neither Charlie nor the woman recognized my joke, and it was in fact as though it had never existed. The voice adopted a peevish tone: 'Who gave you men permission to enter Mr. Morris's room?'

'The door was unlocked,' Charlie lied.

'So what if it was? You cannot simply enter another man's rented quarters and speak into his wall piece.'

'You have our apologies for that, ma'am. We were to rendezvous here some days ago, only our travels were delayed. As such, we were in a hurry to visit with Morris, and threw caution to the wind.'

'He made no mention of any rendezvous.'

'He wouldn't have.'

'Hmm,' said the voice.

Charlie continued: 'You say he has left with a bearded man. Was this person called Warm? Hermann Warm?'

'I never asked the man's name, and he never offered to share it with me.'

'What color was his beard?' I asked.

'Is that the brother again?'

'Was it a red beard?' I asked.

'It was red.'

'How long has Morris been away?' said Charlie.

'Four days today. He paid up until tomorrow morning. When he said he was leaving early I offered him a partial refund but he would not take it. A gentleman, that one.'

'And he left no word for us?'

'He did not.'

'Did he say where he was going?'

'To the Illuminated River, he told me. He and the red-bearded man had a laugh about it. I do not know why.'

'You are saying they were laughing together?'

'They were laughing at the same time. I assumed they were laughing at the same thing. I searched for the river on a map but couldn't find it.'

'And Mr. Morris did not appear to be under duress? As though his departure was forced, for example?'

'It did not seem so.'

Charlie studied this. He said, 'The friendship is a curiosity to me.'

'To me, also,' the voice agreed. 'I'd thought Mr. Morris didn't like the man, then all at once they became inseparable, spending every minute together locked away in that room.'

'And you are certain he left no instruction for us?'

'I think I would know if he had,' she answered haughtily.

'He left nothing behind at all then?'

'I did not say that.'

Charlie glared into the horn. 'Ma'am, tell me what he left, if you please.'

I could hear the woman breathing. 'A book,' she said finally.

'What kind of book?'

'A book he wrote in.'

'What did he write in the book?'

'I don't know. And if I did know, I would not tell you.'

'Personal writing, is that it?'

'That's right. Naturally, just as soon as I understood what it was I closed it up.'

'What did you learn from your reading?'

'That the weather was not favorable at the start of his trip to San Francisco. I am embarrassed to have learned that much. I respect the privacy of my lodgers.'

'Yes.'

'My lodgers can expect from me the most absolute kind of privacy.'

'I understand. Can I ask you, where is the book now?'

'It is with me, in my room.'

'I would like very much if you would show it to us.'

She paused. 'That I should not do, I don't think.'

'I tell you we are his friends.'

'Then why did he not leave word for you?'

'Perhaps he left the book for us.'

'He forgot the book. I found it tangled in sheets at the foot of his bed. No, he was in a rush to pack and go, always looking over his shoulder. For all I know it was you two he wished to stay ahead of.'

'You will not show me the book then, is that correct?'

'I will do right by my guests, is what I will do.'

'Very well,' Charlie said. 'Will you bring us up lunch with ale?'

'You are staying on with us?'

'For one night, anyway. This room will do fine.'

'What if Mr. Morris comes back?'

'If he left with Warm, as you say, he will not be coming back.'

'But if he does?'

'Then you will make a nice profit in champagne, for it will be a happy reunion indeed.'

'Do you want a hot lunch or cold?'

'Hot lunch, with ale.'

'Two full hot lunches?'

'With ale.'

The woman signed off, and Charlie returned to lie on the bed. I asked him what he made of the situation and he said, 'I don't know *what* to make of it. We will need to get a look at the book, of course.'

'I don't believe the woman will share it.'

'We will see about that,' he said.

I opened a window and leaned out into the salty air. The hotel was located on a steep incline and I watched a group of Chinese men, in their braids and silk and muddy slippers, pushing an ox up the hill. The ox did not want to go, and they slapped its backside with their hands. Their language was something like a chorus of birds, completely alien and strange, but beautiful for its strangeness. Likely they were only cursing. There came a knock at the door and the stout, lipless hotel woman entered with our lunches, which were tepid, if not actually hot. The ale was cool and delicious and I drank half of it in a single pass. I asked the woman what I had spent with this long sip and she scrutinized the glass. 'Three dollars,' she estimated. 'Both meals together are seventeen.' It seemed she hoped to be paid at once, and Charlie stood and handed her a double eagle; when she began fishing the change from her pocket, he caught her wrist, telling her to keep it as payment for our rudeness in entering Morris's room without permission. She kept the money but did not thank him and in fact appeared displeased to be receiving it. When Charlie produced a second double eagle and held this in her direction, her face grew hard.

'What's this?' she asked.

'For the book.'

'I have already told you, you cannot have it.'

'Of course, ma'am, you would keep it; we only wish to look it over awhile.'

'You will never lay eyes upon it,' she said. Her hands were red and balled and she was thoroughly insulted. She stomped from the room, in a hurry I suspected to tell some or all of her employees of this latest moral victory, and Charlie and I sat together to eat our lunch. I became sorrowful at the thought of this woman's fate; to my concerned expression he told me, 'You can't say I didn't try with her,' and I had to admit it was the truth. The food, I might mention, was unremarkable in every way other than its cost. When the woman returned to collect our plates, Charlie stood to meet her. Her head was high, her expression superior, and she said, 'Well?' Charlie did not answer, but dropped to a crouch and buried his fist in her stomach, after which she fell back onto a chair and sat bent over, drooling and coughing and generally struggling to regain her breath and composure. I brought her a glass of water, apologizing and explaining that our need of the book was no trifling matter, and that one way or the other we would have it. Charlie added, 'We hope no more harm will come to you, ma'am. But understand we will do whatever it takes to get it.' She was in such a state of muted outrage I did not think she heard the logic in our words, but when I escorted her to her room, she handed over the journal all the same, and without any further episode. I insisted she take the extra double eagle and in the end she did take it, which I like to think lessened the indignity of her catching such a terrific punch, but I do not suppose it did, at least not so very much. Neither Charlie nor I was predisposed to this manner of violence against a physical inferior—

'yellow violence' some would call it—but it was a warranted necessity, as will be shown in the proceeding pages.

What follows is a verbatim transcription of all pertinent sections of the journal of Henry Morris, as related to his mysterious partnership with Hermann Kermit Warm and the defection from his post as the Commodore's scout and longtime confidant.

✸ *Approached by Warm today, quite out of the blue, and*
after having scarcely laid eyes upon him for nearly a
week. I was passing through the hotel lobby and he snuck
to my side, lifting my arm by the elbow like a gentleman
helping a lady over patchy terrain. This surprised me,
naturally, and I broke off with a start. At this, he looked
hurt and demanded, 'Are we engaged to be married or
aren't we?' It was nine o'clock in the morning but he was
drunken, that was plain. I told him to leave off following
me, which surprised him and me both, for though I had
sensed a body spying on me these last few days and
nights, it was a distant feeling and I had not formulated
the words in my own mind. But I saw by his guilty

expression that he had been following me, and I was glad to have stood my ground with him. He asked if I would loan him a dollar and I said I would not. Upon receiving my answer he popped his top hat, frayed and dusty, and left the hotel with his thumbs hooked in his vest, his head tilted proudly back. Crossing past the awning, he stepped into the street, and the bright warmth of the sun. This gave him pleasure, and he extended his arms as if to soak in the light. A team of horses was pulling a load of garbage up the hill and Warm climbed casually onto the back of the cart, this accomplished so nimbly as to have gone unnoticed by the driver. It was a graceful exit, I could not deny it, though generally he is looking all the worse than when I first laid eyes on him, not so much from drink as overall misuse of self. He smells ghastly. I should not be surprised if he expires before those two from Oregon City arrive to put him down.

✷ *One of the odder days I have yet passed. This morning, Warm was once again waiting in the lobby. I spotted him before he did me, and I made a study of his markedly improved appearance. His clothes had been cleaned and mended and he had bathed. His beard was combed, his face scrubbed, and he looked to be an altogether different person from the man who had accosted me twenty-four hours earlier. Presently he spied me at the base of the stairway and hurried across the lobby to take up my hand, offering his sincerest apologies for his behavior on the previous day. He looked touched, genuinely, when I accepted this, which in turn touched me, or gave* me pause, for here was an unknown version of a man I had thought I knew, and knew well. To my increased amazement he then asked if he might treat me to lunch, and though I was not hungry I took him up on this, curious as I was to learn what change of fate had befallen this previously destitute and grubby individual.

We retired to a restaurant of his choosing, a charmless garbage chute of a lopsided shack called the Black Skull, where Warm was enthusiastically greeted by the owner, a rank-smelling man with a black-and-red-checkered leather eye patch and not a single tooth in his head. This dubious personage asked Warm how his 'work' was progressing, and Warm replied with a single word, 'Glowingly.' This made little sense to me but tickled the owner acutely. He showed us to a far table with a curtain, bringing us two bowls of tasteless stew and a loaf of bread, tangy with threat of mold. No bill was ever presented to us, and when I asked Warm about the nature of his and the owner's alliance he whispered that it was not yet realized but that he had 'every faith it would come to nothing.'

After lunch, when the owner had cleared the table and drawn the curtain for us, Warm's jovial composure changed, and he became stiff and serious. He took a half minute to gather his thoughts and at last looked me in the eye, saying, 'I have been watching you, yes, it is the truth. I began to do this at first with the thought of learning your weaknesses. Let me admit it to you then. I have thought about killing you, or having you killed.' When I asked him why he would wish such a thing he said, 'But of course the moment I saw you I knew you were the Commodore's man.' 'The Commodore?' I said vaguely. 'Whatever in the world is that?' He shook his head at my novice playacting, dismissing it out of hand, and returned to his speech. 'My feelings for you quickly changed, Mr. Morris, and I'll tell you why. You haven't a dishonest bone in your body. Typically, for example, when a man wishes another man a good morning, he will smile just as long as he is facing the other person, but as soon as he passes by, the smile immediately drops from his face. His smile had been a false one. That man is a liar, do you see?' 'But everyone does that,' I said. 'It is only a small civility.' 'You do not do it,' he told me. 'Your smile, though slight, remains on your lips long after you have turned away. You take a genuine pleasure in communing with another man or woman. I saw this happen time and again and thought, if only I could have a person like that on my side, I would see my every idea through to completion. I meant to broach this very subject during my visit of yesterday morning, but my purpose was mislaid, as you will recall. I was nervous to face you, frankly, and I thought a drink would give me courage.' He lowered his head at the memory. 'Well,' he said, 'this morning I awoke in my hovel suffering extreme shame. This was not a new occurrence for me, but today there was something wholly disabling about it. The shame had a heaviness I had never experienced, and hope to never experience again. It was as though I had hit a wall, reached my very limit of self-loathing. Some would call this an epiphany. Call it what you will. But I faced the day today and have vowed to change my life, to cleanse my body, to cleanse my mind, to share my secrets with you, because I know

you are a good man, and because a good man is the thing
I need most in my life, just now.'

Before I could respond to the passionate oration,
Warm pulled from his pockets several loose, much-
abused papers, and he laid these before me, imploring
me to look upon them, which I did, finding page after
page of scribbled, intricate numerical lists, figures, and
scientific calculations imparting I did not know what.
At last I had to admit my ignorance to him. 'I'm afraid
I have no idea what all of this represents,' I said. 'It is
the bedrock of a momentous discovery,' he told me. 'And
what is the discovery?' 'It is perhaps the most significant
scientific event of our lifetime.' 'And what is the event?'
Nodding, he collected the papers into an untidy stack,
pushing this away beneath his coat. With the corners of
the pages peeking over his lapel, he chuckled, regarding
me as though I were a very clever man indeed. 'You are
asking for a demonstration,' he said knowingly. 'I am
not,' I responded. 'You will have one, all the same.' He
pulled a watch from his coat and stood to leave. 'I have
to go now, but I will visit you in the morning at your
hotel. I will make my demonstration, at the conclusion
of which I will have your opinion, and your decision.'
'Decision in regards to what?' I asked, for I had no clue
what he was actually proposing. But he only shook his
head and said, 'We can discuss it tomorrow morning. Is
this agreeable with your calendar?' I told the funny man
it was, and he gripped my hand, hurrying off to some
other crucial location. I watched him pushing through
the restaurant, and I saw that he was laughing. And
then he was gone.

✳ *No sooner had I risen from bed than Warm knocked on my door. His appearance had improved further in that he was wearing a new top hat. When I commented on this he removed it to show me the hat's every detail, the interior stitching, the softness of its calfskin band, and what he called its 'general richness and fineness.' I inquired what he had done with his old hat and he became cagey. I pressed him and he admitted to dropping it over an unsuspecting pigeon sunning itself in the street. The pigeon could not escape from under the weight, and so Warm had the guilty pleasure of watching the topper run away from him, rounding a corner for parts unknown. As he told me this story I spied a covered crate at his feet. I asked what this was for, and he raised his finger, and said, 'Ah.'*

He readied himself for the enigmatic demonstration, and soon the crate's contents sat on the small dining table in the center of my room. Here is what I saw before me. A low-sided wooden box, approximately three feet long by two feet across, a burlap sack containing fresh, strong-smelling earth, a red-velvet sack, and a tin canteen, placed upright. The curtains were drawn and I crossed over to open them, but Warm said he preferred them as they were. 'It is necessary both for reasons of privacy and for the demonstration to come off most effectively,' he explained. I returned to the table and watched him pour two-thirds of the earth into the box, smoothing and packing it until it lay level. He then passed me the velvet sack and asked that I inspect its contents. I found it to be filled with gold dust and said as much. He took the sack back and emptied the dust into the box. Of course this shocked me, and I asked what he was doing. He would not say, but instructed that I should commit to memory the shape of the dust (he had poured it out in a tidy circle). He covered this over with the remaining one-third of the earth and spent a full five minutes packing it down, slapping it with his hands so that it was firm as clay. He expended no small amount of energy doing this and was perspiring freely by this point. Now he fetched my washbasin and held this over the earth, slowly pouring the water out so that it nearly met the rim of the box. Having accomplished these curious tasks, he stood back smiling at my doubtless puzzled expression. At last he said, 'Here is a model of a prospector's river diggings. Here we have in miniature that which has driven half the world mad. The principal challenge for the prospector is this: How does he get at that which he knows is just beneath his feet? The only answers to the question are hard labor, and good fortune. The former is taxing, the latter, unreliable. For several years now I have been searching out a third method, a surer, simpler one.' He held up the canteen and unscrewed its top. 'Correct me if I am wrong, Mr. Morris, but with this formula I believe I have accomplished just that.' He handed the canteen to me and I asked if I were meant to drink it. 'Unless you were after a painful ordeal of death, I would advise against it,' he told me. 'It is not a tonic?' I asked. 'It is a diviner,' he said, and how strange his voice was as he spoke these words, how odd and haunted, his throat constricted, his pulse fluttering at his temples. Bowing his head then, he emptied the canteen into the box. It was *a stinking, purplish liquid. It was thicker than the water but quickly assimilated and disappeared into it. Thirty long seconds passed us by and I stared hard at the water but could see no difference. I raised my eyes to watch Warm's. His lids were half closed, and I thought he looked somewhat sleepy. I opened my mouth to offer him my condolences, for his experiment was apparently a failure, when I noticed in his eyes the reflection of a gathering, golden glow. When I returned my attention to the box my heart leapt into my throat, for there before me, I swear before God in heaven, the ring of gold was illuminated and shining through the heavy layer of black earth!*

My reaction to the demonstration was one of complete amazement, and my many sputtering declarations and questions pleased Warm to no end. He soon fell to explaining his plans for the liquid, which are as follows. To dam a secluded section of river and under cover of night, fill the waters with the formula—in greater quantity, obviously—and then, once it has taken hold, to wade the river and remove the gold at his leisure. The glowing, he explained, lasted only precious minutes, but in that time he might cull what would take him weeks were he to use the traditional methods of extraction. Once he had played out a particular segment of river he would move to another, then another, this repeated until he made his pile, and then he would sell the formula's secret ingredients for a million and spend the rest of his days in what he called the 'silken arms of glad success.' By this point I was fairly reeling. All told, it was the most singularly impressive invention I had ever heard of. My only remaining question was slow in coming. I did not want to offend the man or undo the high feelings in the room but it was something that needed addressing, and so I simply came out with it. 'Why is it you are being so candid with me?' I asked. 'How do you know I will not betray your confidences?' 'I have already explained my reasons for engaging you,' Warm replied. 'I need another man to see this plan through, and I believe you are that man.' 'But I am currently receiving a wage to keep watch over you, that you might be killed!' I exclaimed. 'Yes, that's a fact, but let me ask you this. What did the Commodore give as his reason for wanting me dead?' 'He says you are a thief.' 'And what is it I have stolen?' 'This he did not mention.' Warm spoke emphatically. 'He could not say, because it is a bald lie. He wants me dead for the reason that I would not give over the ingredients of my gold-finding liquid. Six months back I approached him in Oregon City, requesting funding for a trip to California. I gave a demonstration similar to the one you have just seen and made him an offer I thought was most generous. He would underwrite an expedition, and in return would receive half of the profit. At first he agreed, and promised me full cooperation and support. But when I would not share the recipe he became enraged, and pointed a pistol at my face. He was drunken, and could not focus. When he swayed I snatched a paperweight from his desk and threw it at him. A lucky shot, knocked him dead in the forehead and brought the great man to his knees. As I beat my hasty exit, taking those carpeted steps three at a time, I heard his voice come booming after me. "You are not free of me, Warm. My men will take your formula by force and cut you down to size!" I believed him. And I was not surprised when you arrived, Mr. Morris. What surprised me, and what surprises me still, is that a gentleman such as yourself would elect to spend his lifetime abetting a killer and bully.'

The story rang true, all the more so when I remembered the Commodore's bandaged head wound from six months past. Warm's words gave me pause, then, and I paced the room awhile, taking stock of things and pondering the possibilities. At last I asked him, not a little desperately, 'But what do you actually expect of me in all this? What can you possibly hope I'll accomplish for you?' 'It is clear, to my mind,' he said. 'I would like for you to go into business with me as a fifty-fifty partner. You will invest whatever money you have toward our maiden expedition, for the cost of food alone would eradicate my small savings. I will need to borrow your quarters to prepare the formula in bulk, and you will assist me in preparing it. Also you will assist me in the actual physical labor once we have set up camp at the river. But most important, you will become the face and voice of the operation, for you have a gift of communication that has proven elusive to me. You will deal with patents and lawyers and contracts and every horrible manner of man-made entanglement— just the type of thing I would bumble terrifically. That will all come later, though. For now, we would enter the wilderness together and see how the formula actually works.' 'And what do you think the Commodore would make of my newfound allegiance?' I wondered. 'Do you understand fully what you are asking of me?' At this, he approached and laid his hands on my shoulders. 'You *are no errand runner for a tyrant, Mr. Morris. You are a better man than this. Come with me into the world and reclaim your independence. You stand to gain so much, and riches are the least of it.' My heart became heavy at these words, and Warm, understanding my need to dissect the matter, left me to my thoughts, and said he would return in the morning for my answer. I sat forlornly upon the bed, the box still resting on the table, its glowing light growing ever dimmer, and then disappearing entirely.*

✷ *It is hours later, and I am still sitting here. The answer lies before me, it is plain to see it, but it is so bold as to be unfathomable. I have no one to turn to in this, and will have to answer the call on my own. I am extremely uneasy.*

✷ *I did not sleep hardly at all last night, and when Warm returned this morning I formally agreed to take part in his expedition to the River of Light. I am convinced now of his genius, and though I am loath to abandon my post I have elected to follow my heart and do just this. What am I living for, after all? I look upon my past with disgrace. I was herded and instructed. But I will be herded and instructed no more. Today I am born anew, and my life will become my own again. It will be different ever after.*

There was a concentrated silence as Charlie and I sat digesting this remarkable story. I approached the dining table and dragged a finger across its surface. There was a dusting of soil resting upon it; when I showed my trembling hand to Charlie he tossed the journal aside and said, 'I believe it. I believe it all. The Commodore's instruction was explicit on one point: Prior to killing Warm I was to obtain by whatever manner of violence necessary what was described to me only as "the formula." When I asked him what the formula was, he said it was none of my affair, but that Warm would know what I meant, and that once I had it I was to guard it with my life.'

'Why didn't you speak to me about this before?'

'I was told not to. And anyway, what could it have meant to

you? It was so vague, I myself hardly gave it a thought. There is always some cryptic obscurity present in the Commodore's orders. Do you remember the job before last, where I first blinded the man before killing him?'

'The Commodore said to do that?'

Charlie nodded. 'He said the man would understand it, and that I should let him "sit awhile in the dark" before putting my bullets in him. This formula business seemed to be more of the same, so far as I could see.' He stood away from the bed and moved to the window, clasping his hands at the small of his back and peering up the hill. He was silent a minute or more, and when he finally spoke his voice was solemn and soft: 'I have never minded cutting down the Commodore's enemies much, brother. It always happens that they are repellent in one way or the other. Lesser villains, men without mercy or grace. But I do not like the idea of killing a man because of his own ingenuity.'

'I don't, either. And I'm very glad to hear you say it.'

He exhaled through his nostrils. 'What do you think we should do?'

'What do *you* think we should do?'

But neither of us knew what to do.

The Black Skull was just as Morris had described it, a

lean-to fabricated of scrap wood and tin, situated in a slim alley between two much larger brick buildings, giving it the appearance of being slowly crushed. The interior was similarly unimpressive or negatively impressive: Mismatched chairs and tables were scattered about the room, and a stovepipe leaked acrid smoke from what looked to be a most disorganized and ill-fated kitchen. We entered unhungry and remained so, the smell of horse meat being thick on the air. The checkered eye patch man from the diary was standing in the corner with a tall and picturesque woman, incongruously well dressed in a bright green sleeveless silken gown. These two were engaged in some manner of entertainment and did not notice us as we took up our position at their side.

The woman was a stunning picture, and the gown was the least of it. Her arms were so very beautiful and fine I found myself wanting instantly to put my hands on them; her face, too, was uncommonly lovely, with a handsome Indian profile and a pair of green eyes that when she set them upon me made me jerk my head away, for it was as though she were looking through my body to a point across the room, and when she did this I felt my core doused in ice-cold water. The proprietor glanced at us automatically and nodded before returning to their sport, which I will now describe:

The woman held her palms out. In her right hand was a small piece of fabric, the same that her dress was made of, its edges sewn with a length of heavy golden thread. I do not know why but there was something magnetic about that bit of cloth; I found it pleasing to gaze upon, and a smile appeared on my face. I noticed the proprietor was also staring and smiling. Charlie was staring but his face remained in its typical unfriendly countenance.

'Are you ready?' the woman asked the proprietor.

He focused his eyes steadfastly on the fabric and his entire being became stiff. He nodded and said, 'Ready.'

Just as soon as he uttered the word, the woman began passing the cloth back and forth, snaking it through her fingers and across the knuckles, working with such speed and cunning that the fabric was lost to the naked eye. Now she balled her hands to fists and held them before the proprietor, addressing him in a low and monotone voice: 'Pick.'

'Left,' he said.

The woman opened her left hand: No cloth. She opened the right to reveal the green and gold square; it had been bunched in her grip but was unfolding itself to lay flat. 'Right,' she said.

The proprietor handed the woman a dollar and said, 'Again.'

The woman held out her hands, palms facing up. 'Are you ready?'

He said that he was. They played another round and this time I focused more intently. The proprietor must have noticed this, for when the woman brought up her fists, he invited me to choose. I believed I knew where the cloth was and gladly joined in. 'It is there,' I said. 'The right hand.' The woman opened her fist and it was empty. 'Left,' she said. I dug into my pocket for a dollar, that I might take a turn.

'I have not finished my engagement with her,' said the proprietor.

'Let me have a single play.'

'You just have had one.'

'Let us go one and then the other.'

He grunted. 'I have engaged her for the time. You may take your turn after I'm through, but for now I need to concentrate completely.' He turned back to the woman, passing her another dollar. 'All right,' he said, and her hands began their slippery movements. Accepting my role of nonparticipant, I paid attention to the woman's hands just as closely as I was able. I do not think I ever paid such close attention to one particular thing in my life. When her hands came to rest I would have bet every penny I had that the cloth was in her left hand. 'The left hand,' said the proprietor, and I twitched in anticipation. Alas, the woman unballed her fist and it was empty, and the proprietor jumped up in anguish. He actually performed a small jump. I hid my feelings as best I could, but inwardly I too was crestfallen. Charlie had been following along with the game; he was partially amused and partially annoyed.

'What is the purpose of this?' he asked.

'To find the bit of cloth,' said the proprietor innocently.

'But what is its appeal? How often do you win?'

'I have never won.'

'And how many times have you played?'

'Many, many times.'

'You are throwing your money away.'

'So is everyone throwing their money away.' He regarded us more closely, now. 'What do you two *want*, can I ask? Are you here to eat?'

'We are looking for Warm.'

At the name, the proprietor's face dropped, and his eyes filled with hurt. 'Is that a fact? Well, if you find him, you send him my regards!' This was spoken so bitterly that Charlie was moved to inquire, 'You have some dispute with him?'

'I fed him many times over after he dazzled me with his trick of lights and shadows. I should have known he would run out on our bargain.'

'What was the bargain, exactly?'

'It is a personal matter.'

I said, 'You were to escort him to the River of Light, is that it?'

He tensed, and asked, 'How did you know about that?'

'We are friends of Warm,' said Charlie.

'Warm has no friends besides me.'

'We have enjoyed a long and healthy friendship with him.'

'I'm sorry, but I do not believe you.'

'We are his friends,' I said, 'and we know he has others, also. He recently dined here with a Mr. Morris, for example.'

'What, the dainty little fellow?'

'They have gone to the river together, is what we have heard.'

'Warm would never entrust his secrets to a fancy man like that.' But he pondered this a moment and apparently came to believe it as fact. He sighed. 'My spirits are low today. I would like to be alone to play this game. You gentlemen have a seat if you want to eat. If not, you will leave me in peace.'

'Do you have any notion where he was planning on setting up his operation?'

The man did not answer. He and the woman began another round of play. When her fists became still he said, 'Right hand.'

'Left,' said the woman.

He paid out another dollar. 'Again,' he said, and the woman's hands resumed their dancing.

'We have thought to visit him at his claim,' I said.

The woman held up her fists and the proprietor exhaled sharply. 'It is the left.'

'Right,' she said.

'Will you tell us when it was you saw him last then?' I said.

'Did you not hear me say I wished for solitude?' he asked.

Charlie pulled his coat back to reveal his pistols. 'I want you to tell us everything you know, and right now.'

The proprietor was not surprised or alarmed by this. 'Hermann spoke of the day you men would come. I did not believe him.'

'When did you see him last?' I asked.

'He came in four or five days ago. He had a new hat to show me. He said he would fetch me the next morning to make for the river. I sat here, in this very room, like an ass, for several hours.'

'But he never said which river, never gave a clue?'

'He has always spoken of following his river upstream to the fountainhead.'

'His river where he had a claim you mean?'

'That's what I mean.'

'Why do you not go there?'

'Follow after him? And then what? Force myself into their company? No, if he had wanted me to go, he would have come for me. He has made his decision to travel with the other man.'

Charlie found the proprietor's attitude distasteful. 'But what of your agreement?' he asked. 'What of the gold?'

'I don't care about money,' the proprietor answered. 'I don't know why. I should pay more attention to it. No, I was looking forward to an adventure with a friend, is the long and short of it. I had thought Warm and I were close companions.'

These words brought an expression of disgust to my brother's face. He buttoned his coat and retired to the bar for a drink. I stayed behind to watch the man lose another dollar to the woman, then another.

'It is hard to find a friend,' I said.

'It is the hardest thing in this world,' he agreed. 'Again,' he said to the woman. But he was tiring, it was clear. I left them to their game. My brother had drunk a brandy and was waiting in the road for me. We walked in the direction of Morris's hotel, passing the livery where we had stabled Tub and Nimble. The hand spied me walking by and called out. 'It is your horse,' he said, beckoning for me to enter. Charlie said he would take in the sights and return in half an hour, and we parted ways.

As I entered the stable I found the hand, a stooped and bowlegged old freckle-spotted bald man in coveralls, inspecting Tub's eye. I stood next to him and he nodded a hello, saying, 'He has an uncommonly agreeable personality, this one does.'

'What about that eye?'

'Here is what I wanted to talk to you about. It's going to have to go.' He pointed and said, 'Two doors down and there's an animal doc.' I asked how much the procedure might cost and he told me, 'Twenty-five dollars, is my guess. You'll want to check with the man himself, but I know it'd be close to that.'

'The entire horse is not worth twenty-five dollars. An eye shouldn't cost me more than five, I wouldn't think.'

'I'll take it out for five,' he said.

'You? Have you done it before?'

'I have seen it done on a cow.'

'Where would you do it?'

'On the floor of the stable. I will drug him with laudanum; he will feel no pain.'

'But how would you actually remove the eye?'

'I will use a spoon.'

'A spoon?' I said.

'A soup spoon,' he nodded. 'Sterilized, of course. Dig out the eye, snip away the tendons with scissors—that's how it was with the cow. Then the doc filled the eyehole with rubbing alcohol. This woke the cow up! Doc said he didn't give it enough laudanum. I'll give your horse plenty.'

Stroking Tub's face, I said, 'There isn't any medicine I might give him instead? He has had a tough time of it already without being half blind.'

'A one-eyed horse isn't worth much to a rider,' the hand conceded. 'Your wisest course might be to sell him for his meat. And I have horses for sale out back. Would you like to see them? I'd give you a fair deal.'

'Let's go ahead with the eye. We will not be riding very far, and perhaps he will still be of some use to me.'

The hand gathered the tools for the operation and placed these atop a quilt he had lain on the ground beside Tub. He brought out a ceramic bowl filled with water and laudanum; as Tub drank this the hand called me to his side. As if in secret, he whispered, 'When his legs begin to buckle I want you to push with me. The idea is that he falls directly onto the blanket, understand?' I said that I did, and we stood together, waiting for the drug to take hold. This did not take long at all and in fact happened so quickly it caught us off guard: Tub's head dropped and swayed and he stumbled heavily toward the hand and myself, pinning us against the slatted sides of the stable. The hand became frantic under the weight; his face grew red as clay and his eyes bulged as he pushed and cursed. He was scared for his very life, and I found myself laughing at him, squirming around with not the slightest sense of dignity, something like a fly in honey. The hand was humiliated and then infuriated by my lightheartedness; his squirming became all the more frenzied and wild. Fearful the man might faint or otherwise harm himself, I reached up and slapped Tub's backside as hard as I was able; he winced and stood away from us and the hand shouted, 'Push, goddamnit, push!' I choked off my laughter and put all my weight against Tub's ribs and belly. Between my efforts and the hand's, in addition to Tub's woozy attempt to regain his footing, we pushed him clear to the other side of his stable, cracking and snapping the slats as he crashed against them. Now the hand grabbed my arm and yanked me back just as Tub, rebounding off the wall, fell to the ground, his head perfectly placed on the quilt, out cold. The hand was panting and sweat covered, and he regarded me with the most sincere contempt, his twisted fists pinned to his denim hips. 'Can I ask you, sir, just what in the hell it is that you're celebrating?' He was so very upset, standing there before me, it took no small amount of self-control not to laugh again. I managed it, but barely. Speaking penitently, I told him, 'I'm very sorry about that. There just seemed something funny about it.'

'To be crushed to death by a horse, this is your idea of carefree entertainment?'

'I am sorry to have laughed,' I said again. To change the subject I pointed at Tub and said, 'At any rate it was a dead shot. Right on the quilt.'

He shook his head and growled lowly, phlegm percolating in his throat. 'Except for one detail. He is lying on the wrong side! How am I to get at the eye, now?' He spit the phlegm on the ground and watched it. He watched it a long while. Whatever in the world was he thinking about? I decided to regain the hand's trust, if only to do right by Tub, for I did not like the idea of the old man performing such a delicate operation while he was angry.

There were several lengths of rope on the wall at the rear of the stable, which I removed and tied to Tub's ankles, that I might pull him over. The hand surely knew what I was doing but did not offer his help, and began instead to roll a cigarette. He did this with great seriousness, as though it required the extent of his concentration. Tying off Tub's ankles took five minutes, during which time the hand and I shared not a word, and I was becoming annoyed with him, feeling his sullenness was exaggerated, when he approached with a second cigarette, this rolled for me. 'Don't ash in the hay, will you?' There was a single pulley hanging above the stable; we ran the two lengths of rope through the swivel, one over top of the other. With the both of us pulling it was not difficult to turn Tub over. After our working and smoking together the hand and I were friends again. I could see why he had been angry. He did not understand about my laughing. But we were very different kinds of people, and many of the things I had come to find humor in would make your honest man swoon.

Tub lay dozing and breathing, and the hand went to fetch a spoon that had been sitting in a pot of boiling water in his kitchen. Returning to the stable, he tossed the steaming utensil back and forth to avoid burning himself. His hands, I noticed, were filthy, though our alliance was so tentative I dared not comment. Blowing on the spoon to cool it, he instructed me, 'Stay away from the rear of this animal. If he comes to the way that heifer did, he'll kick a hole right through you.' He pushed the spoon into the socket, and with a single jerk of his wrist, popped the eye out of its chamber. It lay on the bridge of Tub's nose, huge, nude, glistening, and ridiculous. The hand picked up the globe and pulled it to stretch the tendon taut; he cut this with a pair of rusted scissors and the remainder darted into the black socket. Holding the eye in his palm, now, he cast around for a place to put it. He asked if I would take it and I declined. He went away with the eye and came back without it. He did not tell me what he had done with the thing and I did not ask.

He took up a brown glass bottle and uncorked it, glugging the contents into Tub's eye socket until the alcohol spilled over, leveling to meet the rim. Four or five pregnant seconds passed when Tub's head shot back, arching stiffly, and he made a shrill, raspy noise, '*Heeee!*' and his hind legs punched through the rear wall of the stable. Seesawing on his spine, he regained his footing and stood, panting, woozy, and less an eye. The hand said, 'Must sting like the devil, the way it wakes them up. I gave him one hell of a lot of laudanum, too!'

By this time Charlie had entered and was standing quietly behind us. He had bought a bag of peanuts and was cracking their shells and eating them.

'What's the matter with Tub?'

'We have taken his eye out,' I told him. 'Or this man has.'

My brother squinted, and started. He offered me his peanut bag and I fished out a handful. He offered the bag to the hand, then noticed the man's outstretched fingers were slick, and pulled it away, saying, 'How about I pour you out some?'

The hand opened his palm to receive his share. Now we were three men eating peanuts and standing in a triangle. The hand, I noticed, ate the nuts whole, shell and all. Tub stood to the side, shivering, the alcohol draining down his face. He began urinating and the hand, crunching loudly, turned to face me. 'If you could pay out that five dollars tonight, it would be a help to me.' I gave him a five-dollar piece and he dropped it into a purse pinned to the inside of his coveralls. Charlie moved closer to Tub and peered into the empty socket. 'This should be filled with something.'

'No,' said the hand. 'Fresh air and rinses with alcohol are what's best.'

'It's a hell of a thing to look at.'

'Then you should not look at it.'

'I won't be able to control myself. Couldn't we cover it with a patch?'

'Fresh air and rinses,' answered the hand.

'When will he be fit to travel?' I asked.

'Depends on how far you're going.'

'We are headed to the river diggings east of Sacramento.'

'You will be traveling by ferry?'

'That I don't know. Charlie?'

Charlie was walking around the stable and smiling at some discreet amusement. He had had another drink or two, judging by his friendliness and happiness. Anyway, he had not heard my question, and I did not press him for an answer. 'Likely we will be traveling by ferry,' I said.

'And when were you planning on going?'

'Tomorrow, in the morning.'

'And once you arrive at the diggings, you will be sleeping out of doors?'

'Yes.'

The hand thought about this. 'It is too soon to go,' he said.

I patted Tub's face. 'He appears alert.'

'I am not saying he cannot do it. He is a tough one. But if he were my horse I would not ride him for a week, at least.'

Charlie returned from his perambulations and I asked for more peanuts. He held the bag upside down: Empty. 'What is the most expensive restaurant in town?' he asked the hand, who whistled at the question, scratching simultaneously his forehead and genitals.

The Golden Pearl was simply bathed in wine—red heavy velvet, with hundred-candle chandeliers over each table, bone china plates, silk napkins, and solid silver cutlery. Our waiter was an immaculate, ivory-skinned man in a night-black tuxedo with blue silk spats and a ruby lapel pin that all but blinded a man to look upon it. We asked for steak and wine, preceded by brandy, an order that pleased him fundamentally. '*Very* good,' he said, writing with a flourish on his leather-bound pad. '*Very, very* good.' He snapped his fingers and two crystal snifters were placed before us. He bowed and retreated but I had every faith he would soon return, that he would see us through our dining experience with the utmost charm and agility. Charlie took a sip of the brandy. 'Jesus, that's nice.'

I took a short drink of it. It tasted entirely separate from any brandy I had ever drunk. It was so far removed from my realm of the brandy-drinking experience I wondered if it might not be some other type of spirit altogether. Whatever it was I enjoyed it very much, and promptly took another, longer drink. Attempting to sound casual about it, I said, 'Where are we in terms of our being in the Commodore's service?'

'What do you mean?' he asked. 'We are continuing on with the job.'

'Even though he has misled us?'

'What do you propose we do, Eli? There isn't any point in severing ties with him until we investigate this so-called River of Light. Even if we were not working for him, I would still be set on investigating.'

'And if Warm and Morris are successful? Do you plan to rob them?'

'I don't know.'

'If they are not, I suppose we will kill them.'

Charlie shrugged, his attitude light and carefree. 'I really don't know!' he said. The waiter brought out our steaks; Charlie pushed a forkful into his mouth and groaned at its delicious taste. I also took a bite, but my mind was on something else. I decided to broach it at once, while Charlie was in a high mood. I said, 'It occurred to me that if we never spoke of finding Morris's diary, no one could think us incorrect in returning to Oregon Territory.'

At these words Charlie swallowed, and his gladness from a moment earlier vanished from his face. 'What in the hell are you talking about?' he asked. 'Would you explain it to me, please? Firstly, what would we tell the Commodore when we got back?'

'We would tell him the truth, that Morris defected with Warm, their whereabouts unknown. We could never be expected to find them without any clue to lead or guide us.'

'At the very least, the Commodore would expect us to check Warm's claim.'

'Yes, and we could say we did and found nothing. Or if you would rather, we could actually visit the place on our return trip. We know Warm won't be there, after all. My point is, if it's only the diary's contents that impels us to continue, then let us burn the book and carry on as though we never laid eyes upon it.'

'And what if the diary isn't the only thing that impels us?'

'It is the only thing that impels me.'

'What is your actual proposition, brother?'

I said, 'Between the Mayfield stash, and our savings back home, we have enough to quit the Commodore once and for all.'

'And why would we do something like that?'

'It seemed you were for it, before. You have never thought about quitting?'

'Every man that has ever held a position has thought about quitting.'

'We have enough to stop it, Charlie.'

'Stop it and do what?' He picked a piece of fat from his teeth and flung this onto his plate. 'Are you *trying* to ruin my dinner?'

'We could open the store together,' I said.

'What *the*? What *store*?'

'We have had a long go of it, and we both have our health and some of our youth left. Here is our chance to get out.'

He was becoming progressively frustrated by my words, and would shortly drop his fist on the table and lash out at me, truly. But just as he was reaching the point of actual anger, some inner thought calmed him and he returned to sawing his steak.

He ate with a full appetite while my food turned cold and when he was finished he called for the check and paid for both plates, despite the cost. I was prepared, then, for him to say something hurtful at the conclusion of the meal, and he did. Draining the last of his wineglass he spoke: 'We have established, anyway, that you wish to stop. So stop.'

'Do you mean to say I would stop but you would continue on?'

He nodded. 'Of course, I would need a new partner. Rex has asked for work in the past, perhaps he could come along.'

'Rex?' I said. 'Rex is like a talking dog.'

'He is obedient like a dog.'

'He has the brains of a dog.'

'I could bring Sanchez.'

At this I coughed, and a trickle of wine flowed from my nostril. 'Sanchez?' I sputtered. 'Sanchez?'

'Sanchez is a good shot.'

I held my stomach and laughed. 'Sanchez!'

'I am merely thinking aloud,' Charlie said, reddening. 'It might take some time to find someone suitable. But you've made your decision, and that is fine by me. It will be welcome news to the Commodore, also.' He lit a cigar and sat back in his chair. 'We will continue with this job and part ways after its completion.'

'Why do you say it like that? Part ways?'

'I will stay on with the Commodore and you will turn clerk.'

'But do you mean to say we won't see each other?'

'I'll see you when I come through Oregon City. Whenever I need a shirt, or some underthings, I will be there.' He stood and stepped away from the table and I thought, Does he actually want me to stop, or is he merely tricking me into continuing by goading me along? I studied his carriage for the answer to this; I received a clue when his brow unknotted and his spine went slack—he was pitying me, in all my wounded wretchedness. He said, 'Tomorrow morning we will ride out to find Warm and Morris. Let us finish the job and see where we stand afterward.' He turned and walked from the restaurant. The elegant waiter appeared beside me, inhaling windily as I stood to go, for my meal was all but untouched, and he was insulted that such beautiful food should go to waste. 'Sir!' he called after me, his tone richly indignant. 'Sir! Sir!' Ignoring him, I walked into the wildness of the San Francisco night: Swaying lanterns on passing carts, a whip's constant recoil, the smell of manure and burned oil, and a ceaseless, all-around caterwauling.

I returned to the room to sleep and saw no more of Charlie until morning, when I awoke to find him fully dressed and washed, clean shaven and pink cheeked; his movements were sharp and alert and I felt a hopefulness that this change in his temperament was related somehow to our argument of the previous evening, that he had elected to remain relatively sober and to rise early so I might by association have a better time of it, and that we might view the job from the moral standpoint. But now I saw his pistol handles were gleaming in their holsters—he had cleaned and polished them, as was his habit prior to the completion of an assignment. His decision to pass a peaceful night without excessive drinking was not done to please or soothe me but so that he might be fully present for the probable murder of Warm and Morris. I rose from the bed and sat at the table across from him. I found I could not face him, and he said, 'It will never do, your pouting like this.'

'I'm not pouting.'

'It's pouting, all right. You can pick it up again just as soon as the job's done, but for now you're going to have to cork it.'

'I tell you I'm not.'

'You can't even look at me.'

I looked. And it was as though there was nothing in the world wrong with him, his manner was perfectly at ease. I imagined what he in turn was seeing in me, hair wild, rubbery belly pushing against an unclean undershirt, eyes red and filled with hurt and mistrust. It came over me all at once, then: I was not an efficient killer. I was not and had never been and would never be. Charlie had been able to make use of my temper was all; he had manipulated me, exploited my personality, just as a man prods a rooster before a cockfight. I thought, How many times have I pulled my pistol on a stranger and fired a bullet into his body, my heart a mad drum of outrage, for the lone reason that he was firing at Charlie, and my very soul demanded I protect my own flesh and blood? And I had said Rex was a dog? Charlie and the Commodore, the two of them together, putting me to work that would see me in hell. I had a vision of them in the great man's parlor, their heads enshrouded in smoke, laughing at me as I sat on my comical horse in the ice and rain outside. This had actually taken place; I knew it to be the truth. It had happened and would happen again, just as long as I allowed it.

I said, 'This is the last job for me, Charlie.'

He answered without so much as a flinch: 'Just as you say, brother.'

And the rest of the morning in that room, packing and washing and preparing for our travels—not another word exchanged between us.

The hand met me at the stable door.

'How is he?' I asked.

'He slept well. Not sure how he'll ride, but he's doing better than I figured he might.' He handed me a bottle of alcohol. 'Twice a day,' he said. 'Morning and night, till you run out. Make sure you tie him to something when you do it. Just douse him and run, is my thought.'

'Have you doused him today?'

'No, and I do not plan to. I did it just the once to show you the way, but from here on, it's all yours.'

Wanting to get it over with, I unstopped the bottle and took a step toward Tub when the hand said, 'I wish you'd take him outside. I just barely got the first hole covered without him kicking a new one.' He pointed and I saw his pitiable patch job, the damaged timber gone over with scraps. I led Tub out and tied him to a hitching post. His socket had crusted blood and pus around its rim, and without the eye to hold its form the lid sagged at its center. I poured in a good amount of the alcohol and stepped clear of him. *'Heee!'* said Tub, kicking and bucking and urinating and defecating. 'Sorry,' I said. 'I'm sorry about that, Tub. Sorry, sorry.' His discomfort passed and I retrieved the saddle from the stable. Charlie led Nimble out and stood beside Tub and I.

'Ready?' he said.

I did not answer but climbed onto Tub. His back and legs had more give than before, his muscles stringy with fatigue; also he was confused by the loss of half his sight, and he craned his neck to the left to see from his right eye. I backed him into the road and he walked in a tight, full circle, then another. 'He is getting his bearings,' I said.

'It is wrong to ride him so soon,' said Charlie, climbing on Nimble. 'You can see he needs rest.'

I pulled hard on the reins and Tub ceased his spinning. 'Let's not pretend you care for his well-being all of a sudden.'

'I don't give a damn about the horse. I'm talking about what's right for the job.'

'Oh! Yes! Of course! The Job! I nearly forgot about it! Our preeminent purpose! Let's talk about it some more! I will never tire of the subject so long as I am living!'

I found my lip was quivering; my feelings were so deeply injured that morning, looking at my brother on his fine, tall horse, and knowing he did not love me the way I had always loved and admired him and looked up to him; my lip quivered and I found myself shouting like this so that people walking past made comments and stared.

'The Job! Yes! The Job! But of course that's what you were referring to!'

Charlie's eyes hooded with contempt, and shame enveloped me like a fever. Without a word he turned and rode off, cutting through the crowded streets and disappearing on the far side of a covered wagon. I scrambled to regain sight of him but Tub continued to crane his neck and walk sideways; I jabbed him with my heels and the pain righted him, but his breath was ragged as we ran, and my shame redoubled. I very much wanted to simply quit then, to stop and walk away from Tub, and from the job, and Charlie, to return on a new horse for my pile in Mayfield and construct a separate life, with the pale bookkeeper or without, just as long as everything was restful and easy and completely different from my present position in the world. This was my dream, and it was a powerful, vivid one, but I did nothing to enact it, and Tub continued his running and wheezing and I made it to the beach and rejoined Charlie, falling in beside him as we headed for the ferry landing. We passed the spot where the horse belonging to the man with the winch had died. The animal was partially skinned, with a good portion of its meat hacked away. Crows and gulls fought over what was left, hopping and pecking, the clammy flesh gone purple, the wind coating it in sand, and the flies insinuating themselves where they could. I felt San Francisco standing behind me but I never looked back, and I thought, I did not enjoy my time here.

The ferry was a smaller-sized paddle wheeler called *Old Ulysses* that had a corral at its foremost end that housed horses alongside sheep and cows and pigs. Just as soon as Charlie tied off Nimble he left me; I did not follow after him but stayed behind to pet Tub and say sweet things to him, offering him comfort with my nearness and kindness, belated as it was. I had a plan to stay down there for the entire eight-hour voyage but the water was rough and the pigs became seasick (only the pigs became seasick), and I found it necessary to take in the air topside. I never once saw Charlie and nothing of consequence happened for the rest of the trip, except for this: I asked a woman if she had the time, and she looked me up and down and said, 'I have no time to share with you,' and walked away. I bought some mealy apples from a blind man and fed these to Tub as the boat was shoring up in Sacramento. His legs were trembling. It was late afternoon.

Charlie and I rode clear of civilization and entered into a forest of oak trees, dense and damp and impossible to navigate incautiously. It was slow going, made all the more so by the fact of our not speaking. I thought, I will not speak first. Then Charlie spoke first.

'I would like to discuss our methods for dealing with Warm.'

'All right,' I said. 'Let us cover the angles.'

'That's it. Starting with our employer. What might he want us to do?'

'Kill Morris first, quickly, and without malice. From Warm, extract the formula, then kill him, also, but slowly.'

'And what would we do with the formula?'

'Return this to the Commodore.'

'And what would he do with it?'

'He would claim to be its author, and he would become ever more infamous and rich.'

'And so the actual question is: Why are we doing this for him?'

'But this is just what I have been getting at.'

'I want to talk it through, Eli. Answer me, please.'

I said, 'We are doing this for a wage, and out of your reverence for a powerful man whom you hope to one day usurp or somehow become.'

Charlie made a stretched-out face that said: I did not know you knew that. 'All right. Let us assume that is true. Would it make sense then to empower the Commodore? To enable him in such a significant way?'

'It would not make sense.'

'No. Now, would it make sense for us to follow the Commodore's instruction just shy of the last? Just shy of handing over the formula?'

'To kill the two innocent men and steal their hard-won idea for ourselves?'

'Morals come later. I asked if it would make sense.'

'It would at least make sense, yes.'

'Fine. Now, let us discuss the consequences of disobeying the Commodore.'

'It would be unpleasant. I should think we would be hunted all our lives.'

'Unless?' he said, lips upturned. 'Unless?'

'Yes,' I said. 'We would have to kill him.'

'Kill him how?'

'What do you mean?'

'Lie in wait for him? Make it known we are after him? Go to war with his lieutenants? He has men in most every outpost and town, remember.'

'No, the only way would be to get it over with right off. To head back just as if we were still working for him, then kill him in his house, and flee.'

'Flee where? Who would come after us if the man himself was dead?'

'I would be surprised if he did not have explicit orders to be carried out in case of untimely passing.'

Charlie nodded. 'He absolutely does. He has spoken to me about it in the past. "If my blood is spilled prematurely, there will be an ocean of blood spilled in response to it." So: How might this inform our plans?'

I said, 'The only way would be to kill him in total secrecy.'

'Total secrecy,' Charlie agreed.

'We would have to arrive under cover of night and shoot him as he sleeps. After this, run into the wild and hide away for many days, then return empty-handed, as though coming from San Francisco, claiming to have missed the formula, to have lost Morris and Warm. We would act very surprised when we learned of the Commodore's death, and we would offer our services in tracking down and killing any of those possibly involved.'

'That is all fine, except for the last part,' he said. 'If the Commodore is murdered, accusations will fly in every direction, and there will be a good deal of violence because of it. I would be surprised if we were not accused; and it would be suspicious if we in turn did not level accusations of our own. A lot of blood work then, and for what? When the man with the money is already gone?'

'What is your thought, brother?'

'What if the Commodore simply died in his sleep? A pillow over the face, is all.'

'Yes,' I said, 'that's the way. And we would have the formula, also.'

'We would have it, but would not be able to use it for a time.'

'We could live off the Mayfield stash, plus our savings.'

'Or we could find a private river and work with the formula anonymously.'

'It would be a difficult thing to keep hidden.'

'Difficult but not impossible. We would likely have to bring a few more into the fold. I don't know how Warm thinks he will be able to dam a river with just the two of them.'

'Let us return to the moral question,' I said.

'The moral question,' said Charlie. 'Yes, let's.'

'I've never much liked Mr. Morris on a personal, man-to-man basis. Or should I say he has never much liked or respected us, which colors my feelings for him. But I will admit to having a certain respect for him.'

'Yes, I feel the same way. He is honorable. Even with this abandonment of his post he is.'

'He is that much more honorable because of it, is my way of seeing things. And as for Warm, I can't help it. I admire him for his intelligence.'

'Yes, yes.'

'Well, I don't know what else to say.'

'You would rather not kill them.'

'That's what it is. I have been thinking about the last job, where we lost our horses. Do you recall those men we were up against? All they were after was blood and more blood, and it made no difference to them whose it was. They were living just to die. And our role was ironclad the moment we stepped onto their property.'

Charlie paused, remembering. 'They were a rough bunch, it's true.'

'It felt right to me, because whether or not they had wronged the Commodore they were evil men, truly, and they would have killed us if we hadn't moved first. But these two, Warm and Morris. It would be more like killing children or women.'

Charlie was quiet. He was thinking about the two futures, the immediate and the distant. I had more to tell him but did not interrupt, as I felt I had said enough to make my point clear. I was relieved we had had this talk, and that Charlie was not outwardly opposed to my way of thinking. I was also relieved the bad feelings from San Francisco were abating or had abated. But then we often came about our truces through this kind of clinical discussion.

Darkness fell before we could locate Warm's claim, and we camped under the oaks. I doused Tub and he screamed, kicking and bucking; when the pain passed him he lay down on the ground to pant and stare at nothing. His appetite was poor but I still believed he had a good deal of life left in him, that he would soon begin his recuperation. As I drifted away to sleep I watched the treetops bowing and clashing in the wind. I could hear the river but could not place it; one moment I felt it was to the north, another moment I was certain it was to the south. In the morning I discovered it was to the east. We found Warm's claim after lunch and decided to spend the night there, that Tub might be rested for a full day's ride, and that Charlie and I might focus ourselves for what lay ahead of us.

The claim was an attractive and comfortable site, and we camped above the river on a grassy sandbank. A small sign posted at the foot of the claim line read: THESE WATERS ARE THE TEMPORARY PROPERTY OF HERMANN KERMIT WARM, AN HONEST MAN ON SPEAKING TERMS WITH MOST EVERY ANGEL IN HEAVEN. THOSE WHO DIP THEIR PANS IN HIS OWN PRIVATE STRETCH WILL FIND THEMSELVES SWARMED, INSULTED, TAPPED WITH SHARP HARPS AND LIKELY LIGHT-NING, TOO. Vines were painted elaborately around these words. Warm had taken his time with the project.

Fat trout hung in the current and Charlie shot one in the head for our dinner. Upon receiving the bullet the fish issued a cloud of blood and steered sideways as the current pulled him down river. Charlie waded in and picked the fish up by the tail, flinging it through the air and onto the bank where I was sitting. I gutted and skinned it and fried it in pork fat. It was four or more pounds and we ate all but the head and innards. The thick green grass made for excellent bedding and we both slept well. In the morning a man stood over us, small and grizzled and smiling, a happy prospector reentering civilization with his hard-won pouch of dust and flakes.

'Good morning, gentlemen,' he said. 'I was just about to make a fire for my coffee when I smelt your smoke. I'd be happy to share a cup, if I might borrow your heat.'

I told him to go ahead and he stoked the coals, setting his blackened kettle directly atop the embers. He spoke to himself as he did this, offering hushed words of encouragement and grace: 'Good, good. Tidy, tidy. Very nicely done.' Every half minute or so he suffered a fit of twitches and I thought, He has been alone in the wilderness for too long, and has become two people.

'You are heading into San Francisco?' asked Charlie.

'You bet I am. Four months I've been away, and the closer

I get I can't hardly believe it. I got it all worked out to the last detail.'

'Got what all worked out?'

'All the things I'm going to do.' We did not ask that he elaborate, but he needed no invitation to continue: 'First thing I'm going to do is rent a clean room, up high so I can look down and see everything as it passes. The second thing I'm going to do is call for a piping hot bath. Third thing is I'm going to sit in it with the window open and listen to the town. Fourth thing I'm going to do is have a shave, to the bare cheek, and a haircut, close-cropped and parted. Fifth thing I'm going to do is buy a new outfit from the hat to the boots. Shirt, undershirt, pants, stockings, all of it.'

'I have to go to the toilet,' Charlie interrupted, and he walked away into the forest.

The prospector was undisturbed by my brother's rudeness and in fact did not appear to notice it. He was staring into the fire as he spoke; he probably would have continued talking even if I had left: 'Sixth thing I'm going to do is eat a steak as big as my head. Seventh thing I'm going to do is get very, very drunk. Eighth thing I'm going to do is get a pretty girl and lie down a while. Ninth thing I'm going to do is talk with her about her life, and she'll ask about mine, and we'll go back and forth like this, civilized and properly. Tenth thing I'm going to do is no one's business in the world but my own. Eleventh thing I'm going to do is send her away and stretch out in the clean, soft bed, like this.' He stretched out his arms as wide as he was able. 'Twelfth thing, boy, I'm going to sleep and sleep and sleep!'

Now the water was boiled and he poured us each a cup of coffee, the taste of which was so poor it actually startled me, and it took my every bit of politeness not to spit the liquid out.

Dredging my finger along the bottom of the cup, I brought up a mound of grit. I smelled and then licked this and identified it as dirt. People will often describe something as 'tasting like' dirt, but this was not the case, here—my cup held earth and hot water, nothing more. I believe the man, through some lonely prospector mania, had begun brewing dirt and tricking himself into believing it was coffee. I had a mind to broach the subject with him but he was so pleased to be sharing, and I did not want to upset his pride; at any rate, who did I think I was to try and undo what had surely taken many days and nights to become fact for him? I decided to wait until his next fit of twitches and then pour out the dirt-water while he was not looking. Charlie came back from the woods and I informed him with secret looks that he should not drink the 'coffee'; when the prospector offered him a cup he declined. 'More for us,' the prospector told me, and I weakly smiled.

'I am wondering if you've seen a couple friends of ours,' Charlie said. 'They would have been heading upriver a few days ago. Two men, one bearded, one not.'

'Had a good deal of gear with them?' he said.

'The one had a red beard.'

'That's right. Had a good deal of gear with them. Two mules loaded down with twice what Benny's carrying.' He pointed to his mule, Benny, standing next to Tub and Nimble. I did not think a mule could carry any more than what he was.

'What type of gear?' I asked.

'Pans, canvas, rope, timber. All the usual. Only thing strange was they had four twenty-five-gallon casks, two per mule. The redhead said they were filled with wine. Wouldn't sell me a drop, the miser! I like a drink as much as anyone, but hauling that much into the wild's just the type of greediness that'll ruin you. You can work a mule to the point where he won't ever recover. These two were well on their way, it looked like to me.'

'Any idea where they were headed?'

'They were keen to know the location of a beaver dam I told them about. I'd only brought it up as a place they'd want to stay away from, but they had to have every detail.'

'Where is it?' asked Charlie.

'Now you got the same look in your eye they had! And I'll tell you just what I did them: That stretch isn't worth your time. Those beavers'll strip every bit of wood from your camp just as soon as you look away, and whatever you put in the river—a rocker or cradle or anything—is as good as gone. A damned nuisance, is all they are. Hey, that's a good one! Get it? *Dam-ed?*' He suffered a fit of twitches and I poured out my dirt-water into the grass. The moment his fit ceased he spied that my cup was empty and made me another, encouraging me to drink. I held the cup to my mouth, clamping my lip on the edge, thus allowing none of the liquid into my mouth.

Charlie said, 'If our friends were headed there, we would like to pay them a visit.'

'Well, you can't say I didn't warn you. But you'll know you're close when you pass a camp of men four or five miles up from here. Do not stop in hopes of making friends, for this group has no interest in socializing. In fact they are downright rude. But no matter. Two miles more, and you'll see the dam. You can't miss the thing it's so big.' He hefted the kettle to pour himself another cupful of his brew and I noticed he winced at the effort. I asked if he was injured, and he nodded. He had fought an Indian with knives and won, he said, but the Indian had taken a piece out of him, which weakened him, and he had lain beside the corpse for long hours before he could summon the strength to stand. He pulled back his shirt to show us the divot beneath his breast. Its edges were scarring but it was still scabbed at its pit—a nasty wound. I would have put its age at three weeks. 'Got me a good one, there. I guess I got him better, though.' He stood away from the fire and returned to Benny, strapping his cup and kettle to the mule's load.

'Where is your horse?' asked Charlie.

'That's what I was fighting the Indian about, didn't I say? He stole away my pal Jesse the one night while I was sleeping. When he came back the next for Benny, I was ready to go. Well, it's a fine day for walking. And if Old Ben can do it, so should I be able to.' He tipped his hat to us. 'Thanks for the company. I'll raise a drink for you, down in town.'

'Hope you see all your plans through,' I told him, and he smiled a crazy smile and said, 'Heh!' He turned and walked away, with Benny bringing up the rear. Once he was out of ear-shot, Charlie asked, 'What was wrong with the coffee?' I passed him my cup; he took a tentative sip and discreetly spit it out. His face had no expression. 'This is dirt,' he said.

'I know it is.'

'The man brews and drinks dirt?'

'I don't think he thinks it's dirt.'

Charlie lifted the cup and took another sip. He pushed this around in his mouth, and again he spit it out. 'How could he not think it's dirt?'

I thought of this twitching prospector and the chicken-holding prospector and the dead, headless prospector and said, 'It would seem to me that the solitude of working in the wilds is not healthy for a man.' Charlie studied the surrounding forest with a kind of suspicion or mistrust. 'Let's move on,' he said, turning to fold his bedroll.

Tub was looking badly, and I was loath to douse him, as I thought the energy the dousing would expend was energy necessary to get us to the beaver dam. He was breathing hard and would not drink water and I said to Charlie, 'I believe Tub is dying.' He gave Tub a brief inspection; he did not say he agreed with me but I could see he did. He said, 'It is only another few miles, and hopefully we'll be there long enough that Tub can rest up and regain his strength. Better give him his alcohol, and let's get started.' I explained I thought it best to skip the dousing, and this gave Charlie an idea. He fetched a bottle from his saddlebags; his face wore a smile as he showed it to me. 'Don't you remember? The tooth doctor's numbing liquid?'

'Yes?' I said, not understanding.

'Well? How about giving Tub a splash of this prior to the alcohol? Just pour it in and let it sit awhile. It'll take the edge off that sting, I'll bet you.'

I was not sure the liquid would be effective without being injected, but I was curious enough that I went along with Charlie and poured a small amount of the medicine into Tub's eyehole. He started and became stiff, expecting the pain from the alcohol, I thought, but the sting never arrived and he returned to his panting. Now I rushed up and doused him with the alcohol, and again he grew rigid, but he never screamed, he never bucked or urinated, and I was pleased Charlie had thought of it; and he, too, was happy with himself, and he patted Tub's nose and seemed to genuinely wish him well. At this, we set off upriver. There was an auspicious feeling between us that I hoped we might hold on to.

The camp south of the beaver dam was a blighted af-
fair, little more than a fire pit and scattered bedrolls, with tools
and wood scrap littered randomly in the area. At the edge of
the camp stood three rough-looking men, glaring as we came
near. They were a filthy group even by prospector standards,
their beards matted, faces blackened with soot or mud, their
clothing stained and unkempt; everything about them was dark
and dingy in fact, save for the color of their eyes, which were a
uniform shade of the most striking blue. Brothers, I thought.
Two of them held rifles at the ready; the third was armed with
pistols in holsters. Charlie called to them, 'Has any of you seen a
pair of men heading north some days ago? One of them bearded,
the other not?' When none among them answered, I said, 'They

had two mules with them, burdened with casks of wine?' Still no reply. We passed them by and I kept an eye on their movements, for they struck me as the types who might shoot a man in his back. Once they were out of sight, Charlie said, 'Those were not your typical prospectors.'

'They were killers,' I agreed. Likely they were hiding from something in their collective past, making do in the meantime by working the diggings, and judging by their looks they were not having much of a time with it.

Another mile up the river and Tub began hacking and coughing. Through my legs I could feel a hollow dryness rattling his rib cage, and I noticed long tendrils of thick blood dropping from his lips into the river. I reached down and touched his mouth with my palm; when I brought up my hand I saw the blood was black. I showed this to Charlie, who said we were close enough to the dam that we might make a temporary camp and approach Warm and Morris on foot. We dismounted and led the horses into the woods. I found a shady spot for Tub and the moment I removed his saddle he lay down on the ground. I did not think he would get up again, and I was sorrowful for having treated him so poorly. I set out my bowl next to him, filling this with water from my canteen, but he would not drink. I poured out some feed onto the ground but he had no interest in this either, he only lay there panting.

'I don't know where we're going to get you another horse out here,' said Charlie.

'He may improve with rest,' I said.

Charlie stood behind me, waiting. I was crouched before Tub, stroking his face and repeating his name in hopes of comforting him. His empty eyehole blinked, caving in on itself; his bloody tongue hung out of his mouth, dripping thickly into the dirt. Oh, I felt very low about it all of a sudden, and I did not like myself in the least.

'We have to go now,' said Charlie. He put one hand on my shoulder and the other on his pistol. 'Do you want me do it.'

'No. Let's just go, and leave him.'

We walked away from the horses and to the north, to see about Warm, at last.

Morris and Warm's camp was walled in on both sides by steep, densely forested hills. We stood at the apex of the westernmost rise, looking down upon their well-groomed settlement: The horses and mules stood shoulder to shoulder in a line, a small fire smoldered before their crisp canvas tent, and their tools and saddles and bags lay in neat stacks and rows. It was late afternoon and there was a chill in the air; the sun cast an orange-white light against the trees and reflected off the river's surface, a silvery, spidery vein. Down shore of the camp sat the humpbacked beaver dam, the water before it pooling in a lazy circle. Who could say whether the formula worked or not, but here was a fine location to test it.

I saw some movement from within the shelter and presently

Morris appeared, crouching to breach its opening, and looking so unlike the fashionable and perfumed person I had known in the past I did not at first recognize him. His linens were sullied with mud and salt rings, his hair a perfect mess; his pants and sleeves were rolled back, the exposed flesh stained wine-purple. A grin was fixed to his lips and he was continually speaking, presumably to Warm, still in the tent, but he stood at such a distance from us we could not hear what he was saying. We descended on their camp at a diagonal route, walking cautiously, with care not to upset any rocks and send these tumbling down to alert the men of our approach. Nearing the base of the hill, we lost sight of the camp in a shallow; cresting this we could hear Morris's voice and discovered he was not speaking to anyone at all, but singing a happy-worker tune. Charlie tapped my shoulder and pointed at the tent; from where we stood we could make out the interior, which was empty. At the same moment I saw this, there sounded a curt instruction from above my and Charlie's heads: 'Keep those hands out or it's a bullet in the brain for the both of you.' We looked up to find a feral, gnome-like individual sitting on the branch of a tree. He had a pistol, a baby dragoon, pointed at us. His eyes were shimmering and victorious.

'This will be our Hermann Warm,' said Charlie.

'That is correct,' said the man, 'and your knowing my name leads me to know yours. You are the Commodore's men, isn't that right? The fabled Sisters brothers?'

'That's right.'

'You have come a long way to get me. I am on the verge of feeling flattered. Not quite there, but close.' I shifted where I stood and Warm spoke sharply: 'Move like that again and I'll kill you. You think I am fooling around, gentleman, but I have you cold and will pull the trigger, make no mistake.' He meant what he said, and it was as though I could feel the precise, heated spot where the bullet would enter my skull. Warm, like Morris, was barefoot and wearing his pants rolled up; also the flesh of his legs and hands was stained purple and I thought, Has the gold-finding solution been effective? I could not tell from his expression, for he only looked fierce and protective. Charlie noticed the purple staining also and asked, 'Have you been making wine, Warm?'

Rubbing his ankles together, cricketlike, Warm answered, 'Not by a long shot.'

'Then are you a richer man today than yesterday?' I asked.

Suspiciously, he said, 'The Commodore spoke to you about the solution?'

'In his vague way, yes,' said Charlie. 'But we learned the hard facts from Morris.'

'I doubt that very much,' Warm said.

'Ask him yourself.'

'I believe I will.' Without looking away from us he whistled shrilly, twice and briefly; in the distance came an identical noise and Warm performed the whistling once more. Up through the trees came Morris then, bounding boyishly over the rise and smiling still, until he saw Charlie and me, wherein he froze, and his face washed over in unqualified terror. 'It's all right, I've got them,' said Warm. 'I climbed up for a look-see downriver, and lucky I did, too. Saw these rascals creeping along in the direction of our camp. They have been made aware of our little experiment here, and they're trying to tell me it was you who told them about it.'

'They are lying,' said Morris.

Charlie said, 'It wasn't just you, Morris. The one-eyed man at the Black Skull let us know where you planned to camp. But it was your diary that proved indispensable.'

Watching Morris's face, I witnessed his tortured recollection. 'The bed,' he said wretchedly. 'I'm sorry, Hermann. Goddamn me, I'd completely forgotten it.'

'Left it behind, did you?' said Warm. 'Don't take it too bad, Morris. It's been a busy time, and we've been working hard, and anyway the blame should be shared. Didn't I let that cyclops in on our plans? And for what? A few bowls of rancid stew.'

'Still,' said Morris.

'Don't give it another thought,' Warm said. 'We got to them before they got to us. That's the important thing. The question now is, what to do with them?'

Morris's face went blank. 'The only thing is to shoot them.'

'Would you look at that?' said Charlie. 'A week in the wilderness and the little man's out for blood.'

'Wait now,' said Warm.

'There is no other way,' Morris continued. 'We'll bury them and be done with it. It will be a month before the Commodore stages any further action against us, and by then we will be long gone.'

'I should definitely feel more at ease with their threat eliminated,' Warm ventured.

'Shoot them, Hermann. Get it over with.'

Warm pondered this. 'It upsets my stomach to think of it.'

'Can I say something?' I asked.

'No,' said Morris. 'Hermann, shoot them. They are going to move.'

'If they move I really will kill them. You there, the big one, go ahead and speak.'

I said, 'Let us into your fold to work with you. We have quit our posts with the Commodore and have no allegiance to him any longer.'

'I don't believe you,' said Warm. 'Your very presence here betrays you.'

'We are here because of what we read in the diary,' said Charlie. 'We want to see your River of Light.'

'You want to poach it, is what you mean to say.'

'We are the both of us impressed with your enterprise and strength of mind,' I told him. 'And we are sympathetic to Morris's decision to quit the Commodore. As I said, we have made the same decision, and were impelled to visit you.'

My words, spoken sincerely, gave Warm pause, and I sensed him watching and wondering about me. When he finally replied, however, his tidings were not in my favor: 'The problem is that even if you are split from the Commodore—which I doubt is the truth—but even if it is so, I have no faith in your motivations. Simply put, you are a pair of thieves and killers, and we have no place for you in our operation.'

'We are not thieves,' said Charlie.

'Merely killers then, is that it?'

'You are both haggard from the work,' I said. 'We will assist you with the labor and offer our protection, also.'

'Protection from whom?'

'From whomever should come up against you.'

'And who will protect us from you?'

'Let us into your fold,' said Charlie. His patience had left him and his tone was demanding, which sealed it for Warm, who no longer spoke, and when I looked up I could see his head listing back as he trained his barrel at Charlie. I was moving to draw my pistols when Warm, still listing and finally listing too far, lost his balance and fell backward from the branch, somersaulting through the air and disappearing mutely into a swath of tall ferns. Morris, unarmed, spun and ran through the trees; Charlie raised a pistol in his direction but I reached up and caught his arm. He raised his other pistol but Morris had ducked out of sight. He broke away from me to give chase but Morris had had too much of a head start to be caught and Charlie abandoned this, doubling back to where Warm had dropped—except the man was no longer there, having snuck away undetected. Charlie looked impotently at the flattened ferns, then up at me. A moment passed and he burst into baffled laughter, his face pale and disbelieving. This meeting with Warm, despite the brandishing of pistols, had been so different from our earlier experiences that he could not help but be amused by it. His amusement soon receded, however, and as we returned to our camp to regroup he became simply angry.

Tub was missing when we returned. He had been so weak it did not occur to me to tie him off, but while we were gone he had stood and walked away. I followed the trail of plump, dust-covered blood orbs leading over the short hill that walled in our camp; the far side of this was near vertical and he had fallen, sliding fifty yards under his own weight before coming to rest at the root of a wide sequoia. He was butted up to this by the spine and his legs were pointed ignobly skyward and I thought, What a life it is for man's animals, what a trial of pain and endurance and senselessness. I considered climbing down to check on him, for if he was still drawing breath it would only be proper to put a bullet in him, but his still features illustrated the arrival of unmistakable death, and I turned away from him, back to camp to find Charlie stocking his ammunition.

Tub's death proved useful in diffusing Charlie's upset, concerned as he was for my well-being, offering me encouraging words, a promise to go halves on a new horse, one who would be just as fit as Nimble or better. I went along with his comforts, acting solemn and thoughtful, but in truth I was not particularly unhappy about Tub's passing. Now that he was gone it was as though my sympathy for him too was gone and I was looking forward to my life without him. He was a kindhearted and good animal but he had been a significant burden to me; our lives were not suited as mates. Many months later I became sentimental about him, and this feeling is still with me today, but at the time of his actual demise I experienced merely a lifted weight.

'Are you ready?' Charlie asked.

I nodded that I was. Knowing the answer, I asked anyway: 'What will our course of action be?'

'Force is the only way,' he said.

'Surely they must know that we could have killed them both but didn't.'

'I would have killed them, if you had not interfered.'

'For all they know, though, we elected not to.' Charlie did not respond and I offered, somewhat lamely, 'If we were to enter their camp without arms, our hands in the air.'

'I refuse to honor the statement with a reply.'

'I am only hoping to discuss each possibility.'

'There are but two. To leave them in peace or to visit them again. And if we visit them again, force will be necessary. They would have killed us before if it had not been for their clumsiness, and now there will be no hesitation on their part. Morris will be armed, and there will be no talking between us and them.' He shook his head. 'Force is the only way out of this, brother.'

'But if we were to return to Mayfield,' I began.

'We've already been through that,' Charlie interrupted. 'If you want to go, go, but you will have to walk back to Sacramento for a new horse. It is your choice to make. I will see this job through with or without you.'

I made the decision to go with Charlie, then. I thought, He's right. We tried to enter into their camp peaceably, but they would not have us. It was all the mercy I could hope for from my brother, and the opportunity to visit the River of Light was too unusual for either of us to turn away from it. My attitude about this decision was that it would be the last bit of bloodshed for my foreseeable future, if not the rest of my life; I told Charlie this and he told me that if the thought brought me comfort I should embrace it. 'But,' he said, 'you're forgetting about the Commodore.'

'Oh, yes. Well, after him then.'

Charlie paused. 'And there will likely be some killing related to the Commodore's death. Accusations leveled, debts owed, that sort of thing. Could be quite bloody, in fact.'

I thought, Then this will be the final *era* of killing in my lifetime.

'It is getting dark,' Charlie said. 'We should strike out now, in case they're planning to beat a retreat. We can come at them the long way around, from the eastern hilltop. It will be fish in a barrel, you watch.' He began urinating on the fire. I watched the light from the dying flames flickering over his cheeks and chin. He was feeling merry. Charlie was always happiest when he had something to do.

We took an annular course around Warm and Morris's camp, crossing the river a half mile up and doubling back, creeping to the summit of the tall hill opposite their settlement. Through the trees we could make out the glowing embers in their fire pit, the kegs of formula sitting up from the waterline, one of them toppled and emptied while the remaining three stood untapped. I could see neither man but their animals remained and I assumed they were either hiding beneath their shelter or else nearby in the woods, armed and waiting for a fight. Morris, I thought, was likely engaged in desperate prayer and repentance; though I scarcely knew the man I decided Warm was probably feeling bolder, more adventuresome, driven by an attitude of rightness and a demand upon himself to see the plan through, come what may. But whatever was going on in their minds, they were nowhere to be seen, and their camp was quiet as the grave.

The dam by comparison was bustling with the inscrutable industry of the nocturnal beavers, numerous, fat, and slick coated in the milky moonlight. They ducked and swam and rose, issuing low groans, communicating some beaver lament or perhaps a sentiment of encouragement; they strode up the shore, pulling twigs and branches back into the water and ferrying these to the dam, atop of which sat the fattest of the bunch, looking over the others as if supervising their efforts. 'That one there is the boss man,' I said to Charlie. He had been watching them also, and he nodded.

Presently the portly beaver lumbered free from the dam and moved onto the shore, stepping cautiously at first, as though he did not trust the ground to support his weight, but his trepidation was short-lived, and now he entered into the camp itself, traveling without hesitation or fear, and heading directly for the kegs of formula. Sticking his head into the spent keg, he recoiled at its fumes, then moved on to one of the full and upright barrels. Standing upon his hind legs, he sunk his teeth into the rim, attempting to topple it and, I suppose, drag or roll it into the river. I found the scenario more amusing than anything but Charlie was very focused and anxious about it, for he knew the beaver's unwelcome attentions would bring about a reaction from Warm and Morris, if they were in fact watching. Sure enough, a moment passed and there came a faint *clack-clack* sound from the bottom of the valley. Charlie nodded excitedly: 'There? You heard it?' The sound was repeated, and then again, and I could make out the blurred black shapes of stones flying through the air and toward the tenacious rodent, who had by this time succeeded in upsetting the keg. We traced the stones' point of origin to a sheltered grouping of trees and bushes twenty yards back from the camp on our side of the river—Warm and Morris were hidden at the base of the same hill we stood upon, and without a word, Charlie and I began creeping down to catch them from behind. 'I will take care of Morris,' he whispered. 'Keep Warm under your pistol, but you mustn't shoot him unless it's an absolute necessity. Give him one in the arm, if need be. He will still be able to work—and he will still be able to talk.'

My very center was beginning to expand, as it always did before violence, a toppled pot of black ink covering the frame of my mind, its contents ceaseless, unaccountably limitless. My flesh and scalp started to ring and tingle and I became someone other than myself, or I became my second self, and this person was highly pleased to be stepping from the murk and into the living world where he might do just as he wished. I felt at once both lust and disgrace and wondered, Why do I relish this reversal to animal? I began exhaling hotly through my nostrils, whereas Charlie was quiet and calm, and he made a gesture that I should also be quiet. He was used to corralling me like this, winding me up and corralling me into battle. Shame, I thought. Shame and blood and degradation.

We were close enough that I could see the spot where Warm and Morris were tucked away, and the indistinct shape of their arms as they tossed their stones. I imagined how their hiding place would look when it was brightly and momentarily lit from our muzzle flashes; each leaf and stone would be sharp and clear and I could envision the men's frozen expressions, their terrible surprise at having been discovered.

Charlie suddenly clapped his hand on my chest to halt me. His eyes examined my eyes and he said my name searchingly;

this removed me from the above-described mentality and re-turned me to the actual earth. 'What?' I said, frustrated, almost, by the interruption. Charlie held up his finger and pointed and said softly, 'Look.' I shook my head to awaken my true self and followed the line of his finger.

South of the camp there came a line of men in the dark, and I knew just as soon as I saw their rifle-toting silhouettes it was the blue-eyed brothers from downriver. Thinking back on my brief interaction with the men, I remembered the slightest shift in their stances at my mention of Warm's wine casks, and now the barrels were just what they moved toward. The beaver was at the waterline with his hard-won prize, but a kick in the belly from the largest brother and he was soaring through the air, landing with a plop in the river. Outraged, he began slapping his tail on the surface of the water, alerting his fellows of this latest danger; they instantly ceased their labors and returned to the safety of the dam interior where they might huddle together without threat of mayhem and brutishness. The boss-man beaver was the last to vacate the scene and his movements were sluggish. I thought he was probably winded after the boot to the stomach—or was he nursing his wounded pride? There was something human about those little beasts, something old and wise. They were cautious, thoughtful animals.

The largest brother rolled the barrel upriver and set it beside its mates before moving to look inside the tent. Finding it empty, he called out a loud 'Hullo!' I thought I detected some restrained laughter from Morris and Warm, and I looked quizzically to Charlie. The laughter grew louder, becoming hysteric, and the brothers shifted on the sandbank, looking at one another uneasily.

'Who is there?' said the largest brother.

The laughter died away and Warm spoke: 'We're here. Who's *there?*'

'We are working a claim downriver,' the brother answered. Kicking a keg, he said, 'We want to buy some of this wine from you.'

'Wine's not for sale.'

'We'd give you San Francisco prices.' He shook his purse to illustrate this, but there was no reply, and the brother looked searchingly into the darkness. 'Why are you hiding in the shadows like that? Are you afraid of us?'

'Not particularly,' said Warm.

'Then will you come out here and speak with us like men?'

'We will not.'

'And you refuse to sell to us?'

'That is correct.'

'What if I simply took a barrel?'

Warm paused to think of the answer. At last he said, 'Then I will send you home less a ball, friend.' Now I could hear Morris's crazed laughter—the last sentence had tickled him to the depths of his soul and he submitted wholly, overtaken by his joy. Charlie, smiling, said, 'Warm and Morris are drunk!'

The brothers came together on the sandbank to speak in private. After their conference of opinion, the largest stepped away from the others, nodding. He said, 'Sounds like you have had your fair share tonight, but before the sun comes up your spirits will turn low, and your heavy blood will force you into sleep. You can count on us returning then, you men. And we will have your wine, and we will have your lives, also.' There was no response to this, no laughter or mocking retort, and the brother took a step downriver, his chin in the air, very dramatic and proud. He was having sovereign-type thoughts, it was plain. His words, at any rate, were sufficiently theatrical as to give the jolly duo below us pause; but now I could hear Morris and Warm speaking in a hurried back-and-forth, lowly at first, but soon giving rise to an outright argument at full volume, their words heated and cross. Morris's pleading voice came clearly as he cried: 'Hermann, no!' Just after this was the report of Warm's baby dragoon, and I saw the largest brother was dropped with a fatal shot to the face.

In a flash then, the other brothers fell to a crouch and began firing in the direction of Morris and Warm; and the drunken pair returned fire, shooting wildly, likely with their heads down and eyes closed. Charlie offered me his swift instruction: 'Take them both down. It's all for nothing if they murder Warm.' From our elevated angle the two remaining brothers proved to be the most elementary game. Less than twenty seconds had passed before they were lifeless in the sand, just beside their leader.

The staggered echoes of our gunshots jumped away over the hills and treetops, and there came from the base of the valley the whooping war cry of Warm. Unaware we had assisted them, he believed they alone had murdered the brothers, and was feeling roisterous about it. Charlie called out to them: 'That was none of your shooting, Warm, but my brother's and mine, do you hear me?' This brought Morris and Warm's celebration to an abrupt end, and they fell once more to hissing at each other, disagreeing and worrying beneath their shrubs and foliage.

'I know you can hear me calling you,' said Charlie.

'Which one's that talking?' asked Warm. 'The mean one or the fat one? I don't want to talk to the mean one.'

Charlie looked at me. He gestured that I should speak and I stepped forward to do this. I hoped to appear purposeful and serious in my movements, but I was embarrassed, and he was embarrassed for me. I cleared my throat. 'Hello!' I said.

'That the fat one?' asked Warm.

'Eli is my name.'

'But you are the bigger one? The huskier of the two?'

I thought I could hear Morris laughing.

'I am husky,' I said.

'I don't mean it unfavorably. I myself have a problem pushing away from the table. Some of us are simply hungrier than others, and what is there to be done about it? Are we meant to starve?'

'Warm!' I said. 'You are drunken, but we need to speak seriously with you. Do you think you can manage it? Or perhaps Morris can?'

He said, 'What do you wish to discuss?'

'The same as before. Of our joining forces and working the river as one.'

Charlie reached over and pinched me, hard. 'What are you doing?' he whispered.

'Our position has changed with this new bit of killing,' I told him.

'I can't see that anything has changed. They are still waiting in the dark with pistols to shoot us down.'

'Let me just see what the reaction is. I believe we can achieve what we wish without spilling any more blood.'

He sat back against a tree, thinking, and chewing his lips. Again he pointed into the darkness that I should speak, and I did: 'If you can't see it through to discuss the venture you will force our hand into action, Warm. I mean this in all honesty when I say we do not want to kill either one of you.'

Warm scoffed. 'Yes, you demand that we should share our

profits with you, and if we choose against this, well, you will be obligated to kill us. Do you see how your proposal might be lacking, from our point of view?'

I said, 'I am proposing we *earn* a part of the profits. And anyway, if we wanted you dead, do you think we would have cut down those men you see before you?'

Morris said something I could not make out, which Warm translated: 'Morris says he thinks he got the one on the left.'

'He did not.'

Warm did not speak to me for a time, and I could not hear him speaking with Morris.

'Is either of you injured?' I asked.

'Morris's arm was grazed. He is still fit, despite a burning feeling.'

I said, 'We have medicine that will eliminate that burning. And we have alcohol to clean the wound. We will work the river alongside you, and we will protect you against bandits or intruders. Think of it, Warm. We had you cold earlier today; if we had wanted you dead, you would be dead.'

Another long silence, where I could not make out the slightest murmur from Morris or Warm. Were they searching their very souls for the answer? Would they allow the heretofore bloodthirsty Sisters brothers into their exclusive fold? There arose a gathering noise then, which at first I could not identify, and when I did identify it I questioned if I was truly hearing the sound, it was so incongruous to the present situation: Hermann Warm was whistling. I did not know the tune, but it was the type I had always enjoyed, slow and maudlin, the lyrics to which would have dealt in heartbreak and death. The whistling became louder as Warm quit his hiding place and walked into the open, across the convex spine of the beaver dam and up the sandbank to his camp. He was a very talented whistler, and the song plummeted and soared, quivering in the air and disappearing into the hush of the river. It went on and on, and Charlie, without speaking a word, stood and began walking down the hill. I did not know the plan and neither could he have known the plan. Warm did not know the plan and Morris could not know it. There was no plan. But I found myself likewise hiking down, and with no thought to conceal our approach. Warm was facing us now, looking up the hill in our direction, searching us out, the song on his lips growing ever more tremulous and romantic. His arms were spread, the way an entertainer spreads his arms, as if to envelop an audience.

We walked across the dam and onto the shore. Warm's tune gave out as we stood face-to-face. He was a wild-looking man, shorter than me by a full foot, and he stank of alcohol and bitter tobacco. His shoulders and arms were thin and he was thin hipped but his belly was great and round and he was not afraid of us in the least, which is to say he was not afraid of death, and I thought I liked him very much; and I could see by the show of whistling, of standing in the clear the way he had that Charlie was also impressed with his boldness and strength of character. Warm offered his hand, first to Charlie and then myself, and we took turns having a shake and solidifying our alliance. After this there was a gap in time where no one knew quite what to say or do. Morris, not yet prepared to socialize, had stayed behind in the bushes with the whiskey.

We stoked the fire and sat to discuss our partnership.
Charlie was for dumping a barrelful of the formula that night
but Warm demurred, saying he and Morris were drunk and exhausted besides. Morris, I should say, eventually emerged from
his hiding place, gripping his arm in discomfort but hoping to
appear nonchalant or cavalier about it. You could see he was
troubled by our joining up with them; I watched Charlie watching him and was concerned about what my brother might say
or do to the man. It was a relief when he greeted Morris without malevolence, extending his hand and saying he hoped they
would let bygones be bygones. Morris shook Charlie's hand re-
flexively; looking at me, he shrugged, and passed over a long silver flask. His mustache was frayed at its ends and his eyes were

red and swollen and he said, 'I'm tired, Hermann.' Warm regarded him with fondness. 'It has been a long one, has it not, my friend? Well, why don't you go sleep it off. We'll all have a rest and regroup as a quartet in the morning.' Morris said no more, but retired to his tent. I had a drink of whiskey and handed the flask to Charlie. He took a drink and passed it to Warm. Warm took a short sip and screwed the top on tight, hiding the flask away in his coat pocket as if to say: That is enough of that. He licked his palm to smooth his hair and tugged on his lapels to straighten them. He was working through a fog, making an attempt at seriousness.

It was decided my brother and I would keep half of whatever we culled from the river, and that the remainder would go to what Warm called the Company.

'The Company being you and Morris,' Charlie said.

'Yes, but it's not as though the profits will be spent at the saloon. They will be used to finance future excursions, similar to this one, though more ambitious, and so more costly. Anyway, if this goes as I believe it might, the Company will grow quickly, with several operations under way simultaneously, and there will be opportunities to become further involved should one prove himself trustworthy. As for now, why don't we wait and see if you and your brother can make it through this modest expedition without slitting my and Morris's throats, eh?'

Fair enough, I thought. Warm began itching his ankles and shins and I asked him, 'Did you pull very much from the river last night?'

He said, 'We were so tickled with the spectacle that a good amount of time was wasted simply staring and wading and laughing and congratulating each other, when we should have been working. But in the quarter hour we labored before the gold ceased its glowing we removed what would have taken us a month if we had panned it. The formula works, all right. It works just as well as I had hoped or better.' Looking over his shoulder at the river, Warm was contented to be thinking of his successes, and I felt a powerful envy as I watched him. He was reaping the benefits, both monetary and spiritual, of his hard labors and intelligence, and it made me think of my own path, which by comparison was so much the more thoughtless and heartless one. Charlie was also studying Warm, though his expression read less of admiration than enigmatic curiosity. Warm I do not think noticed our attentions to his person, and continued with his story: 'It was just the prettiest thing I have ever seen, gentlemen. Hundreds upon hundreds of pieces of gold, each of them lit up, bright as a candle flame. I will call it the most pleasing work I've taken part in, stepping up and back in the water and sand, picking out the golden stones and plunking them into the bucket.' His eyes were sharp and focused at the memory; a shiver ran through me as I gazed at the river and imagined it as he had described. 'Twenty-four hours,' he said, 'then you will see for yourselves.'

Once again he began scratching his shins, more fiercely than before; I noticed in the firelight the coloring of his skin had darkened, and that the flesh was agitated and raw. He nodded his head at my curious expression and told me, 'Something I did not account for, it's true. I knew the formula to be caustic, but I had assumed it would do no harm once diluted in the river. In the future we should equip ourselves with a kind of covering for our feet and ankles.' Morris called to him from the tent and Warm excused himself; when he returned he wore a grim face and confided in us that Morris was having some difficulty acclimating himself to life out of doors. 'God knows I am indebted to him, but you should have seen his face when I forced him to leave his powders and scents in San Francisco. How he made it to California from Oregon City carrying all those bottles and boxes is beyond me.'

'How is his arm?' I asked.

'The bullet only nicked him, and he is in no danger that I can see, but morale-wise he is doing poorly. Your both being here is weighing on his mind, and his legs are bothering him, more than mine, even. But you said something about medicine? It would put him at ease, I think, your making good on the offer of help.'

Charlie sent me back to our camp to collect our effects while he and Warm hammered out the final details of the consortium. When I returned with Nimble, weighed down with both our saddles and baggage, Charlie had dragged the three dead brothers nearer the fire, which I understood at once but which Warm, standing by, could not fathom. 'Would it not be best to haul them into the forest?' he said. 'I should not like to look at their faces in the morning.'

'The sun will never shine upon them,' Charlie answered, and he pulled one of the men directly over top of the flames.

'What are you doing?' said Warm.

'How are you fixed for lamp oil?'

Now Warm understood. He fetched his supply of oil, and I in turn gave him the alcohol and numbing medicine. He left to tend to Morris while I assisted Charlie in disposing of the corpses. We coated them head to foot in the oil and they were soon all three of them burning exultantly, their bodies stacked and blackened at the base of the blaze and I thought, So much for the calmer life. Warm's face appeared at the entrance of the tent to watch the gruesome spectacle. He looked sad. After a time he said, to no one, 'I have had enough of this day, today.' His head disappeared, and I was alone once more with my brother.

Watching him roll out his blankets, I wished to ask him what was in his heart just then, for I wanted so badly to trust him, that he had at last made a moral decision, but I could not think of the correct words to say, and I was fearful of what the answer might be, and besides that I was spent, and just as soon as I laid my head on the ground I dropped into the most impenetrable kind of dreamless, leaden sleep.

When I awoke, the sun was upon my face, the river sound was in my ears, and Charlie was not beside me. Warm stood stiffly over the bonfire ash pile, a long stick in his hand, half raised as though set to strike. He pointed out the gray-black skull of one of the dead brothers and said, 'See it? Now, watch.' He tapped the top of the skull and the entire visage collapsed to dust. 'There is your civilized man's last reward.' His words had an embittered edge to them, so that I was moved to ask, 'You are not the God-fearing sort, Warm?'

'I am not. And I hope you aren't, either.'

'I don't know if I am.'

'You are afraid of hell. But that's all religion is, really. Fear of a place we'd rather not be, and where there's no such a thing as suicide to steal us away.'

I thought, Why did I bring up God so soon after waking? Warm returned his attentions to the ash pile. 'I suppose the brain cooks down to nothing?' he mused. 'The heat converts it to water, which then evaporates. Just a slip of smoke and away floats the precious organ onto the breeze.'

'Where is Charlie?'

'He and Morris went to have a swim.' Warm found another skull and likewise tapped and collapsed it.

'They went together?' I asked.

Looking upriver, he said, 'Morris was complaining about his legs and your brother said he thought a dip might soothe the burning.'

'How long ago did they leave?'

'Half an hour.' Warm shrugged.

'Will you take me to them?'

He said he would. He was not alarmed and I did not wish to alarm him but I tried to hurry him along as much as possible, acting as though I were overheated and ready for a swim myself. Warm was not a man who liked to rush, however; in fact he appeared to insist upon stopping and dissecting most every little thing. Pulling on his boots, he wondered, 'What do you imagine happened to the first man who wrapped his bare feet in leaves or leather, to protect himself? Likely he was pushed from the tribe, emasculated.' He laughed. 'He was probably showered with stones and killed!' I had nothing to add to this, but Warm did not need any reply from me, and he continued his speech as we set off upriver: 'Of course in those times people's feet were covered in the very toughest calluses, so the desire for footwear was likely more for appearance than comfort or necessity, at least in the warmer climates.' He pointed out an eagle flying nearby; when the bird swung down and collected a heavy fish from the river, Warm applauded.

His legs were troubling him and I offered my arm, which he took, with thanks. The sand was soft and deep and he asked me once and then again if we might rest, and though I was loath to hesitate anymore than was necessary, I was also hesitant to explain my reasons for hurrying. But Warm deduced it; he chuckled and asked me, 'You do not trust your brother completely, do you?' In the context of our tentative business alliance, and because Charlie was currently alone with Warm's weakened comrade, here was a serious question, and yet his expression spoke only of amusement, as though we were engaging in the lightest type of town gossip.

'He is a difficult one to pin down,' came my sideways answer.

'Morris, I think, actually despised your brother before your helping us last night. And yet this morning they were walking arm in arm. What do you make of it?'

'I don't know what to say, other than it is out of character for him.'

'You do not think his assistance is wholesome?'

'I am surprised to hear it, is all.'

Warm paused to scratch at his shins, and I could see his skin had become considerably darker, with blisters beginning to bloom upward toward the kneecap. His scratching grew more furious, so that he fairly shredded his own flesh with his fingernails; I believe he was frustrated about the formula acting as an irritant, and thus marring the beauty of his plans. At last he fell to slapping his legs to quiet the maddening itch, and this seemed to bring him some relief. Straightening his pant legs, he asked me, 'But you don't really think Charlie would *kill* old Morris, do you?'

'I do not know. I hope not.' He put his arm on mine and we continued upstream. I said, 'I'll admit it feels unusual to speak this way with you.'

He shook his head. 'Best to keep it out in the open, as far as I'm concerned. And isn't it already? And really, what can Morris and I do about it? We would rather you and your brother *not* kill us, but we're at your mercy more or less, aren't we?'

'It's quite a group you've assembled, Warm.'

Gravely, he said, 'Dodgy, isn't it. A dandy and two infamous murderers.'

I began to laugh, and Warm asked me what was funny. 'You, and your purple legs and hands. Morris and my brother, and the men piled high in the fire. My dead horse tumbling down a hill.'

Warm appreciated the sentiment, and stood awhile to beam at me. 'Touch of the poet in you, Eli.' He said he would like to ask me something personal, and I granted him permission, and here is what he wished to know: 'It is a question I put to Morris some time ago, but now I am wondering the very same thing about you, which is how you came to work for a man like the Commodore.'

I said, 'It's a long story. But basically, my brother knew violence from a young age, thanks to our father, who was a bad man. This brought about many problems for Charlie, one of these being that whenever he was insulted he could never engage in your average fight with fists or even knives, but had to see each episode through to death. Well, you kill a man, then his friend or brother or father comes around, and it starts all over again. So it was that Charlie sometimes found himself outnumbered, which was where I came in. I was young, but my temper was always high, and the thought of someone causing harm to my older brother—up until then he had been a very good and protective brother—was enough to make me partway insane. As his reputation grew, so did the number of his opponents, and so did his need for assistance, and in time it was understood that to come up against one of us was to do battle with both. It turns out, and I don't know why this is, and have at times wished it were not so, but yes—we had or have an aptitude for killing. Because of this, we were approached by the Commodore, who offered us positions in his firm. At first this was more muscle work—debt collection, that type of thing—than outright murder. But as he took us further into his confidence, and as the wage increased, it soon devolved to it.' Warm was listening intently to the story, and his face was so serious I could not help but laugh. I said, 'Your expression tells me your opinion of my profession, Warm. I am inclined to agree with you. At any rate, and just as I was saying to Charlie, this job is my last.'

Warm ceased walking, and turned to watch me with a lost, fearful look on his face. I asked him what was the matter and he said, 'I believe you meant to say the job *before* was your last. For you do not plan to see this one through, isn't that the case?'

We had just cleared a curve in the river; looking up, I saw Charlie, naked, stalking from the water to his clothing on the shore. Morris lay floating just behind him, belly up, his body still. When Charlie turned toward us, his face broke into a smile, and he waved. Now I saw Morris was sitting up, unmolested, and he too waved and called to us. My heart was pounding hard; it felt as though the blood was draining right out of it. Returning my attentions to Warm, I answered him, 'It was only a mix-up of words, Hermann, and we are through working for the man. I give you my word on it.'

Warm stood before me then, looking into me; his manner conveyed several things at once: Sturdiness, wariness, fatigue, but also an energy or glow—something like the center of a low flame. Is this what they call charisma? I do not know, exactly, except to say Warm was more *there* than the average man.

'I *believe* you,' he said.

We made our way to the others, with Morris calling from the water, 'Hermann! You must come in! It really is a great help.' His voice was high pitched, and he was outside of himself, removed from his personal constraint of rigidness and seriousness, and very much pleased to be. 'The gay little baby,' Warm commented, dropping onto his backside in the sand. Squinting in the sunlight he looked up and asked, 'Help me with my boots, Eli, please?'

In the evening I found myself resting before the fire

with Warm, waiting for the sky to darken that we might use the gold-finding formula most effectively. To pass the time, he encouraged me to speak of my life, to recount for him my many dangerous adventures, only I had no wish to do this, and in fact wanted to forget about myself for a moment; I turned the questions back upon him, and he was all the more forthcoming than I. Warm enjoyed speaking of himself, though not in a proud or egotistical way. I think he merely recognized the tale as an uncommon one, and so was pleased to share it. As such, his life story was revealed to me in a single sitting.

He was born in 1815 in Westford, Massachusetts. His mother was fifteen years old and ran off after giving birth, just as soon as she was strong enough to carry herself away. She left Warm to the care of his father, Hans, a German immigrant, a watchmaker and inventor. 'A great thinker, a tireless puzzler and problem solver. He could never crack his own private problems, however, and there was no shortage of these. He was . . . *difficult* to be around. Let me just say that Father had some unnatural habits.'

'Like what?' I asked.

'Ugly things. A specific area of deviancy. It is too unpleasant to speak of. The visual would put you off your feed. Best to move along.'

'I understand.'

'No, you don't, and be glad of that. But here was the reason he left Germany, and from what I gather he left quickly, under cover of night, taking a near-total financial loss in transit. He hated America on sight and continued to hate it with all his being until his death. I remember him looking out at that beautiful autumnal Massachusetts landscape and spitting on the ground, saying, "The sun and moon shame themselves by shining their lights upon it!" Berlin was a great metropolis and playground for him, you see. He felt relegated and undermined here, and that his new audience was not as respectful as the one he knew back home.'

'What did he invent?'

'He made small, practical improvements on existing inventions. A pocket watch with a compass built into its face, for example; another that he designed exclusively for ladies—a smaller model cast in a teardrop shape and painted in pastel colors. He was well paid and well liked before scandal ruined him, and he was forced to expatriate. When he arrived in America, dressed strangely and speaking almost no English, he found himself unwanted by even the lowliest watch companies, whom he believed were far beneath him; as he fell into poverty his mind grew darker, when it was already shades darker than your average man. Increasingly his inventions became diabolical, nonsensical. At last he focused his every energy on the refinement of torture and killing devices. The guillotine, he said, was the mechanical embodiment of man's underachievement and aesthetic sloth. He updated it so that instead of simply removing a person's head, the body would be cut into numberless tidy cubes. He named the great sheet of crisscrossing silver blades *Die Beweiskraft Bettdecke*—The Conclusive Blanket. He invented a gun with five barrels that fired simultaneously and covered three hundred degrees in one blast. A hail of bullets, with a slim part, or what he called *Das Dreieck des Wohlstands*—The Triangle of Prosperity—inside of which stood the triggerman himself.'

'That's not a bad idea, actually.'

'Unless you are fighting five men at once who happen to be standing directly in front of each barrel, it is a terrible idea.'

'It shows imagination.'

'It shows a complete disregard for safety and practicality.'

'Anyway, it's interesting.'

'That I will not deny, though at the time—I was thirteen years old—his work brought me little in the way of amusement. Actually, his inventions filled me with horror; I could not shake the notion he wanted to try them out on me, and even now I dare say this was not mere paranoia on my part. So I was not entirely unhappy when he packed a bag and left one spring morning, without any instruction or good-bye—not so much as a pat on the head from the old man. He later committed suicide, with an ax, in Boston.'

'An ax? How is that possible?'

'I don't know. But here was what the letter said: *Woefully sorry to report your Hans Warm killed self with ax on 15th May. Possessions forthcoming.*'

'Perhaps he was murdered.'

'No, I don't think so. If there was ever anyone who could find a way to kill himself with an ax, it was Father. They never did forward his things. I have often wondered what it was he held on to, there at the end.'

'And after he left you, then what happened?'

'I was alone for two weeks in our cabin when my mother arrived, standing in the doorway, twenty-eight years old, pretty as a picture. She had heard I'd been abandoned and came to fetch me back to Worcester, where she had been living all the while. She was awfully sorry to have left me, she said, but she had been deathly afraid of my father, who would drink too much and menace her with knives and forks and things. It was very much a forced or one-sided romance, was my understanding. She could not discuss their time together without revulsion. But that was past, and we were the both of us well pleased to be reunited. The whole first month in Worcester she simply held me and cried. This was the sum total of our relationship at the beginning. I wondered if it would ever stop.'

'She sounds like a kind woman.'

'Indeed she was. There were five years of blissful relations where our life was a kind of perfection. She had been given a legacy by her family in New York, and so I always had enough to eat, and my clothes were clean, and she encouraged me in my pursuit of knowledge, for even at that tender age, curiosity in most everything was strong in me, from mechanical engineering to botany to chemistry—yes, clearly that! Unfortunately this contented existence was not to last, for with my transformation to manhood it became clear to her that I was my father's son, both in looks and temperament. I became obsessive with my studies, hardly ever leaving my room. When she tried to guide me toward healthier pastimes I was consumed by an anger that frightened the both of us. I took to drinking, not too terribly much at the start, but enough that I would become abusive and belittling, just as my father had. Having been through all this before, my mother understandably found my behavior repellent, and she removed her affections in wretched stages until there was nothing left between us, nothing but for me to go, which is what I did, taking my small sack of money and heading to St. Louis, or should I say my sack ran out in St. Louis, which forced me to cease traveling. It was wintertime, and I feared I would perish from cold or sadness or both. I sold my horse and married a fat woman I did not love, or even like, named Eunice.'

'Why would you marry someone you didn't like?'

'She had an enormous potbellied stove in her cabin that emanated heat like the coals of hell. And by the looks of her she held a stockpile of food that might feed the both of us through to the spring. You're smiling, but I assure you these were my lone motivations: Warmth and nourishment. I so longed for any manner of comfort, I would have married an alligator if only it would share its bed. And I might as well have married an alligator, for all the kindness Eunice showed me. She had no grace or charm whatsoever. She had noncharm, or anticharm. A bottomless well of antagonism and hostility. And she was terrifically ugly. And she smelled like rotten leaves. A brute, to put it briefly. When the money from my horse sale ran out, and when she understood I had no plans to copulate with her, she pushed me from the bed and onto the floor, where the heat from the stove burned my topside, while the draft coming up through the boards froze my bottom. Also, my hopes for a bountiful dinner table were soon dashed. Eunice was as protective as a mama bear about her biscuits. She gave me the occasional bowl of watery stew, so let's say she wasn't all bad, but the good was there in such measly quantities you had to keep a sharp watch lest you miss it entirely. But as I said, it was miserably cold, and I had made the decision to dig in my heels and pass the winter in that cabin, one way or the other. After the weather broke I would rob her and run away into the sunshine—I would have my last laugh. She recognized my plan, however, and got me one better before I could see it through. I came home from the saloon and found a large and angry-looking man sitting at the dinner table. He had a plateful of biscuits before him. I understood right away. I wished them good luck and left.'

'That was sporting.'

'I returned an hour later and tried to set the cabin alight. The man caught me huddled over my matchbox and kicked me so hard in the backside it lifted me from the earth. Eunice saw it all from the window. That was the only time I saw her laugh. She laughed a long time, too. Anyway, I am embarrassed to say it, but after this hurtful episode I became disenchanted, and turned for a time to common thievery. I could not get my mind around my misfortune, was the thing. Only months earlier I was alone with my books, clean and sheltered and well fed, happy as could be. And now, through no fault of my own, I found myself sneaking into barns at night and burrowing under manure-matted hay so as not to freeze to death. I said to myself, Hermann, the world has raised up its fist and struck you down! I resolved to strike back.'

'What did you steal?'

'At the start I was after the bare necessities. A loaf of bread here, a blanket there, a pair of wool socks—small things that no man should be denied. But with every passing crime I became more stealthy and cocksure and also greedy; after a time I began to take away anything I could get my hands on, just for the malicious pleasure I derived from it. I stole items I could never conceivably use. A pair of women's boots. A crib. At one point I found myself running from an abattoir with a severed cow's head in my arms. What for? What functional purpose might it serve? When it became too heavy I dropped the thing into a river. It bobbed along, then caromed off a rock and sank out of sight. Stealing became like a sickness. I think I saw it as a way to extract revenge against everyone who was *not* shivering and famished and alone. It was around this point my drinking began to take hold of me, body and spirit. You talk about your slippery roads.'

'My father was a drinker. And Charlie is, also.'

'It is something that plagues me still, and perhaps will always plague me. Of course it would be best to cork the bottle forever. I have recognized the problem. I know it doesn't agree with me. Why not stop? Why not put an end to it? No, that would make too much sense. That would be entirely too reasonable. Oh, it's a slippery road, all right, make no mistake about that. Well, days and months passed me by and I became dirtier and more depraved all the while, inside and out. You will meet some down-on-their-luck types who take pride in their pared and scrubbed nails, men who will boast of their once-per-week baths, financial hardships be damned. They attend church services regularly and sit patiently in the pews, awaiting their change in fate without a trace of bitterness, beards combed down just so. Let me say that I was not one of these. In fact I was the far opposite. I became increasingly drawn to filth. More and more I desired to lay and grovel in it, to actually *live within in*. My teeth fell out, and this pleased me. My hair dropped away in patches and I was glad. I was the raving and maniacal village idiot, in short, only the village was not a humble, thatched-roof township, but the United States of America. Finally I was seized by an unshakable preoccupation, namely the belief that I was actually composed of human waste.'

'What?'

'A living mold of waste, was my notion. Excrement. My bones were hardened excrement. My blood—was *liquid* excrement. Do not ask me to elucidate. It is something I will never be able to explain. I was suffering, if I'm not mistaken, from scurvy, which added together with the drinking and mental agitation brought about this queer idea.'

'Living waste matter.'

'I delighted in the thought of it. My favorite pastime was to push through a crowd, touching and groping the bare arms of unescorted women. The sight of my own grime on their pale wrists and hands was just as satisfying a thing as I could think of.'

'I don't suppose you were very popular.'

'I was a popular point of discussion. Socially, though? No, I was not well thought of. But then I rarely stayed in one place long enough to become more than an alleyway myth. Mania or no, I was not a fool, and I knew enough that I should strike and move on at once, before any violence came against me. I would steal a horse and head for the next town, only to start my contamination campaign all over again. My days were ordure and ugliness and the blackest kind of sin, and I was only half living, just barely hanging on, waiting and hoping, I think, for death. And then one morning I woke up and found myself in a most curious place, and would you care to guess where that was? Don't say jail.'

'I was going to say it.'

'Let me just tell you then. I awoke with the king mother of all whiskey headaches on a cot in militia barracks. I was washed and my beard had been shaved clean. My hair had been cut back and I wore a soldier's uniform. The reveille was screaming in my ears, and I thought I would die, literally, of fright and confusion. Then a bright-faced soldier came by and gripped me by the arm. "Wake up, Hermann!" he said. "You miss roll call one more time you'll wind up in the stockade!"'

'What in the world had happened?'

'That was precisely what I wanted to know. But put yourself in my position. How would you find the answer to this?'

'I suppose I would ask someone.'

Warm affected a serious posture and voice: 'Pardon me, my good man, but would you mind telling me how it is I came to join the militia? It is only a slight detail, but I just can't seem to put my finger on it.'

'It would be an awkward way to start a conversation,' I admitted. 'But what else was there to do? You could not simply go along with it.'

'But that is exactly what I did do. Fell right in line, as a matter of fact. You must understand, Eli, that I was disconcerted in the extreme. As a drunkard, I was used to losing an hour or two here and there, or even an entire evening. But how much time had passed for me to join the militia and establish relationships with the other soldiers, all of whom appeared to know me well? How could I not recall so drastic a change? I decided to keep my head down and go with the crowd until I could figure things out.'

'And did you ever?'

'It was all the doing of the bright-faced soldier, named Jeremiah. Every once in a while, out of boredom, he liked to go into town and find the very lowest sort of alcohol-muddled scallywag. He would fill him with drink, extract personal information, and then, once the man was totally incapacitated, drag him back to the barracks, outfit him in a military uniform, and put him to bed. This is what happened to me.'

'Were you very angry when you understood you'd been tricked?'

'Not particularly, because by the time I found out, I was glad to be there. Life in the militia brought about many positive changes in my life. I was forced to bathe regularly, which I did not like at the start, but I endured, and this return to the habits of cleanliness successfully killed my bedeviling excrement obsession. I was fed, and the cots were comfortable, the barracks warm enough, and there was usually at least a little something to drink at night. We played cards, sang songs. A sturdy group of men, those soldiers. A bunch of orphans, really, alone in the world, passing time together, with nothing much to do. In this manner, six or seven uneventful months rolled by, and I was beginning to wonder how I might get out of there when I had the good fortune to befriend a lieutenant colonel named Briggs. If I had not come to know him, then you and I would not presently be sitting about, waiting for the river's riches.'

'What happened?'

'I will tell you. I was passing by his quarters one evening when I noticed his door, which usually was not only closed but bolted shut, was now ajar. Like many of the other soldiers, I had developed a curiosity about him, because while your typical officer was very much the taskmaster and bellower, Briggs was shy and retiring, a slight, gray-haired man with a faraway gaze, forever locked in the privacy of his room doing God only knew what. Mysteries are scarce in the militia; I found I could not help but investigate. I opened the door and peered in. Tell me then, Eli, what do you think I saw?'

'I don't know.'

'Take a stab.'

'I really don't know, Hermann.'

'Not much for guessing, eh? All right, I'll just say it. I saw our man Briggs, standing alone, deep in thought, and he was wearing a crisp cotton smock. On the table before him were burners and beakers and all manner of laboratory paraphernalia. Scattered around his room were numberless bulky, heady tomes.'

'He was a chemist?'

'A hobby chemist, and not a very keen one, I came to learn. But the sight of his effects took hold of me. Without hardly knowing what I was doing I entered fully into his quarters and stood before the equipment, staring over it as if hypnotized. By this time Briggs had noticed my gawking person; he blushed and cursed me, damning my impertinence and ordering me from the room. I begged his pardon but he would not hear me, and he pushed me out the door. That night I found I could not sleep. The nearness to the books and equipment reawakened my hunger for study and learning; it came over me like a fever, and at last I rose from my cot and wrote Briggs a letter by candlelight, explaining about my past and my father's, and essentially demanding that he take me on as his assistant. I slid the missive under his door and he called for me the next morning. He was wary, but once he understood my seriousness and the depth of my knowledge we struck a bargain, which was that I would assist him in his experiments, and as payment for this he would allow me access to his effects and books, and I should be allowed a certain amount of time to work on my own in his room. I gladly quit my usual nights of cards and bourbon and dirty stories and set up what was, at least for militia barracks, a fairly ambitious laboratory. Guided then, by my own sense of intuition, and also by the books Briggs happened to have in his library, I was led to the realm of Light.'

Warm paused to pour himself a cup of coffee. He offered me a cup and I declined. He took a small drink and returned to his story.

'The years that had passed me by since I last studied, how many had they been? And all that time I did little else but abuse and mistreat myself. I had had no sustenance to speak of, neither physical nor mental, and as I sat and cracked a book that very first evening I was visited by a concern that my brain might not recognize words the way it had in the past. The brain is a muscle, after all, and I would have to retrain it, wouldn't you think? Eh? Well, I had a nice surprise then, which was that my mind, unbeknownst to me, had all the while been improving itself of its own accord, waiting for the day I might dust it off and use it again. Now that day had arrived and my brain, as though worried I might only shelf it once more, attacked every page of every book with a magnificent strength and vitality. It was all I could do to keep up, but thankfully I did, and received my reward some months later when the idea for the gold-finding formula came to me, or should I say hit me, for it was just as though I were knocked on the chest with a heavy stone—I actually fell back in my chair. Poor Briggs didn't know what was wrong with me. At first I couldn't speak. Then I jumped for the ink and paper and would not be moved for an hour.'

'What did he think of the idea?'

'That I do not know, for I never told him—and he never forgave me for not telling him. It was not that I mistrusted him personally, but that I didn't think any man could keep this information to himself. It was simply too much weight to carry. Of course, this offended him terrifically, and he banished me back to the barracks, where I tried for a time to continue my work. When this proved impossible—the men were fond of hiding or otherwise defacing my notes—I began to plan my escape by desertion. But when one of my bunkmates beat me to it, and when he was apprehended and shot the selfsame day he struck out, then the thought of desertion lost its appeal for me. At last I was beginning to feel desperate, fearful my grand idea would vanish into thin air, and I turned to Jeremiah, the man responsible for my being there. I told him, "Jeremiah, I want to quit this place. Tell me, please, what should I do about it?" He put his hands on my shoulders and said, "If you want to leave here then you should turn and walk away. Because, Hermann, you are not actually in the militia." I had never formally joined, it turns out, never signed my name to anything. That night they threw me a party. I left in the morning and set up a modest laboratory nearby. It took me near a year of trial and error before I had the desired results. First I managed to illuminate the gold, but only for a brief instant. When I figured out a way to sustain the glow, something in the formula turned the gold gray. At one point I accidentally burned my shack halfway to the ground. It was not easy, is what I am saying. When at last I found myself pleased with the effects, this coincided with the news of the gold strike in California and I came west on the Oregon Trail. This spit me out in Oregon City and led me to your man the Commodore. From there, I believe, you know the story.'

'More or less.'

Warm scratched his hands and legs. Gazing upward, he spoke over his shoulder: 'What do you think, Morris? Sky dark enough to suit you?'

Morris called back, 'Give us another minute, Hermann. The wretch has painted himself into a corner, and I'm closing in for the kill.'

'We will see about it,' said Charlie.

They were playing cards in the tent.

Four men all at once removing their pants beside a
river in the nighttime. The fire was tall behind us and we had
had three drinks of whiskey apiece, this being just the proper
amount for the task at hand, we decided—enough to offset
the coldness of the water, but not so much that we would not
be able to focus on the work, and later on, to remember it. The
lead beaver was sitting lumpily atop the dam, scrutinizing us,
and scratching himself with his hind legs like a dog; the formula
had wreaked its havoc upon his flesh, also. But where were his
comrades? It seemed they were hiding out or otherwise resting.
When my feet touched the water I began nervously to laugh but
suppressed this, feeling that outright gladness was not correct, or
was disrespectful; to what or whom, I cannot say, but I had the

impression we were all of us holding our breath, much in the same way, and for the same vague reasons.

One of the kegs had been rolled to the shore, its top opened, ready to be poured. I caught a lungful of the formula's scent and my chest flashed with an instant, burning heat. Morris was standing shy of the river, watching the water with a look of dread.

'How about your legs, Morris?' I asked.

Regarding his shins, he shook his head. 'Not good' was his answer.

Warm said, 'I put a pot of water on the fire, and laid out some scrub soap for us to wash ourselves just after. Morris and I failed to think of this last time, hence our present troubles.' Turning to Morris, he said, 'Can you stand another night of it?'

'Let's get it over with,' Morris muttered. His legs were rashed to the thigh now, his skin rubbed raw and covered over in fat blisters, these filled with a brownish liquid and drooping slightly under their own weight. He was having trouble supporting himself upright, and as he hobbled closer to the water's edge I wondered, Why are we putting him through this? 'Morris,' I said, 'I think you should not do any work tonight.'

'And forfeit the winnings to you all?' he scoffed, but his tone, the weakness in his throat, betrayed any good humor. He was frightened, and Warm was quick to second my thought. 'Eli is quite right. Why not sit back and rest, for now. You will still receive a share of whatever I pull.'

'And from me, also,' I added.

Warm and I looked to Charlie. His charity was slower in coming, but eventually he, too, nodded and said, 'Me, also, Morris.'

'There, you see?' said Warm.

Morris hesitated. His pride had been awakened and he did not want to quit. 'What if I were to pull only from the shallows?'

'It's good of you to suggest it,' Warm said, 'but that might disable you permanently. Best to sit back now, and let us do the work. You can make up for it next time around, eh? What do you say?' Morris did not answer, but stood apart from us, looking morosely at the sand. Brightening, Warm said, 'Last time, the glowing was concentrated on this side of the river where we poured the formula. But if you were to agitate the waters, with a tree branch, say, from atop the beaver dam, you would likely increase the field of illumination.'

Morris was pleased with the idea, and we found a long branch for him to work with. Warm led him by the arm and installed him at the center of the dam, shooing the beaver back into the water before continuing on his own to the farther shore, which would be his area of focus. Now he called for Charlie and me to dump the first keg into the waters, warning us not to let any of the formula rest upon our flesh. 'You can see that it's painful enough watered down; the raw liquid itself might burn a hole clean through you.' He pointed out the second keg, positioned at the shoreline, twenty yards up river. 'As soon as the first is emptied, dash up and empty the other.'

'What of the third keg?' asked Charlie. 'Would it not be best to dump them all and be done with it?'

'We are already pushing our luck with two,' answered Warm.

'If we were to finish tonight we could leave in the morning and get Morris to a doctor.'

'We would all of us need doctors. Keep focused, Charlie, please. After you two empty the second barrel we'll let Morris mix it all. Once you see the glow, take up your buckets and get to work, quickly!'

Charlie and I squatted before the keg to lift it. My hands were shaking terribly, I was so nervous all of a sudden; my shoulders twitched and quivered and I thought, I have not felt this way since I lay down with a woman for the very first time. And it was just the same type of divine excitability: I was tortured with giddiness in anticipation of that river coming to life. Charlie noticed my shivering and ducking and asked me, 'All right?' I said I thought I was. I gripped the bottom lip of the keg with my fingers, digging into the hard-packed sand. We counted three and slowly hefted the heavy barrel into the air and began taking our cautious, crabwise steps, easing into the running river. The shock from the cold made Charlie hiss, and then laugh, which made me laugh, and we ceased moving for a moment that we might both laugh together. The moon and bright stars hung above our heads. The formula swayed and rolled in the barrel. Its surface was black and silver, and the river was black and silver. We tilted the keg and the dense liquid dropped from the lip. I could not remember ever feeling quite so bold.

From the moment we started pouring we took small backward steps in the direction of the sandy bank. The keg swirled its fumes and vapors and once more I caught the scent in my nose and lungs; I retched and nearly vomited, it was so strong and overpowering. The heat attacked my eyes and they were instantly awash in tears.

Once we were clear of the water we tossed the barrel and dashed upriver for the second. We hefted and dumped this and I stood back on the sand to wait. On the far shore, Warm instructed Morris to begin his stirring. When the frail man could not keep a sufficiently brisk pace, Warm foraged a branch for himself and agitated the waters by slapping the surface over and over, just as quickly and violently as he was able. I heard a noise at my back and turned to find Charlie cracking open the third barrel with a hatchet.

'What are you doing?' I asked.

'We will dump them all,' he said, grunting as he wrenched back the top of the keg.

Warm took notice and shouted across the river: 'Leave off with that!'

'We will dump them all and be done with it!' said Charlie.

'Leave off!' Warm cried. 'Eli, stop him!'

I came closer but Charlie was already lifting the keg on his own. He took several weighted steps before misplacing his balance and stumbling; the thick fluid crested the lip and ran down the front of the barrel, covering and coating his right hand over the knuckles. This began in a matter of seconds to attack his flesh and he dropped the keg at the waterline, where the current pulled the formula out and to the dam.

Charlie was bent over in pain, his jaw clenched and locked, and I took up his wrist to study his injury. There were blooming blisters across the knuckles and upward to the wrist—I could actually see the blisters rising and falling, as though they were breathing, the way a bullfrog takes air into its throat. He was not frightened, but angry, his nostrils flaring like a bull's, with spit running down his chin in a long, elastic ribbon. His eyes, I thought, were magnificent; their reflection in the firelight revealed the very embodiment of defiance, of clarified hatred. I took up the heated water from the fire and doused his hand to rinse it, afterward fetching a shirt to wrap him. Warm did not know what we were doing, or that Charlie had had an accident. 'Hurry, you men!' he called. 'Can't you see? Hurry up over there!'

'Can you hold a bucket with it?' I asked Charlie.

He attempted to close his hand and his forehead folded in sheer pain. The tips of his fingers, sticking from the dressing, were already bloating and it occurred to me this was his shooting hand—something I imagine he had thought of the moment the formula had been spilled. 'I can't close it,' he said.

'But can you still work?'

He said he believed he could and I fetched a bucket, sliding the handle past his hand and onto his forearm. He nodded, and now I took up a bucket for myself, and we turned to face the river.

In the time we had been distracted with Charlie's injury the formula had taken hold, its glow so bright I had to shield my eyes. The river bottom was illuminated completely, so that every pebble and mossy rock was visible. The flakes and fragments of gold, which moments earlier were cold and mute, were now points of the purest yellow-and-orange light, and just as distinct as the stars in the sky. Warm was working away, his hand dipping into the river, his head darting up and back in search of the larger pieces. He was methodical about it, working intelligently, efficiently, but his face and eyes, lit from the river glow, revealed the highest, most supreme type of joy. Morris had exhausted himself and could no longer stir; he planted his long stick into the dam and leaned against it, gazing over the waters with an expression of calm, almost narcotic satisfaction. I looked at Charlie. His face had softened, gone slack, his pain and anger removed, forgotten, and I saw his throat drop as he swallowed. My brother was overwhelmed. He looked into my eyes. He smiled at me.

In the static world of hard facts and figures it was approximately twenty-five minutes before the gold ceased glowing, but the moments that passed while we worked the river were neither brief nor long, were in fact somehow removed from the very restriction or notion of time—we were outside of time, is how it felt to me; our experience was so uncommon we were elevated to a place where such concerns as minutes and seconds were not only irrelevant but did not exist. This feeling, speaking personally, was brought on not only by the wealth our ever-growing piles of gold represented, but also from the thought that this experience was born of one man's unique mind, and though I had never before pondered the notion of humanity, or whether I was happy or unhappy to be human, I now felt a

sense of pride at the human mind, its curiosity and persever-
ance; I was obstinately glad to be alive, and glad to be myself.
The gold from our buckets shone in dense shafts of light, and
the branches and limbs of the surrounding trees were bathed
in the glow of the river. There was a warm wind pushing down
through the valley and off the surface of the water; it kissed my
face and caused my hair to dance over my eyes. This moment,
this one position in time, was the happiest I will ever be as long
as I am living. I have since felt it was too happy, that men are
not meant to have access to this kind of satisfaction; certainly
it has tempered every moment of happiness I have experienced
since. At any rate, and perhaps this is just, it was not something
we could hold on to for very long. Everything immediately after
this went just as black and wrong as could be imagined. Everything after this was death in one or the other way.

Traveling back across the dam, Morris made a misstep
and tumbled into the deepest part of the river. He fell fully
under the water and did not come up. The gold had by then
ceased glowing and my brother and I were sitting in the sand
beside the fire, hurriedly cleaning ourselves with the water and
soap Warm had laid out. My discomfort from direct contact, I
should say, had been minimal at first; between the coldness of
the river, which tingled the flesh, and also my own excitement
and fast-moving blood, I was not aware of any untoward sensation. But by the time the gold once again went mute I felt an ex-
panding heat which became my total concern and focus. Now I
was moving just as quickly as I could, dousing and scrubbing my
hands and legs and feet. Charlie could only work half as fast and

I came to his aid once I had washed myself. I had just finished with his legs when I heard Morris shout out. When I looked up he was dropping through the air.

Charlie and I ran to the shore, by which time Warm had moved to the center of the dam, his heavy bucket pulling at his right side. He stared helplessly at the river and Charlie called to him that he should use Morris's stick, still wedged in the dam, to pull him clear, but Warm did not seem to hear this. He set his bucket beside his feet, and his face was grim. He took a broad step and leapt from the dam into the poisoned waters. He resurfaced with Morris under his arm. Morris was limp but breathing, his eyes closed, mouth hung open, water lapping into his mouth over his tongue.

As they cleared the river, Charlie and I came nearer to help them but Warm shouted that we must not touch them, and we did not. They lay on the sand, panting and spent, and I ran for the water pot, hefting it to the shore. First I doused Morris, who moaned, and then Warm, who thanked me, but with the pot soon empty and the men in need of a more thorough washing, Charlie and I dragged the two upriver, beyond the formula waters, and laid them in the shallows. I fetched the raw soap and we knelt at their sides, scrubbing the men and splashing them and telling them all would soon be well, but their discomfort only grew and they became increasingly vocal about their pain. Now they were writhing and tensing and shuddering as though they were being slowly immolated, and indeed I suppose that is just what they were being.

We pulled them clear of the water. I took the last of the numbing medicine and covered their faces and scalps with it. Their eyes were coated in a gray-white film, and Morris said he could not see. Then Warm said he could not see. Morris began to weep, and Warm searched out his hand. They lay together holding hands and crying and moaning and drifting away and then suddenly, alertly screaming—both of them at once as though their pains were synchronized. I gave Charlie a secret look that asked: What should we do? His secret response: Nothing. And he was right. Short of killing the men, there was not a thing in the world we might do for them.

Morris died at dawn. Charlie and I left him on the shore and carried Warm into his tent. He was delirious, and as we laid him on his cot he said, 'What did we pull, Morris? What time is it?' Charlie and I did not attempt to answer; we let him alone to sleep or to die. The sky was low with clouds and we slept beside the fire through to the afternoon. When it began drizzling rain over us I sat up and noticed two things at once: Morris was no longer newly dead but dead-dead, his body stiff and cruel and bloodless and somehow light or weightless, resembling a piece of driftwood more than a man; and second, the beavers had climbed out of the water and died on the shore just shy of our camp. That is to say, nine dead beavers in a line on the sand. There was something decorative about this, but also ominous or forbidding. They lay on their bellies, their eyes closed, with the leader in the center, slightly ahead of the others. I did not like to think of the group emerging silently from the waters, marching toward me and my brother as we slept. Did they have it in their beaver minds to swarm and attack us? To ruin us just as we had them with our evil man-made concoctions? Thankfully, I would never know the answer to this.

I felt badly that Morris had died so soon after making the decision to correct his life and abandon the Commodore. I wondered if during his final moments he felt his death was deserved, if he wished he had never left his post, if he passed with compunction and disappointment. I hoped not, but thought he likely had, and I hated the Commodore for his impact then. I hated him as vividly as I have ever hated anyone, and I made a particular decision about him. The decision did not make me feel better but I knew it would eventually, and so it put the matter mostly to rest for the present, despite a lingering bitterness, that our night of shared glory had ended in such a tangle of grotesqueness and failure.

I stood and inspected my legs. Hours before, as I had dropped away to sleep, I was fearful I would awaken to find them covered in the liquid-filled blisters, but there was nothing of the kind. From the midthigh down the skin looked as though it had been burned by an afternoon in the sun; they were warm to the touch and there was a degree of discomfort but it was not at all like Morris's legs had been, and I did not believe my condition would worsen with time.

Charlie was asleep on his back, eyes wide open, and with a full erection pressing against the front of his pants, which despite my not wanting to know about the thing I took as a sign of wellness. I thought, Who knows in what extraordinary form good tidings might arrive in our lives? I pulled back one of his cuffs and saw that his legs looked just as mine did, red and without hair, but healthy. His hand, however, was much for the worse, with his purple fingers threatening to burst they were so plumped up. The sight of this, along with the beavers, and also Morris made me lonesome; I wished to wake up Charlie to speak with him but decided it best to let him rest.

It occurred to me I had not cleaned my teeth since San Francisco, and I crouched at the waterline upriver, scrubbing my tongue and gums and teeth and spitting out the foam like buckshot across the surface of the water. I heard Warm's voice and looked back at the tent. 'Hermann?' I called, but he said nothing more. I moved to the beavers and hefted them one by one, holding them at their tails and flinging them into the water south of the dam. They were heavier than I expected them to be, and the texture of their tails did not feel like the appendage of a living being, but something crafted by man. Charlie had sat up to watch as I tossed out the final few. In spite of the peculiarity of my work, he said nothing about it, and in fact he looked somewhat bored. Forgetting his injury, he reached up to swat a fly from his face and winced at the pain of his fingers knocking together. I tossed out the last beaver and returned to sit beside him. He attempted to unwrap his dressing but it had stuck and dried to his gummy flesh, and when he peeled the cloth back, along with it came a layer of skin from his knuckles and fingers. It did not look to hurt him, any more than he was already hurting that is, but it frightened and disgusted him, and me, also. I said I thought we should soak the entire thing in what was left of the alcohol before removing the dressing and he answered that he would rather wait until after he ate. I made us a small breakfast of coffee and beans. I took Warm a plate but he was sleeping, and I did not wake him. His entire body was red and purple and the blisters on his legs were doubled in number and all of them had burst, coating his skin in the brown-yellow liquid. His toes were black and a death-smell emanated from him; I thought he would likely pass over before the sun set. When I came away from the tent, Charlie was pouring the alcohol into one of Warm's pots, and there was another pot of boiling water on the fire with a cotton shirt dancing in its roiling bubbles. He had taken the shirt from Morris's saddlebag, he said, and looked to me for a reproach, but of course I had none to give him. He submerged his hand in the alcohol and a fat, Y-shaped vein rose up and pulsed on his forehead. He needed to scream but did not; when the pain subsided he held his hand before me and I removed the dressing. The flesh came away as before, and his hand as I saw it was ruined. Charlie looked at it but said nothing. I pulled Morris's shirt from the water with a stick; once it was cooled I wrapped the hand, covering the fingers this time, that we would not have to see them and think about what they meant.

I decided to bury Morris, away from the river where the sand and soil met. This took me several hours and was accomplished with a short-handled spade of Warm's. I did not and still do not understand the reason for this tool's existence in comparison with its long-handled counterpart. I will say that digging a grave with it was absolutely a self-torture. I did the work alone, except that Charlie helped me drag the body up the beach and drop it into the hole, but mostly my brother sat away by himself, and twice he walked upriver far enough that I lost sight of him. I did not press him, and he remained attendant for the actual filling in of the grave.

We had Morris's diary on hand (why did we not return this to him when he was living? It had not occurred to us, is why), and I struggled with the question of whether or not I should bury it with him. I asked Charlie his opinion on the matter but he said he did not have one. In the end I decided to hold on to the book, my thought being that his story was a unique one, and so best to keep his words aboveground where they might be shared and admired. It was a graceless and miserable thing to see Morris's crooked body at the bottom of that pit. He was filthy and purple and obscene to look at. It was no longer Morris but I spoke to the thing as though it was, saying, 'I am sorry, Morris. I know you would have preferred a more stylish affair. Well, you impressed us with your show of character. For whatever it's worth, you have my brother's and my respect.' Charlie was unmoved by my speech. I was not sure he had been paying attention enough to hear it. I was fearful I had been overly dramatic. Public speaking, it goes without saying, was not something I typically engaged in. Recalling my *bomboniere* from the Mayfield bookkeeper, I removed this from my coat pocket and dropped it into the pit, with Morris—a measure of grandness, was my idea. It unfurled across his chest, shining and blue and fine. I asked Charlie if we should mark the spot with a cross and he said I might ask Warm. When I entered the tent I found Warm awake and somewhat alert. 'Hermann,' I said. He blinked his milky eyes and 'looked' in my general area. 'Who's there?' he asked.

'It's Eli. How are you feeling? I am happy to hear your voice.'

'Where is Morris?'

'Morris has died. We have buried him up from the river. Do you think we should mark his grave or leave him be?'

'Morris . . . died?' He began to shake his head back and forth, then to silently weep, and I went away from the tent.

'Well?' said Charlie.

'I will ask again later.'

I thought, I have had enough of grown men crying.

We combined the entire pull of gold, which between our four-man effort from the night before and Morris and Warm's initial two-man affair made for near an entire bucket's worth. This represented a fortune and I could scarcely lift the thing of my own strength. I asked Charlie to lift it but he said he did not want to. I told him it was very heavy and he said he believed me.

In a fit of practicality, and with my thoughts moving inevitably to the future, I began to look over Morris's horse. He was a sturdy animal, and despite a pang of guilt I put my saddle on him and rode him up and down through the river shallows. He was a smooth rider and something of a gentleman. I had no particular feeling for him but I thought it was likely to follow if we spent any amount of time together. I decided I would win him over with kindness and sugar and trust. 'I am going to adopt Morris's horse,' I said to Charlie.

'Oh,' he answered.

Warm was too unwell to transport, and anyway I did not think he could be saved even if we moved him. He was scarcely aware of my nearness but I did not want to leave him to die alone. Charlie brought up the fact that we did not know the recipe for the formula and I said I knew that and what did he think we should do, torture the dying man for every last instruction and ingredient? His tone was somber, and he said, 'Don't talk to me like that, Eli. I've lost my work hand in this. I am only telling you what is on my mind. After all, Warm may very well want us to know it.' He was looking away as he said it; and I had never heard him speak this way, even when we were boys. I thought he sounded something like me, actually. He had never been afraid before, that I could remember, but now he was, and he did not know what it meant or what to make of it. I told him I was sorry I had jumped on him about the formula and he accepted my apology. Warm called out my name, and Charlie and I entered his tent. 'Yes, Hermann?' I said.

He was flat on his back, his eyes directed upward at the crest of the tent. His chest was rising and falling unnaturally quickly, and he was wheezing and breathing heavily. He told me, 'I am ready to dictate Morris's tombstone.' I fetched a pencil and paper and knelt by his side; when I told him to go ahead he nodded, cleared his throat, and spit straight into the air, a thick globule that doubled back in a graceful arc and landed on the center of his forehead. I do not think he noticed this, or perhaps he did not care. Either way, he did not clean himself or ask to be cleaned. He said: 'Here lies Morris, a good man and friend.

He enjoyed the finer points of civilized life but never shied from a hearty adventure or hard work. He died a free man, which is more than most people can say, if we are going to be honest about it. Most people are chained to their own fear and stupidity and haven't the sense to level a cold eye at just what is wrong with their lives. Most people will continue on, dissatisfied but never attempting to understand why, or how they might change things for the better, and they die with nothing in their hearts but dirt and old, thin blood—weak blood, diluted—and their memories aren't worth a goddamned thing, you will see what I mean. Most people are imbeciles, really, but Morris was not like this. He should have lived longer. He had more to give. And if there is a God he is a son of a bitch.' Warm paused. He spit again, this time to the side, onto the ground. 'There is no God,' he said, and closed his eyes. I did not know if he wanted the last sentence included on the tombstone and I did not ask, for I had no plans to transfer the speech, as it was clear to me he was not completely in his own mind any longer. But I promised Warm I would write it out just as he had said it, and I believe this consoled him. He thanked Charlie and I and we left the tent to sit before the fire. Charlie, gripping the wrist of his wounded hand, said, 'Don't you think it might be time to go now?'

I shook my head. 'We can't leave Warm to die alone.'

'It could take him days to die.'

'Then we will stay here for days.'

This was all that was said on the matter; and this was the beginning of our new brotherhood, with Charlie never again to be the one so far ahead, and me following clumsily behind, which is not to say the roles were reversed, but destroyed. Afterward, and even today, we are careful in our relationship, as though fearful of upsetting each other. In terms of our previous manner of correspondence I cannot say why it vanished suddenly then, snuffed as it was like a candle. Of course the moment it passed I became fond of it in a sorrowful kind of way, at least in theory or maudlin memory. But the question has entered my mind so many times: Whatever became of my bold brother? I can never say, only that he was gone and has yet to return.

As it happened, anyway, we would not have to wait days for Warm to pass, but hours. Night had fallen and Charlie and I were lying beside the fire, feeling very lazy and heavy, when Warm spoke in a wispy voice, 'Hello?' Charlie said he did not want to go, and I entered the tent alone.

Warm was breathing his last. He knew this and was frightened. I thought, Will he turn religious at the end, and plead for a speedy entry into heaven? But no, the man was too firm in his nonbeliefs for any last-minute cowardice. He did not wish to speak with me but asked after Morris, having forgotten the man was dead.

'Why is he not here?' Warm gasped.

'He died this morning, Hermann, don't you remember?'

'Morris? Died?' His forehead accordioned and his mouth parted, fixed open in anguish, and I stared at his gums, shiny with blood. He turned away, inhaling choppily, haltingly, as though the passage were partially blocked. I shifted my feet and he turned to follow the sound, asking, 'Who's there? Is that Morris?'

I told him, 'It is Morris.'

'Oh, Morris! Where have you been all this time?' His tone was so deeply relieved and moved, I felt a tightening of emotion in my throat.

'I was gathering firewood.'

Warm, invigorated: 'What's that? Firewood? Foraging fuel? That's the idea. We will have a bonfire tonight, light up the entire operation. All the better to sort through our buckets of fortune, eh?'

'All the better,' I agreed.

'What about the others?' he wondered. 'Where have they run off to? That Charlie doesn't much like the hard work, I have noticed.'

'No, he would rather stand by.'

'Not much for cleaning up, is he?'

'No, he's not.'

'But he has turned out a good man, you can't say otherwise.'

'He's a good man, Hermann, you were right about it.'

'And the other, Eli, where has he gone?'

'He is out there somewhere.'

'Making his rounds? Securing the camp?'

'He is in the darkness, out.'

In a lower tone he said, 'Well, I don't know how you feel about it, but I have come to like that one quite a lot, actually.'

'Yes. And I know he likes you, too, Hermann.'

'What's that?'

'I said I know he likes you, too.'

'Do I hear a trace of jealousy in your voice?'

'No!'

'I'm very flattered by it! All these men crowding around, and all of them so decent and honorable. I felt such the outcast, and for such a long time.' At these words, his lips curled in bittersweet sadness, and he closed his eyes; tears bloomed from the closed corners of his lids and I wiped these away with my thumbs. Warm kept his eyes shut after this. They would not open again. He said, 'Morris, if I shouldn't make it through the night, I want you to carry on with the formula.'

'Better not to think of it. You should only rest, now.'

'I had an idea that if you were to coat your flesh with pork fat prior to submersion, that would likely reduce the damage.'

'It is a fine idea, Hermann.'

He gasped. He said, 'Well, I feel we have known each other a long while!'

'I feel just the same.'

'And I'm sorry about your dying before.'

'I am all right, now.'

'I wanted to help you. I thought we could be friends.'

'We are friends.'

'I'm,' he said. 'I'm.' He opened his mouth widely and there came a foreign noise from deep within his insides, as though a solid piece of him had cracked or popped. What was this? I did not think it hurt him, or at least he made no sound of pain. I held my hand to his chest and felt his heart flutter and drop. A column of air pushed from his mouth and his body lurched and grew still, and this was where the clock stopped for Hermann Kermit Warm. His right arm fell from the cot and I lifted it back up. When it fell again I left it to hang and exited the tent. I found Charlie sitting fireside, and all was the same as when I had left him save for one conspicuous detail.

Which was that there were now a half–dozen Indians milling about the camp, rummaging our bags, inspecting the horses and donkeys, and generally searching through our possessions for anything of value they might keep for themselves. The moment I breached the tent an Indian holding a rifle gestured with the barrel that I should sit beside Charlie, and I did this. Neither my brother nor I were armed, our gun belts sitting coiled beneath our saddles on the ground, as was our habit when we were bivouacked. But even if Charlie had been armed I do not know that he would have pulled his pistol. He sat to the side, staring into the flames, casting the rare glance at our visitors but not wanting any part of them.

The bucket of gold sat between us, and I believe this might

have gone undetected if Charlie had not attempted to hide it under his hat, which the Indian with the rifle saw and was made suspicious by. He crossed over and tossed the hat aside; his expression was unsmiling and remained so even when he discovered the bucket's contents. But he found it interesting enough that he called for the others to abandon their investigations, and now they were all squatting around the fire and peering into the metal container. One of them began to laugh but the others did not like this and told him, if I am not mistaken, to be quiet. Another looked at me and addressed me brusquely; I thought he was asking where we had got all the gold. I pointed to the river and he stared at me contemptibly. They emptied the bucket, pouring out equal shares into calfskin bags until it was empty. After this they stood and discussed some serious matter or another, pointing at Charlie and me as they spoke. The Indian with the rifle entered into Warm's tent and gasped. To think of it now, this seems most un-Indian-like, him gasping like that. But he really did do it. He gasped just like an old woman and all but fell out of the tent, his hand clamped over his mouth, his eyes wide with fright and scandal. Shooing his people backward, away from our camp and toward the river, he described what he had seen in the shelter, and they all turned and hurried off into the darkness. I found it odd they did not take our pistols or horses or lives, but it was likely they thought we had some manner of plague or leprosy. Or perhaps they decided the gold was treasure enough.

'Warm's dead,' I told Charlie.

'I am going to sleep,' he said.

And do you know, this is just what he did do, too.

I put Warm into the ground in the morning, with no help from Charlie, though he was once again petulantly present for the burial itself. Warm's lone bag was filled with his diaries and papers and I searched through these for the formula's recipe but could not understand hardly any of what he had written down, this owing less to my ignorance of science and chemistry than to his penmanship, which was atrocious. Finally I gave up and rested the books atop his chest before filling him over with sand and earth. I made no speech this time, and decided I would not mark either one of the side-by-side graves, which I have since wished I had done, illustrating some connection between them as loyal friends, and also mentioning their accomplishments on the river. But I was feeling melancholic and obscurely hexed or obstructed and wanted badly to move on; and so the moment the grave was filled, Charlie and I mounted our horses and left, with the tent standing and fire still smoking. Looking back at the camp I thought, I will never be a leader of men, and neither do I want to be one, and neither do I want to be led. I thought: I want to lead only myself. So that they would not starve to death I had untied Warm's horse and the donkeys. The horse did not move but the donkeys followed after us. I fired a shot over their heads to scatter them and they ran downriver. They were naked, without any sign of ownership on them, and their stumpy legs swiveled back and forth so quickly and efficiently it did not look real to me.

We took a northwesterly route and arrived in Mayfield three days later. During all this time of riding, Charlie and I had little to say to each other, though when we spoke we were civil and not unfriendly about it. I believe he was wondering whom he might be for the rest of his life; and in a way I was wondering the same thing about myself. Reflecting on the last few days I had passed I told myself, If this was indeed my last bit of work, it is just as well to bow out in so dramatic a fashion. I decided I would pay my mother a visit just as soon as I was able, if she was in fact still alive; and I had many invented, conciliatory conversations with her, each of these ending with when she reached her crooked arm over my neck, kissing me above the line of my beard beneath the eye. The thought of this made me tranquil, and the ride to Mayfield, despite our recent hardships, was as pleasant as could be expected. At what was roughly the halfway point I said to Charlie, 'Your left hand is still faster than most men's right.'

'Most isn't all,' he answered, and we returned to silence.

My thoughts about the Indians stealing the gold were complicated. It seemed appropriate in some way that we should not have it—had I not felt a sense of remorse when I hefted that bucket? But I doubt I would have been able to pontificate with such detachment if there was not the pile of gold waiting for us under the stove in Mayfield, a sum that represented for me the realization of all I wanted to be changed in my life. So when I smelt smoke on the wind a mile or two outside of town, I was inhabited by the most powerful type of dread and apprehension. In the time it took Charlie and I to get to the hotel, my feelings pushed past worry and on to anger, which gave way to miserable acceptance. The hotel was burned to the ground, as were the surrounding buildings; in the rubble I spied the potbellied stove, and it was toppled. I stepped through the ash and blackened timber, knowing our treasure was gone, and when I found it to be unrectifiably so I turned back to Charlie, sitting with hunched shoulders on Nimble in the middle of the sun-blanched road. 'Nothing,' I called.

'Drink,' he called back, which was just as sane and thoughtful a reply as I had ever heard him speak. But with the hotel gone there *was* nowhere to get a drink, or nowhere to sit and become drunk, and we were forced to buy a bottle of brandy from the chemist's and to empty this in the road like common rascals.

We sat on the walkway across from the remains of the hotel and stared at it. The fire had gone out days before but smoke still rose up here and there in wriggling ghost-snakes. When the bottle was half gone, Charlie said, 'Do you think Mayfield did it?'

'Who else?'

'He must not have left at all, but hidden himself away, waiting for us to go. I suppose he got the last laugh then.' I admitted he had and Charlie said, 'I wonder where your girl is.'

'I had not thought of it.' For an instant I was surprised by this, then not.

A person appeared down the road and I recognized him as the weeping man. He was leading his horse, tears streaming down his face, as usual. He did not see us or take notice of us; he was speaking lowly to himself, in a state of catatonic devastation, and I found myself intensely annoyed by him. I picked up a rock and threw it. This glanced off his shoulder, and he looked at me. 'Get away from here!' I said. I do not know why I disliked him so. It was as though I were chasing a crow from a corpse. Well, I was drunk. The weeping man continued on with his miserable voyage. 'I don't know what to do next,' I admitted to Charlie.

'Best not to think of it just now,' he counseled. And then, bemusedly: 'Would you look at this? It is my own true love.' It was his whore approaching. 'Hello, what's-your-name,' he said happily. She stood before us looking damp and raw and red-eyed, the edges of her dress dirtied, her hands trembling. She drew back her arm and threw something at my face. It was the hundred dollars I had left her to give to the bookkeeper. Looking down at the money on the ground, I began to laugh, though I knew it meant the bookkeeper had died. I thought, It must not have been that I loved the bookkeeper, but that I loved the idea of her loving me, and the idea of not being alone. At any rate there was nothing in my heart like sorrow, and I peered up at the whore and said to her pitiful face, 'And so what about that?' She spit and walked away and I picked the coins up from the ground. I gave Charlie fifty dollars and he dropped it into his boot, his pinkie arched elegantly skyward. I dropped mine into my boot as well, and we both laughed as though this were the pinnacle of modern comedy.

We were sitting fully in the dirt now, and the bottle was

nearly empty. I think we would have passed out and slept in the road but Charlie's whore had gone and gathered all the other whores, who presently stood over us in a pack, looking down with scandal and outrage. With Mayfield and then the hotel gone, they were all of them fallen on hard times, with perfume no longer trailing over their heads, their dresses no longer crisp and folded stiff with starch. They started in on Charlie and me, saying unkind things about our characters.

'What a pair.'

'Look at them on the ground like that.'

'Look at the gut on the one.'

'Other one's hurt his hand, looks like.'

'No more killing stable boys for him.'

Over the din, Charlie asked me confusedly, 'What are they so upset about?'

'We chased away the boss man, remember?' To the whores I explained, 'But we didn't burn the hotel down, Mayfield did. At least I think it was him. But I am sure it wasn't us.' This only served to make them angrier, however.

'Don't you talk about Mayfield!'

'Mayfield wasn't so bad!'

'He paid us, didn't he?'

'He gave us rooms, didn't he?'

'He was a bastard, but he wasn't half the bastard as you two.'

'You two are the real bastards.'

'The genuine article, that's the truth all right.'

'What should we do with these bastards?'

'These bastards.'

'Let's get them!'

Now they came upon us, overpowering and pinning us to the ground. Through the wall of bodies I could hear Charlie laughing, and I also found this humorous at the start, but my amusement gave way to upset when I found myself unable to move, and as I watched the darting hands of the whores empty my pockets of all my money. I began then, and so did Charlie start to struggle and berate the whores, but it seemed the more we fought the stronger they became. When I heard Charlie scream out in pain I felt truly panicked—his whore was grinding her heel into his injured hand—and I bit the whore closest to me through her dress, sinking my teeth into her rank and ample belly. She became enraged by this, removing my pistol from its holster and pointing it at my skull above the brow. Now I lay completely still and silent, and the look of hatred was so vigorous in her eyes I was expecting at any moment to witness that bright white light from the deep black pit of the gun barrel. But this never came, and the whores, having had enough, wordlessly climbed off and left us, taking with them our pistols and cash, save for the hundred dollars we had dropped in our boots, where they luckily had not thought to look.

INTERMISSION II

I passed out in the dirt and sun in the half-dead town of May-field. When I awoke it was dusk and the peculiar girl from my prior visit was standing before me. She had a new dress on, and her hair was just-cleaned and wrapped in a fat red bow. Her hands were clasped daintily to her chest and there was an expectant air of tension about her. She was not looking at me but to my side, at Charlie. 'It's you,' I said. She made a quieting gesture, then pointed to my brother, who was holding a water-filled mason jar. At the bottom of this was a swirling dust devil of black granules and I saw that the girl's knuckles were flecked in the poison, as before; when Charlie brought the jar to his lips I knocked it away from his hand. The jar did not break but landed in a pit of mud. The water drained away and the girl made a sullen expression at me. 'Why did you do that?'

I said, 'I have wanted to talk with you, about what you told me before.'

Staring distractedly at the jar, she said, 'About *what* did I tell you before?'

'You said I was a protected man, do you recall it?'

'I recall it.'

'Can you tell me, please, am I protected still?'

She watched me, and I knew she knew the answer but she did not speak.

'To what degree am I protected?' I persisted. 'Will it always be so?

She opened her mouth and closed it. She shook her head. 'I will not tell you.' Her dress hem spun in a wheel as she turned and retreated. I searched around for a rock to throw at her but there were none within reaching distance. Charlie was still watching the jar, propped in the mud. 'I am damned thirsty,' he said.

'She wished to kill you dead,' I told him.

'What, her?'

'I saw her poison a dog before.'

'The pretty little thing. Why in the world would she do that?'

'Just for the evil joy of it, is all I can think.'

Charlie squinted at the purpling sky. He lay back his head and closed his eyes and said, 'Well, world?' Then he laughed. A minute or two passed, and he was sleeping.

END INTERMISSION II

Charlie had his hand cut off by a doctor in Jackson-

ville. His pain by this time had lessened but the flesh had begun to rot and there was nothing else but to remove it. The doctor, named Crane, was an older man, though alert and steady; he wore a rose in his lapel and from the start I had faith in him as a person of principles. When I spoke of my and Charlie's financial straits, for example, he waved away my comment as though the notion of receiving a wage was little more than an afterthought. There was an incident when Charlie produced a bottle of brandy, saying he wished to get drunk before the procedure, which the doctor was against, explaining that the alcohol would cause excessive bleeding. But Charlie said this made no difference, he would have his way and nothing in the world would stop him.

At last I took Crane aside and told him to give Charlie the anesthetic without telling him what it was. He saw the wisdom in my plan, and after successfully sedating my brother everything went as well as such a thing can. The operation took place in the candlelit parlor of Crane's own home.

The rotting had crept beyond the wrist and Crane made his cut halfway up the forearm with a long-bladed saw manufactured, he said, specifically for severing bone. His forehead was shining with perspiration when he was through and the blade of the saw, when he accidentally touched it afterward, was hot enough that it burned him. He had laid out a bucket for the hand and wrist to drop into but his aim or placement was off and it landed on the floor. He could not be bothered to retrieve this, busy as he was caring for what remained of Charlie, and I crossed over and lifted it myself. It was surprisingly light; blood dripped freely from the open end and I held this over the bucket, gripping it by the wrist. My touching Charlie's arm like this would not ever have happened when it was attached, and as such I blushed from the foreignness of it. I found myself running my thumb over the coarse black hairs. I felt very close to Charlie when I did this. I placed the hand and wrist standing upright in the bucket and removed this from the room, for I did not want him to see it whenever he awoke. After the surgery he lay on a tall cot in the center of the parlor, bandaged and drugged, and Crane encouraged me to take in the air, saying it would be many hours before Charlie was conscious again. I thanked him and left his home, walking to the far edge of town, to the restaurant I had visited on the way to San Francisco. I sat at the same table as before and was received by the same waiter, who recognized me, and asked in an ironic voice if I had returned for another meal of carrots and stalks. But after witnessing the operation, and with dried droplets of my brother's blood decorating my pant legs, I was not hungry in the least, and asked only for a glass of ale. 'You have given up food entirely then?' he said, snuffling into his mustache. I found myself offended at his tone and told him, 'My name is Eli Sisters, you son of a whore, and I will kill you dead where you stand if you don't hurry up and serve me what I asked for.' This brought the waiter's gawking and leering to an end, and he was cautious and respectful afterward, his hand atremble as he placed the glass of ale before me. It was out of character for me to lash out in so common and vulgar a way as this; later, as I walked away from the restaurant, I thought, I must relearn calmness and peacefulness. I thought, I am going to rest my body for one full year! Here was my decision, and one that I am happy to say I eventually realized, one that I thoroughly relished and basked in: Twelve months of resting and thinking and becoming placid and serene. But before this dream-life might come to pass, I knew, there was one last bit of business I would have to see through, and which I would see through on my own.

It was ten o'clock at night when we finally arrived at our shack outside of Oregon City. I found the door knocked off its hinges and all our furnishings overturned or destroyed; I walked to the rear room and was unsurprised to find my and Charlie's stash gone from its hiding place behind the looking glass. There had been more than twenty-two hundred dollars tucked into the wall, but now there was nothing save for a single sheet of paper, which I took up, and which read thus:

Dear Charlie,

    I am a bastard I took your $, all of it. I am drunk but I don't think I will return it when I'm sober. Also I took your brother's $ and I'm sorry Eli, I always liked you when you weren't looking at me cockeyed. I am going far away with this $ and you can try to find me and good luck on that score. Any rate you will both earn more, you were always good earners. It's a hell of a way to say so long but I've always been this way and I won't even feel bad about it later. There is something wrong with my blood or mind or whatever it is which guides a man.

—Rex

I folded the note and returned it to the carved-away wall. The looking glass had been dropped and broken, and I pushed around the shards with my boot. I was not thinking but waiting for a thought, or a feeling. When this did not materialize I gave up on it and went outside to pull Charlie down from Nimble. Crane had given him a dropper bottle of morphine and he had been more or less catatonic for the duration of our return trip. I had found it occasionally necessary to tie him to Nimble and lead him by a length of rope. And he was several times jarred from his stupor by the realization his hand was no longer attached to his body. It was something that slipped his mind again and again; when he noticed, he was run through with shock and miserableness.

I walked him to his room and he crawled onto his naked, lopsided mattress. Before he dropped away I told him I was going out, and he did not ask where, and he could not possibly care. He clapped his jaws and held up his bandaged stump to wave it. Leaving him to his drugged slumber, I stood awhile at the entrance of our home, taking stock of our wrecked and meager possessions. I had never had any strong feelings for the place; looking around now at the wine-stained bedding and cracked plates and cups, I knew I would never sleep there again. It was an hour's ride into town. My mind was intent and clean and focused. I had been traveling for many days but was not in the least bit fatigued or compromised. I was not in any way afraid.

The Commodore's mansion was dark save for his half-lit rooms on the top story. The moon was high and bright and I hid beneath the shaded boughs of an ancient cedar that stood on the border of the grand property. I watched a servant girl leave out the back with an empty washtub under her arm. She was angry about something, and as she made for her cabin, separate from the main house, she cursed under her breath. I waited fifteen minutes for her to exit; when she did not, I crossed the yard in a crouch, moving toward the house. She had failed to lock the back door and I crept fully into the kitchen. It was still and cool and orderly. What had the Commodore done to the girl? I stole another glance at her cabin; all was quiet and unchanged, except she had lighted a single white candle and placed this in her window.

I climbed the carpeted stairs and stood outside the Commodore's quarters. Through the door I heard him berating and insulting someone; whom I did not know, for the man only mumbled his apologies, and I could not tell who he was or what he had done wrong. When he had had enough abuse he made to leave the room; as his footsteps drew closer I pressed myself against the wall beside the door hinges. I had no pistol, merely a squat, blunt blade, what I have always heard called a plug blade, and I took this up in my hand. But the door swung open and the man descended the stairs with no knowledge of my being there. He left out the back door and I snuck to a window at the end of the hall to follow his movements. I watched him enter the servant girl's cabin; he appeared in the window, glaring bitterly at the mansion, and I hid in the shadows to witness the hurt in the man's eyes. His hideous face was descriptive of a violent life, and yet there he stood, bullied and cowed and impotent to defend himself. When he blew out the candle the cabin fell dark and I backtracked down the hall. The door had remained open and I entered.

The Commodore's quarters accounted for the entire top floor of the mansion, and there were no walls in this vast space, no rooms, but the furniture was grouped together as though there were. It was darkened save for the low lights of the occasional table lantern or flickering sconce. In the far corner behind a Chinese folding screen rose a plume of blue cigar smoke; when I heard the Commodore's voice I paused, thinking him not alone. But as I listened I heard no second voice, and deduced he was only speaking to himself. He was resting in the bath and giving an imaginary speech and I thought, What is it about bathing that prompts a person to do this? I gripped the plug blade and walked across to meet him, following a line of rugs so as not to make a sound. I came around the screen, blade aloft, prepared to stick this into the Commodore's naked heart, but his eyes were covered with a cotton cloth and I found my arm dropping in degrees to my side. Here was a man whose influence could be found in every corner of the country, and he sat drunk in a copper bathtub, his body hairless, his chest scooped and bony, an overlong ash dangling perilously from his cigar. His voice was reedy:

'Gentlemen, it is a question often asked, and today I put it to you, and let us see if you know the answer. What is it that makes a man great? Some will point to wealth. Others to strength of character. Some will say it is a great man who never loses his temper. Some that it is one who is fervent in his worship of the Lord. But I am here to tell you precisely what it is which makes a man great, and I hope that you will listen to my words on this day, and that you will adopt them into your hearts and souls, and that you will understand my meaning. For yes! I wish to bestow greatness upon you.' He nodded, and held up a hand, in appreciation at his phantom applause. I took a step closer to him and leveled my blade at his face. I knew I should kill him while I had the chance but I wanted to hear what he had to say. He lowered his hand and took a long drink of his cigar. This upset the ash, which fell into the bath with a hiss; he splashed the water with his fingertips where he imagined the ash had landed. 'Thank you,' he said. 'Thank you, thank you.' He paused, sucking in a chestful of air. Now he spoke with emphasis, and loudly. 'A great man is one who can pinpoint a vacuity in the material world and inject into this blank space an *essence of himself*! A great man is one who can create good fortune in a place where there previously was none through *sheer force of will*! A great man, then, is one who can make *something* from *nothing*! And the world around you, assembled gentlemen, believe me when I say it is just that—nothing!'

In one quick movement I was upon him. Casting the plug blade to the ground I pressed down on his shoulders so that his head dropped beneath the surface of the water. He began at once to splash and flail; he coughed and choked and made a noise that sounded like *'Hesch, hesch, hesch!'* This reverberated against the walls of the bathtub and I felt it tickling through my legs and up into my trunk. The Commodore's life instinct was awakened and his struggling became ever more fierce, but I had all my weight upon him and he was pinned and could not move. I felt very strong, and correct, and nothing in the world could have prevented me from seeing the job through.

His washcloth had fallen away from his face and he stared

up at me through the water, and though I did not want to look at him I thought it would not have been proper otherwise and I matched his eyes with mine. I was surprised by what I saw, because he was only afraid, just like all the others who had died. He recognized me, but that was it. I suppose I had wanted him to see me and lament that he had not shown me the proper respect, but there was no time for that. Speaking practically, I thought there was perhaps an explosion of colors in his mind, then a limitless void, like a night, or all nights stirred together.

The Commodore died. After this I pulled him up so that his head was only halfway submerged, to make it look as though he had drunkenly drowned himself. His hair was pasted over his forehead and his cigar floated near his face and there was nothing dignified about his closing setting. I left through the front door and rode back to Charlie's and my shack, where I found him asleep and in no mood for travel. Despite his protestations I roused him and tied him to Nimble and we rode in the direction of Mother's.

EPILOGUE

There was silver in the dawn, and heavy dewdrops weighed down the stalks of tall grass. Charlie had finished his morphine and lay snoring on Nimble's broad back as we rode up the trail to the property. I had not seen the house in years and wondered if it might be in ruins, and what I would do if Mother was not there. When the house came into view I saw that it was newly painted, and that a room had been added to the rear; there was an orderly vegetable garden with a scarecrow, and the scarecrow looked familiar to me. I recognized it was wearing an old coat of my father's, and also his hat and pants. I dismounted Morris's horse and approached the visage to check its pockets. There was nothing in them but a single spent match. I put this into my own pocket and stepped to the front door. I was too nervous to knock and so for a time merely watched it. But my mother had heard me walk up and met me at the door in her nightgown. She looked at me with not a trace of surprise, and over my shoulder.

'What happened with him?' she asked.

'He has injured his hand, and is tired about it.'

She scowled, and asked me to wait on the porch for a moment, explaining that she did not like for people to see her climbing into bed. But I already knew this and told her, 'I will come when you call for me, Mother.' She walked away and I sat on the railing, swinging my leg and looking all around at the house's every detail. I was feeling tenderhearted and aching about it. Looking at Charlie, slack on his horse, I thought of the times we had had there. 'They were not all bad,' I said to him. My mother called my name and I walked through the house and into the back, the added room, where she lay in her tall bed of brass and soft cotton. She patted her hands over top of the blanket. 'Where are my glasses?' she asked.

'They are in your hair.'

'What? Oh, here. Yes.' She put them on and looked at me. 'There you are,' she concluded. Her face broke into a frown and she asked, 'What happened to Charlie's hand?'

'He had an accident and lost it.'

'Misplaced it, did he?' She shook her head and muttered, 'As though it is only a trifle or inconvenience.'

'It is no trifle to me or him, either.'

'How did he lose it?'

'It was burned, and then infected. The doctor said it would kill his heart if Charlie forwent the surgery.'

'Kill his heart?'

'That is what the doctor said.'

'He used those exact words?'

'Words to that effect.'

'Hmm. And was the operation very painful?'

'He was unconscious for the actual cutting. He says now there is a burning, and that the stump itself itches, but he is taking morphine, which helps. I should think he will be healed soon. The color has returned to his face, I noticed.'

She cleared her throat, and then again. Her head began to tick and tock, as though she were weighing her words; I implored her to speak her mind and she said, 'Well, it's not that I am not happy to see you, Eli, because I am. But could you tell me just what prompted your visiting me after all this time?'

'I felt a need to be near you,' I told her. 'It was very strong, and it overcame me.'

'Yes,' she said, nodding. 'And would you explain to me, please, just what in the world you are talking about?'

This made me laugh, but then I could see she was serious, and I made an attempt to answer honestly: 'What I mean is, all of the sudden, at the end of a long and difficult piece of work, I didn't understand why we should not be near each other, when we were always so close before, you and I, and even Charlie.'

She did not appear to think very much of this answer; or perhaps she did not believe it. As though to change the subject, she asked, 'How have you been in terms of your temper?'

'It will get away from me on occasion.'

'What of the soothing method?'

'I still use the soothing method from time to time.'

She nodded and took up a cup of water from the nightstand. After drinking, she dabbed her face with the collar of her gown;

in doing this, her sleeve dropped and I saw her crooked arm. It had been set improperly and looked irregular, as though it might cause her discomfort; at the sight of it I felt a ghostly pain or what some call a pity pain in my own arm. She caught me looking and smiled. Her smile was beautiful—my mother was a famously beautiful woman when she was young—and she said gladly, 'You look just the same, do you know?'

I cannot state how much of a relief it was to hear her say this, and I told her, 'When I see you, I feel the same. It is when I am away that I lose myself.'

'You should stay here then.'

'I would like to stay. I have missed you very much, Mother. I think of you so frequently, and I believe Charlie does, also.'

'Charlie thinks of himself, is what Charlie thinks of.'

'He is so hard to get ahold of, always breaking away.' I felt a sob growing in my chest but I pushed this back and extinguished it. Exhaling, I gripped myself. Soberly, I said, 'I don't know if I should leave him outside like that. Might I bring him in the house?' I was quiet for a time. I waited for my mother to say something, but she never did. Finally I told her, 'We had many adventures together, Charlie and I, and we saw things most men do not get to see.'

'And is that so important?'

'Now that it is over it seems so.'

'Why do you say that it's over?'

'I have had my fill of it. I am after a slower life, is the thing.'

'You have come to the right house for that.' Pointing around the room she asked, 'Did you see all the improvements? I keep waiting for you to compliment—anything.'

'Everything looks splendid.'

'Did you see the garden?'

'It is fine. The house, also. And you. Are you feeling well?'

'Yes and no and in between.' Thinking, she added, 'Mostly in between.'

A knock on the door, and Charlie entered the room. He took off his hat and hung it from his stump. 'Hello, Mother.'

She watched him for a long time. 'Hello, Charlie,' she said. When she did not look away he turned to me. 'I didn't know where we were at first. The house was so familiar but I couldn't place it.' Whispering, he said, 'Did you see the scarecrow?'

Mother sat watching us with something like a smile on her face. But it was a sad smile, and far away. 'Is either of you hungry?' she asked.

'No, Mother,' I said.

'Neither am I,' said Charlie. 'But I would like to take a bath, please.'

She told him to go ahead and he thanked her, making to leave. As he stood in the doorway to face me his expression was guileless and straight and I thought, There is not the slightest bit of fight left in him. After he had gone, Mother said, '*He* looks different.'

'He needs a rest.'

'No.' She tapped her chest and shook her head. When I explained he had lost his shooting hand she said, 'I hope the two of you don't expect me to lament that.'

'We expect nothing, Mother.'

'No? It seems you are both expecting me to pay for your food and board.'

'We will find work.'

'And what would that be, exactly?'

'I have given some thought to opening a trading post.'

She said, 'You mean you will invest in one? You don't mean

you will work in one? With all the customers, and their questions?'

'I have imagined doing it myself. Can't you picture it?'

'Frankly, I can't.'

I sighed. 'It doesn't matter what we do. Money comes and goes.' I shook my head. 'It doesn't matter and you know it doesn't.'

'All right,' she said, relenting. 'You and your brother can sleep in your old room. If you truly mean to stay on, we can add another room later. And when I say we, I mean you and Charlie.' She reached for a hand mirror and held this up before her. Smoothing her hair she told me, 'I should probably be glad you two are still a united front. Since you were boys, and it was always the same.'

'Our alliance has been broken and mended many times.'

'Your father brought you close.' She lowered the mirror. 'We can thank him for the one thing.'

I said, 'I think I would like to lie down, now.'

'Should I wake you for lunch?'

'What are you making?'

'Beef stew.'

'That's fine, Mother.'

She paused. 'Do you mean: That's fine, don't wake me? Or: That's fine, do?'

'Do wake me, please.'

'All right then. Go and get some rest.'

I turned away from her and looked down the hallway. The front door hung open and presented me with a block of pure white light. Passing under mother's jamb I thought I heard her voice; I swung around and she watched me expectantly. 'Are you all right?' I asked. 'Did you call for me?' She beckoned and I crossed the room. Standing beside her bed, she reached up and gripped my fingers. Now she pulled me to her, hand over hand up my arm as though she were scaling a rope. She hooked her arms around my neck and kissed me below my eye. Her lip was wet and cool. Her hair and face and neck smelled of sleep and soap. I walked away to my and Charlie's old room and lay down on a mattress on the floor. It was a comfortable and clean space, if small, and I knew it would do for a while, and in its way was perfect. I could not recall a time when I was precisely where I wanted to be, and this was a very satisfying feeling.

I dropped into sleep but awoke with a start some minutes later. I could hear Charlie in the next room, washing himself in the bathtub. He was saying nothing and would say nothing, I knew, but the sound the water made was like a voice, the way it hurried and splashed, chattering, then falling quiet but for the rare drip, as if in humble contemplation. It seemed to me I could gauge from these sounds the sorrow or gladness of their creator; I listened intently and decided that my brother and I were, for the present at least, removed from all earthly dangers and horrors.

And might I say what a pleasing conclusion this was for me.

ACKNOWLEDGMENTS

Leslie Napoles
Gustavo deWitt
Gary deWitt
Nick deWitt
Mike deWitt
Michael Dagg

Lee Boudreaux
Abigail Holstein
Daniel Halpern
Sara Holloway
Sarah MacLachlan
Melanie Little

Peter McGuigan

Stephanie Abou

Daniel McGillivray

Hannah Brown Gordon

Jerry Kalajian

Philippe Aronson

Emma Aronson

Marie-Catherine Vacher

Azazel Jacobs

Monte Mattson

Maria Semple

George Meyer

Jonathan Evison

Dave Erikson

Dan Stiles

Danny Palmerlee

Alison Dickey

John C. Reilly

Carson Mell

Andy Hunter

Otis the dog

THE
SISTERS BROTHERS

. . .

PATRICK deWITT

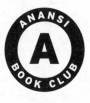

QUESTIONS FOR DISCUSSION
THE SISTERS BROTHERS BY PATRICK deWITT

• • •

1. The western seems to be as popular a genre as it has ever been. How does *The Sisters Brothers* make the western new again?

2. Several odd characters have an impact on the story, including the weeping man, the witch, and the poisonous little girl. What is their function in the story?

3. The novel is full of gems of wisdom as "little victories" from Eli's mother and from Eli: "There were many hardships in our type of life and we took these small comforts as they came. I found they added up to something decent enough to carry on." And, "The creak of bedsprings suffering under the weight of a restless man is as lonely a sound as I know." What is your favourite observation or bit of wisdom in the novel?

4. Which scene in the book was the funniest for you and why? Which character was the funniest? The saddest? The most ridiculous? What did you think of the ending?

5. How did you relate to the character of Eli? How reliable a narrator is he?

6. What is Eli's relationship with money? What about Charlie's? How do you answer Eli's question: "What would the world be without money hung around our necks, hung around our very souls?"

7. When Charlie threatens to put a hole in the dentist's brain if he does not turn over the morphine, Watt's says "At times I feel one is already there." Why do you think he says this? Why does Charlie kill so thoughtlessly and remorselessly?

8. Eli longs for the quiet and peaceful life of a general store owner and the love of a good woman so that he "might improve her time on earth with the devotion of another human being." What do you think are his chances at succeeding in this desire, having finally come out as the "lead man" and having sworn off killing?

9. When asked why the brothers are after Hermann Kermit Warm Eli replies, "He has done something incorrect and we have been hired to bring him to justice." What do you think of his answer?

10. Eli comments that sometimes he feels "a helplessness." Are the fates of the characters in the novel built by their own choices or out of their control?

11. "It is hard to find a friend," says Eli. "It is the hardest thing in the world," agrees the proprietor of the Black Skull, whom Warm has abandoned for his new friend Morris. Is friendship possible in such a harsh environment? Why or why not?

12. Charlie says that Mayfield "has a describing problem." How would you describe this book?

© Danny Palmerlee

ABOUT THE AUTHOR

Patrick deWitt was born on Vancouver Island in 1975. He is the author of the critically acclaimed novel *Ablutions*, which was named a *New York Times* Editors' Choice book. He lives in Portland, Oregon.